Salmonella Men on Planet Porno

Salmonella Men on Planet Porno

Stories

Yasutaka Tsutsui

*Translated from the Japanese
by Andrew Driver*

PANTHEON BOOKS, NEW YORK

Translation copyright © 2006 by Andrew Driver

All rights reserved. Published in the United States by Pantheon Books, a division of Random House, Inc., New York, and in Canada by Random House of Canada Limited, Toronto. Originally published in Japan as *Poruno Wakusei No Sarumonera Ningen* by Shinchosha, Co., Ltd., Tokyo, in 1979. Copyright © 1979 by Yasutaka Tsutsui. English translation originally published with twelve additional stories by Alma Books, Ltd., Surrey, in 2006.

Pantheon Books and colophon are registered trademarks of Random House, Inc.

"Rumours About Me" originally appeared in *Zoetrope: All-Story.*

Library of Congress Cataloging-in-Publication Data
Tsutsui, Yasutaka, [date]
Salmonella men on Planet Porno : stories / Yasutaka Tsutsui; translated from the Japanese by Andrew Driver.
p. cm.
ISBN 978-0-307-37726-5
1. Tsutsui, Yasutaka, [date]—Translations into English. I. Driver, Andrew. II. Title.
PL862.S77A2 2008   895.6'35—dc22   2007051356

www.pantheonbooks.com

Printed in the United States of America
First American Edition
9 8 7 6 5 4 3 2 1

CONTENTS

Acknowledgements

The author would like to thank the following persons for appearing in the title story or allowing their works to be cited in it: Toshitaka Hidaka (zoologist), Akira Miyawaki (botanist), Yasushi Kurihara (ecologist), Kazuki Miyashita (ecologist), Makoto Numata (biologist), Kenzaburo Oe (novelist), Fujio Ishihara (SF writer), Yo Sano (mystery writer), Konrad Lorenz (animal behaviourist) and Edmond Hamilton (SF writer).

Salmonella Men on Planet Porno

The Dabba Dabba Tree

My father came up from the country carrying a curiously shaped bonsai tree.

"This here's a Dabba Dabba Tree," he announced, showing it to me and my wife. "It's a special kind of cedar, see."

"My, what an odd-looking thing," said my wife, examining it with a look of puzzlement.

The tree was about eight inches tall. It was thicker at the base but tapered off towards the top, where the foliage was more sparse. Standing upright, the trunk formed a perfect cone.

"Yes, and what an odd name," I added, watching my father's expression. Perhaps it would shed some light on his reason for bringing the tree.

"Well, it's not just the name that's odd," he said, narrowing his eyes. "If you put this Dabba Dabba Tree in your bedroom at night, you'll have fruity dreams till morning comes!"

"Gosh! I wonder what he means," said my wife.

I whispered in her ear. "Erotic dreams, of course."

"Oh!" she exclaimed, blushing.

My father gave her a lewd look and continued. "You've been married five years but still ain't had kids. That's why I brought you the tree. Put it in your bedroom tonight – you're sure to have some cracking dreams. Go on, have it! It's no good for an old codger like me! Kekekekekeh!" he chuckled like some weird bird, before setting off back to the country.

That night, we took the Dabba Dabba Tree into our bedroom and placed it at the foot of our double bed. Yes, we were still using a double bed even after five years of marriage. Well, our bedroom was rather small. There wasn't enough room for two beds.

"Good night, then."

"Yes, good night."

We dived under the sheets, excitedly turned our backs on each other, and concentrated on getting to sleep. At times like this, you want to be the first to drop off. Otherwise, the sound of your partner's breathing gets on your nerves and keeps you awake. So much the worse if you know she's having an erotic dream. And worse still if she starts talking in her sleep.

Luckily, I nodded off immediately.

And I started dreaming. I dreamt I was in my bedroom, sleeping in my double bed with my wife.

"Yes! A dream!"

I sat up. My wife was slumbering peacefully next to me, completely naked. She can't sleep any other way. I turned my head in puzzlement.

"Great. What's erotic about that?!"

If I made love to her after all this time, there wouldn't be anything erotic about it at all. It would just be dull old reality – whether she was naked or not.

"Well, if this is an erotic dream, I'd better do something erotic!"

I got out of bed and put my shirt and trousers on. Then I slipped on some sandals and went outside. To find a woman worthy of sharing my erotic dream, I'd have to go to the nightlife district. I walked along a dark side-road, then turned into a major thoroughfare. The street shone as bright as day, thanks to the bars and restaurants on either side. There were people everywhere.

"Where are all the tasty women then?" I grumbled. I was feeling rather tired after walking two or three blocks. Having an erotic dream clearly demanded a certain amount of perseverance. I would spot a woman who looked promising from a distance but who, on closer inspection, turned out to be a wrinkled old hag. Or a tall, slender girl with a great figure would be walking in front of me. I'd hurry to catch her up, only to find that she was a complete dog to look at. I'm not usually picky about my women. But now that

I was having this erotic dream, it would have been pointless to go for someone I didn't fancy. I walked on.

Then a girl stepped out of a streetside café. She was dressed in a dark-brown suit and looked like a college student. Wearing little make-up besides her lipstick, she had pale skin, large eyes and a pretty face.

"YES!!!" I exclaimed, blocking her way.

"Can I help you?" she asked, looking me up and down.

"Well, actually…" I replied falteringly, wondering how to explain. "Actually, I've got this Dabba Dabba Tree, you see, and…"

"Oh no. Not you as well!" she giggled. Then her expression changed to a frown. "You're the fourth one tonight. You're going to say you're having an erotic dream because of this 'Dabba Dabba Tree', and you want to have sex with me. Right?"

"What? You mean there are others?" I replied, somewhat surprised. But after all, it *was* just a dream. Who cared? "I mean, er, that's right. I really want to have sex with you."

"In your dreams!" she said with an ironic smile, shaking her head. "I've said the same to all of them. This might be a dream for you, but for me, it's reality! And anyway, I'm still a virgin. I refuse to lose my virginity just to fulfil someone else's dream!"

What was she on about? Well, it didn't matter. It was just a dream.

"Those other three must have been weak-willed. Spineless. And maybe they didn't want you enough anyway," I said. "But I won't give up so easily, d'you hear? This may well be reality for you, but for me it's just a dream. So I don't care what happens! And anyway, I fancy you. I fancy you like mad, so I'm going to make love to you. And if you say no, I'll just have to force myself on you, right here and now."

"What, here in the street?"

"That's right. I don't care who sees us, or where we are. I'm going to pounce on you, and rip that tasteful, well-tailored dark-brown suit off your body, a-a-and then, and then I'm going to pull off your bra, and – and—"

"All right, keep your hair on! Look, you're slobbering!"

"Oh." I quickly wiped my mouth with the back of my hand. "And then, and then, I'm going to pull down your panties—"

"Er – I'm wearing tights."

"I'm going to pull down your panties together with your tights, then I'm going to grab hold of you, throw you onto the pavement and ravish your body by force. Well, you say you're a virgin, and that's a bit unfortunate for you. But hey, it's a dream, it doesn't matter! I'll ravish you, and then—"

"The police might see us."

"I don't care. If they come to arrest me, I'll just shout out at the top of my voice. Then I'll wake up. Mind you… This is reality for you, isn't it. Your clothes will be in a mess and you'll be stark naked. You can't go home like that. What'll you do?"

"I don't know. What do you think?"

"Why don't we find a hotel? I don't really want to rape you here. If the police came, they'd only spoil it."

She hesitated for a moment, observing me with a sideways look. "All right," she answered eventually, with some reluctance. "I'll go with you. After all, it seems I only exist inside your dream. I can't just ignore you, can I."

So we turned off into a side road and wandered around the back streets looking for a discreet hotel. There were none to be found.

"Where are they all?!"

I was getting irritated. If we didn't do it quickly, I might wake up.

"We might find one if we went away from town," she said. "There's a hotel right next to my college."

We went up a hill and at last found a hotel. We entered the lobby and stood at the reception desk. A middle-aged woman with thinning hair came out. "I'm afraid we're full," she said. "But if you'd like to wait five or ten minutes, there's sure to be a vacancy."

I couldn't be bothered to walk around looking for another hotel, so we went into the little waiting room next to the lobby. There, we sat on a sofa waiting for a vacancy. We were alone.

"Are you married?" the girl asked me.

"Yes."

"Really? And what's your wife doing now?"

"Sleeping next to me in our bedroom."

"You mean you're having a dream like this while your wife's sleeping next to you? What sort of a husband are you?!"

"And how do I know what she's dreaming about?!"

As I said that, another couple came into the hotel. I could hear the receptionist repeating the same words in the lobby.

"I'm afraid we're full. But if you'd like to wait five or ten minutes, there's sure to be a vacancy."

As the couple came into the waiting room, I let out a cry. When they saw me, they stopped in their tracks. The woman was my wife. Her partner was our neighbour, Mr Miyamoto.

"Well, well!" said Miyamoto obsequiously.

They sat on the sofa opposite us. Chubby Miyamoto looked down at the floor in embarrassment.

"Well, aren't you having a good time!" my wife said sarcastically.

"Yes, and you too!" I replied. I was going to ask how long she'd been seeing Miyamoto. But it was just a dream. It would be pointless to ask.

"She's pretty," said my wife, indicating my partner with her chin.

"Is this your wife?!" the girl said, hurrying to her feet. "Pleased to meet you. I'm, er—"

"Don't be stupid. You don't have to say anything." I tugged her back down by the edge of her skirt.

The receptionist came in. "We have a vacancy now," she announced. "This way, please."

"Well, excuse us," I said to Miyamoto and my wife as we got up to go.

The receptionist led us to our room. As soon as she'd left, I jumped on the girl, yelling "Come on, then!"

"Don't!" she shrieked. She evaded me and stood at the corner of the bed. "That woman will be back with the tea soon."

"You seem to know a lot about it!"

She blushed.

"Anyway, I can't wait for all that. Let her come in!"

The girl eluded me again.

As we continued our chasing game, the receptionist came in with the tea. "The bath water should be hot now, so please feel free. Good evening." And with that she left the room.

"I want to have a bath," said the girl.

"I can't wait for that," I moaned. "Can't you have one later?"

"Certainly not! I've been perspiring with all that walking around. You should have one after me, too. Look at your face. It's covered in sweat."

"No! I can't wait any longer!" I said, lunging at her.

She darted into the bathroom and closed the door behind her.

"All right, I'll come in with you!" I called out as I banged on the door.

"No!" she shouted. "I'd be too embarrassed."

There was nothing for it. I took off my clothes and sat on the edge of the bed, naked, waiting for her to reappear. I was getting more and more irritated. This dream seemed awfully close to reality. I even started to think it might *be* reality. So, as a test, I dug my fingernail into my right cheek. If this was a dream, it wouldn't hurt.

It hurt.

It hurt so much that it woke me up. In my sleep, I'd dug my nail hard into my cheek.

"DAMN!!!"

My wife was still sleeping peacefully, contentedly next to me. In my rage, I jumped up and punched her on the arm.

"Ow! OW!! What are you doing?!" She sprang up, startled. "Just when I was getting to the good bit!"

"Huh! You think I'm going to let you have all the fun? I'm going to go back to sleep and have the time of my life!"

"You think you're the only one? Watch me!"

We turned our backs on each other with huffs of indignation, and concentrated on getting back to sleep. Luckily, I dozed off in an instant. And I started to dream. I dreamt I was sleeping in our bed at home.

"Yesss!! A dream!"

I slipped out of the sheets. My wife was sleeping naked on the bed.

"Right! Let's get back to that hotel!"

I hunted around the bed looking for my clothes. But my shirt and trousers were nowhere to be seen. Of course they weren't. I'd taken them off in the hotel.

I quickly looked around for another pair of trousers. But I couldn't even wait that long. And anyway, it was only a dream.

"All right! I'll go as I am!"

I raced out of the house stark naked, with nothing on my feet.

I ran along the dark side road and came out onto the main street. As before, it was as bright as day and full of people. Passers-by opened their eyes wide when they saw me running through the street in my birthday suit. A few women screamed.

"Oy, you! Stop!!"

Near the crossroads, a policeman came running after me. "Stop that man! He's gone insane!"

There's always someone who gets in the way, even in a dream. A passer-by stuck out a leg and tripped me, sending me sprawling on the pavement. The policeman jumped on my back as I struggled hard to resist. "This is my dream!" I cried. "Why don't you just disappear!"

The policeman was desperately trying to handcuff me. "He's lost his mind! Help me apprehend him!" he shouted to the watching bystanders.

Four or five men stepped forwards and tried to hold me down. I was punched hard two or three times, but I hardly felt a thing. It was a dream, after all. Still, I couldn't waste any more time messing about like this. If I didn't get away soon, the girl might grow tired of waiting and leave the hotel. So, reluctantly, I decided to wake up again. Even as the policeman and bystanders were holding me down, I shouted at the top of my voice.

The sound of my voice woke me up.

"What now, for God's sake?! What are you shouting for? You've gone and woken me up again! And just when I was getting to the good bit!" My wife, also woken by the sound of my voice, flew at me in a fury.

"You think you're the only one who wants a good dream?!"
I said. I got up, took a fresh shirt and trousers from the wardrobe,
laid them down beside the bed and got back in. "This time I'll get
it right. I'll show you!"

"Well, you're not the only one!"

Once again, we turned our backs in indignation and concentrated on getting back to sleep. Again, I dropped off immediately.
And I started dreaming again.

"Yessss!!! A dream!"

I got up immediately and hurriedly pulled on the shirt and trousers
I'd laid beside the bed. I'd left my sandals in the hotel, too, so I slipped
some shoes onto my bare feet. Then I dashed out of the house. If I
failed to make it with that pretty girl this time, it would be the end
of the world. I ran through the main street with my hair all over the
place. I did knock down the odd passer-by, but this time I managed
to keep running without being challenged. I turned off the main
street onto the dark uphill road that led to the hotel. I raced up the
road panting, my whole body covered in sweat. I caught sight of the
hotel's purple neon sign. My knees were about to give way.

"Where have you been all this time?" said the girl as I rushed
into the room. Dressed in a bathrobe, she was drinking a bottle of
beer she'd taken from the fridge. She looked utterly fed up.

"Sorry about that. Come on, then. Let's get on the bed!"

As I went to embrace her, she turned her face away in disgust.

"No way! You're covered in sweat! Go and have a wash!"

All right. I took off my clothes and went into the bathroom.

When I came back out, she was on her second bottle of beer.
I suddenly remembered that I didn't have any money. I wouldn't
even be able to pay for the hotel room, let alone the beer.

Who cares, I thought. As soon as it was time to settle the bill, I'd
just shout out loud. Then I'd wake up and get away without paying.
The girl would be left behind, of course. She'd be taken away by
the police on charges of not paying for drinks or accommodation.
That would be a bit sad, but it couldn't be helped. If I told her
about it, she'd only refuse me again. Anyway, she was bound to
have some money of her own, even if she was only a student.

Alcohol had given her cheeks a rosy glow, and her eyes were beginning to look glazed. The front of her bathrobe had fallen open, revealing a glimpse of her plump white breasts.

"Come on then, let's get you on the bed. Heheh, heheh, hehe-heheheh!"

I lifted the girl in my arms and laid her down on the bed, where I undressed her.

Her body felt much too realistic for this to be a dream. *If things feel this realistic, I should have had a beer too*, I thought. I'd been thirsty just now and really needed a drink. But I thought it wouldn't taste any good, as it was just a dream. So I decided not to. Anyway, I couldn't get out of bed to have a beer now that I was in the middle of it. I started to get on with the action.

Then the doorbell rang.

The sound of it woke me up.

I was in bed, lying on top of my wife and making love to her.

"What? You??" I groaned. "The last person I wanted to be doing it with!!"

My wife had woken up at the same time. "The feeling's mutual!" she replied with immense displeasure.

The doorbell rang again. It was already morning. Sunlight flooded in through a gap in the curtains, illuminating the Dabba Dabba Tree at the foot of our bed. I'm self-employed, so I don't have to get up early.

"Who could that be? At this time of the morning?"

"Go and find out," said my wife.

"You go!"

"I haven't got anything on."

"Nor have I!"

"You can get dressed more quickly."

I got up, slipped on my shirt and trousers and went to open the front door.

Standing there in the porch was our neighbour, Mr Miyamoto.

"Mr Miyamoto!…" I was going to mention our meeting at the hotel, but I managed to stop myself in time. That was a dream, after all. "What is it? At this time of the morning?"

"Yes, I'm sorry to bother you so early. It's just that I've got this 'Dabba Dabba Tree,' you see," he said. "It's a kind of bonsai tree, and if you put it in your bedroom at night—"

"Yes, yes, yes," I interrupted. "I know, I've got one myself."

"Then you'll know what I mean. As it happens, I'm in the middle of a dream right now. Me talking to you here is actually part of my dream. Now, I've been quite keen on your wife for some time, you see. And I've always wanted to, you know, *have* her, if ever I had the chance. Well, thanks to my Dabba Dabba Tree, I can now fulfil my wish, even if it is only a dream. And that's why I've come over. So without further ado, is your wife at home?"

"She's still in bed, actually."

"So much the better!" he said, and tried to force his way in.

I barred his path in utter incredulity. "Now just you wait a minute! This may be a dream for you, but for me it's reality. I'm not going to let you barge in here and sully my wife's honour just to fulfil your dream!"

"But I really want to make love to her! Otherwise what's the point of having an erotic dream?"

As we stood there arguing, Miyamoto's wife came running up.

"Oh dear! I really am sorry for my husband's selfishness. I said you shouldn't go, didn't I?! Look how much trouble you're causing our neighbour!"

"I know what," Miyamoto said, turning to me. "You can have sex with my wife. Now that's got to be fair, hasn't it?"

"Oh!" gasped his wife. Her face immediately turned a shade of crimson. She looked up at me with fluttering eyes and started to contort her body suggestively. "I'm sure he wouldn't be interested in an ordinary woman like me."

I found it hard to agree, and looked her over. She was a slim, good-looking woman with an oval face and large eyes. Yes, now that I saw her in this light, she was actually quite attractive. I gulped.

"No, no, not at all," I eventually replied. "Quite the opposite, in fact. That is, if *you* don't mind…"

She wriggled in embarrassment. "Well! I never dreamt this would happen. I mean, I don't mind at all, if *you* don't mind…"

"Really? Well, in-in-in that case… um…" I turned to Miyamoto, to make sure it was all right by him. But he'd already slipped into the bedroom. "Right, OK, so let's get… um…"

"Right, yes, let's, shall we? Haha! Who would have thought it? Ho ho ho!" Mrs Miyamoto started to take off her blue-and-white striped dress, revealing a dark blue bra and panties underneath.

I ripped off my shirt and trousers, put my arm around her shoulders and led her into the bedroom. Her whole body was quivering with excitement. Her husband and my wife were already at it on the double bed.

"Er, excuse me, could you move over a bit?"

"Yes, of course."

Miyamoto shifted over to the edge of the bed while still making love to my wife. I flopped down on the other side with Mrs Miyamoto. We threw our arms around each other and started getting down to it.

The two women began to gasp and pant, each spurred on by the other. Then the doorbell rang.

"You go this time," I said to my wife.

"No!" she replied through her panting, shaking her head vigorously. "You go, please!!"

I reluctantly prised myself from Mrs Miyamoto's tight embrace, threw on my shirt and trousers, and went to open the front door. Standing there in the porch was the Lola Cosmetics salesgirl. Now, this woman was stunningly beautiful. I'd always had a secret lust for her.

"Er… Good morning! Is your wife at home?" she asked.

"Oh, it's you! Hehehehch!" I replied slowly. I licked my lips and rolled my eyes over her voluptuous physique, compressed into a suit of pure white. "Yes. Of course she's at home. Anyway, why don't you come in!"

She gave me a dubious look and edged into the hallway, keeping her distance at all times, before closing the door behind her.

"By the way, have you ever heard of the Dabba Dabba Tree?" I asked, still staring lewdly at her body.

"No. What's that?"

She really didn't seem to know. Realizing that it would take a while to explain, I thought hard before telling her the whole story.

"In other words, this is all part of Mr Miyamoto's erotic dream," I added in conclusion. "We are nothing but characters in his dream. So how about it? If we're merely characters in someone else's erotic dream, we might as well do something erotic too. The least we could do is have it off and enjoy ourselves!"

She looked at me as if I were mad. "I never heard anything so ridiculous in all my life. This is someone else's dream?! You must be out of your mind."

"No, you don't understand," I said with a sigh. "I'm perfectly sane. But we're in someone else's dream. Could you please take your clothes off now, quickly."

She opened her eyes wide. "What unbelievable depravity! You, a seemingly respectable householder – a-a-a respectable member of society—"

I'd had enough. So I just pounced on her. "If we don't hurry, Miyamoto will wake up!" This salesgirl was younger and more beautiful than Mrs Miyamoto. She was bound to be a much better sex partner.

As I ripped off her suit, she resisted me with all her strength. "But for us, this is reality!" she cried as she tried to hold me off. "Our lives will continue, even after your Mr Miyamoto wakes up. Then what will you do about these marks on my body?"

"Yes, you've got a point. But there's another way of looking at it. As soon as Miyamoto wakes up, we might simply cease to exist!"

She was wearing a dark brown bra and panties. Her attempts to resist had made her perspire profusely, but when I pulled down her pants, she suddenly seemed drained of all energy. She flung herself onto me with a moan. "You complete bastard," she said, and started to sob.

I lifted her in my arms and carried her into the bedroom. "Er, excuse me, could you move over a bit?" I said to the other three on the bed.

Mrs Miyamoto was still lying there in a state of limbo, just as I'd left her. When she saw the salesgirl, she cried out in despair, "No! You can't leave me like this! Finish me first!"

Miyamoto half-lifted himself off my wife and glared at me. "That's right. Dream or no dream, I won't have you insulting my wife!"

At that moment, the doorbell rang again.

"Sorry. You'll have to excuse me for a moment."

I set the salesgirl down on one side of the bed, returned to the hallway and opened the door. Standing there in the porch was a shabby middle-aged man, with what looked like a Geiger counter dangling from one hand.

"Yes. Can I help you?"

"I'm from the City Sanitation Department. Am I correct in thinking you have a Dabba Dabba Tree?"

"Yes, we do. How did you know that?"

"I thought as much," replied the Sanitation Officer. "This is an Erotic Dream Sensor. It never fails. And now, if you would let me have the tree please." And he strode into the house without so much as a by-your-leave.

"Just you wait a minute!" I called. But the Sanitation Officer walked straight into our bedroom and made for the Dabba Dabba Tree at the foot of our bed. "What do you want it for?" I asked.

"Haven't you read the morning papers? All right, I'll tell you. Recently, these Dabba Dabba Trees have been causing serious social unrest. Because of them, people can no longer distinguish dreams from reality. People have been having sex in the streets, or violating bus conductors in front of their passengers. Men have been accosting female assistants in department stores. Women have been cavorting through the streets stark naked, arousing young men in broad daylight. Girls have been asking complete strangers to go to bed with them. It's a world of sexual violence and wanton depravity. So the government has started to confiscate the Dabba Dabba Trees."

"Oh dear. I didn't realize there were so many," I said with a sigh. "But if that's what the government says, I suppose we have no choice."

"It's not fair!" moaned my wife, who was sitting on the bed listening to us. "We've only had ours one night!"

"Don't worry," said Miyamoto, raising his head from the bedclothes and scowling at the Sanitation Officer. "Because, you see, this is all happening in my dream. If I so choose, this man will no longer be allowed to exist. He will simply disappear!"

The Sanitation Officer pulled a wry face. "So there's another madman in the house, is there?!"

"You don't believe me?" said Miyamoto, standing on the bed. "So be it. I'll prove it to you. I'll prove that this is my dream." And then he shouted out at the top of his voice.

Miyamoto was awoken by the sound of his own voice. And in that instant, everyone else simply ceased to exist.

Rumours About Me

I was surprised to hear my name mentioned on the evening news one day.

"And now, other news," said the announcer. "Earlier today, Tsutomu Morishita asked Akiko Mikawa out for a drink, but was turned down. Mikawa works as a secretary in the same company as Morishita. This is the fifth time Morishita has asked Mikawa out for a date. He's been refused on all but the first occasion."

"W-what? WHAT??" I slammed my cup down on the table as I looked on in disbelief. "What was that? What did he say??"

My face appeared large on the TV screen.

The newsreader continued."It's not yet clear why Mikawa continues to reject Morishita. Hiruma Sakamoto, a friend and work colleague of Mikawa, thinks it's because – although Mikawa doesn't particularly dislike Morishita – she doesn't particularly like him either."

Now a photo of Akiko Mikawa appeared on the screen.

"In view of this evidence, it's thought that Morishita failed to leave any impression at all on Mikawa during that original date. According to well-informed sources, Morishita went straight to his apartment after work today, and is now eating a meal that he prepared by himself. Well, that's all we have on Tsutomu Morishita for today. Now let's go over to our correspondent at the Yakuyoke Hachiman Night Festival in Kobe. I imagine things are starting to hot up now, Mizuno-san?"

"Yes, that's absolutely right."

I sat there open-mouthed, staring at the screen blankly as the next item continued.

I eventually came to my senses. "What was that all about?" I muttered to myself.

I was hallucinating. That was it. I was seeing things. And hearing things. That was the only explanation. I mean, what would be the point in reporting that I'd asked Akiko Mikawa out for a drink and was so spectacularly rejected, as always? The news value was zero.

All the same, it still seemed so real – the pictures of me and Akiko, the captions under the photographs, the newsreader's manner, everything.

"Don't be daft!" I told myself, shaking my head vigorously.

The news ended.

I nodded to myself. "A hallucination. Yes. That's what it was," I said. "But hey, what a realistic hallucination!"

I laughed. My laughter reverberated around my tiny bedsit room.

What if the news had been real, I wondered. What if Akiko Mikawa had seen it, what if my workmates had seen it? What would they have thought? I had myself in stitches just imagining their faces.

Now I was laughing uncontrollably. "Wahahahahahaha, hoohoohoo, hahaha, hee, hee, wahahahahahahahaha!!!"

I climbed into bed, but still the laughter wouldn't subside.

There was an article about me in the morning paper.

MORISHITA REJECTED AGAIN

At around 4.40 yesterday afternoon, Tsutomu Morishita (28, an employee of Kasumiyama Electric Industries, Sanko-cho, Shinjuku, Tokyo) invited Akiko Mikawa (23, a secretary at the same company) out for a drink after work. Mikawa refused, claiming she had to go home early. Morishita was wearing a red tie with green polka dots, which he'd bought in a Shinjuku supermarket the previous day. Morishita later returned to his apartment in Higashi-cho, Kichijoji, and made his own dinner. He is thought to have gone to bed immediately after eating, as usual. This is the fourth time Morishita has been refused by Miss Mikawa.

There was a picture of me next to the article, the same one as had been used on television the night before. But there was no picture of Akiko Mikawa. I was obviously the main subject of this story.

I read the article four or five times while drinking a glass of milk. Then I tore the newspaper up and threw it into the bin.

"It's a conspiracy!" I muttered. "Someone's playing a practical joke on me. My God! All this just to have a laugh!"

Whoever it was, they'd need a lot of money. Even a single copy of a newspaper would be expensive to print. Who could it be? Who would go to such bizarre lengths just to get at me?

I couldn't remember offending anyone that much. Perhaps it was someone else who fancied Akiko Mikawa. But what was the point? She'd done nothing but reject me.

No, this must be someone really perverse, I thought. Trouble was, I couldn't think of anyone who could possibly be that perverse.

Damn! I should have kept the newspaper, I thought on my way to the station. I regretted losing my temper. If I'd kept the newspaper, it might have helped me to ferret out the culprit. It would have been evidence once I'd found him.

I forced myself onto the packed commuter train and found a place to stand in the middle of the carriage. I thought about all the people I knew. Then I caught sight of a newspaper being read by the man standing next to me. It was a different newspaper to mine, but it also had an article about me. And this time, it occupied two whole columns.

I gasped audibly.

The man looked up from his newspaper, glanced back at the photograph next to the article, then looked up again and stared at me. I hurriedly turned my back.

Who had done this?! I was livid. The villain had actually replaced all the morning papers along this line with fake ones. He wanted to make sure the article was seen not just by me but also by everyone else who took the same train as me. In that way, he could make a complete fool of me and vilify my name. And of course, the ultimate intention was to make me lose my mind. I filled my lungs with the stuffy air inside the packed train. The bastard! I wasn't going to play his game! No one was going to drive me mad!

I laughed aloud. "Hahahahahaha! Who's going mad, then?" I shouted. "I'm not!! Hahahahahaha!"

At Shinjuku Station, an announcer was barking over the loud-speakers. "Shinjuku. This is Shinjuku. Change here for the Yamanote Line. The train on Platform 2 is for Yotsuya, Kanda and Tokyo. By the way, Tsutomu Morishita was on this train today. All he's had this morning is a glass of milk. Mind the doors!"

There was nothing unusual about the atmosphere at work. But as soon as I walked into the office, seven or eight of my colleagues started tapping each other on the shoulder, giving me sidelong glances and whispering to each other. They must be talking about me, I concluded.

After clearing a few memos from my desk, I went over to Admin. In the office were four secretaries, one of them Akiko Mikawa. As soon as they saw me, they changed their expressions and started typing feverishly on their keyboards. It was quite obvious – they hadn't been working but talking about me until that very moment.

Ignoring Akiko, I called Hiruma Sakamoto out to the corridor.

"Was someone enquiring after me yesterday?" I asked.

She looked as if she were about to cry. "I'm really sorry," she answered nervously. "I didn't know they were journalists! I didn't think they'd put it all in the newspaper like that!"

"They?! Who?"

"There were four or five men. Of course, I didn't know any of them. They accosted me on my way home and asked all sorts of things about you."

"Hmmm." That got me thinking. The conspiracy was clearly much more sinister than I'd imagined.

Just after lunch, I was called to the Chief Clerk's desk. After issuing a new work assignment, he gave me a knowing look. "I read about it in the paper," he whispered.

"Oh?" I answered, not knowing quite what to say.

The Chief Clerk grinned and brought his face close to mine.

"You can't trust the media, can you. But don't worry. Personally, I couldn't be less interested." The liar. He was loving every minute.

My new assignment took me out of the building and into a taxi. The young cabbie had his radio on at full volume.

"Ginza 2nd Street, please."

"Eh? What's that?"

He couldn't hear me for the music.

"Ginza 2nd Street."

"Ginza what Street?"

"Second. Ginza 2nd Street."

The cabbie finally understood, and the taxi set off.

The music ended. An announcer started talking.

"This is the news at two o'clock. The government this morning ordered all laughing bags to be confiscated from shops throughout the country. Police nationwide have been instructed to clamp down on the illegal manufacture or sale of the bags. Laughing bags are novelty toys that emit a hysterical laughing noise. Today's move follows a dramatic surge in social unrest caused by nuisance calls using the bags. Calls are often made at two or three o'clock in the morning. When the victim answers, the caller makes the bag laugh into the telephone. There have also been reports of a phenomenon known as 'laughing-bag rage'.

"Tsutomu Morishita arrived at work on time this morning. Soon after entering his office, he went to the Administration Department and called Hiruma Sakamoto out to the corridor, where the two were observed in conversation. The precise nature of their discussion is not yet clear. Details will be announced as soon as they're known. Later, Morishita went out on company business, and is currently travelling towards central Tokyo in a taxi.

"The Ministry of Health & Welfare today released the results of a nationwide survey of pachinko game-machine users and designers. The results suggest that playing pachinko after eating eels can be very detrimental to health. According to Tadashi Akanemura, Chairman of the National Federation of Game-Machine Designers—"

The cabbie switched the radio off – he probably wasn't too interested in the news.

Was my name really that well known? I closed my eyes and thought about it. Could I really be so famous, when there was nothing distinctive about me at all? After all, I was nothing but a lowly office worker, a company employee. No one as unremarkable as me could possibly merit attention in the world of the media.

So just how well-known was my name, my face? Take this cabbie. Was he aware that the person mentioned on the news just now was none other than the passenger in the back of his cab? Had he recognized me as soon as I got in? Or did he actually know nothing about me at all?

I decided to test him. "Er, driver? Do you know who I am?"

He checked me out in the rear-view mirror. "Have we met somewhere, sir?"

"No. I don't think so."

"Well then, I don't know you, do I."

There was a pause. "You're not one of them celebrities, are you sir?" he asked at length.

"No. Just an office worker."

"You been on telly?"

"No. Never."

The cabbie smiled wryly. "Then I'm not going to know you, am I sir."

"No," I replied. "I suppose not."

I thought back over the radio news I'd just heard. The announcer knew that I was in a taxi heading for central Tokyo. That meant someone must be following me. They must be watching my every move. I turned and looked through the rear window. The road was full of cars – it was impossible to know which of them was following us. Come to think of it, they all looked pretty suspicious now.

"I think someone's following us," I said to the cabbie. "Can you shake them off?"

"That's a lot to ask, sir, if you don't mind me saying so," he said with a grimace. "Unless you know which car it is. Anyway, you'd have a job shaking anyone off in this traffic."

"I think it's that black Nissan. Look! It's got a newspaper company flag on it!"

"Well, all right sir, if you insist. Though, personally, I just think you're being paranoid, sir."

"I'm perfectly sane," I countered hastily. "Don't go taking me to the madhouse, will you!"

The taxi meandered and roamed aimlessly for a while, as if driven by a sleepwalker, before finally arriving in Ginza 2nd Street.

"Well, I lost the black Nissan at least," the cabbie said with a broad smile. "That must be worth something!"

I reluctantly added five hundred yen to the fare on the meter.

On entering the office of our client in Ginza 2nd Street, I was greeted with uncommon courtesy by a female receptionist whose face I recognized. She led me to a special reception lounge for particularly valued guests. Normally, I'd be called to the duty clerk's desk, and would stand there talking while he remained seated.

I sat myself on a sofa in the spacious lounge and was fidgeting in some discomfort when, to my surprise, the Department Director walked in with his assistant. They both started greeting me with particular formality.

"Suzuki is always most glad of your kind assistance," said the Department Director, bowing deeply. Suzuki was the duty clerk who usually saw me.

As I sat there bewildered, the Department Director and his assistant, far from discussing the business at hand, started to heap sycophantic praise on me. They admired my tie, flattered my dress sense, and even started extolling my good looks. In my embarrassment, I hurriedly handed over the documents I'd been given by the Chief Clerk, passed on his message and quickly took my leave.

As I left the building, I noticed the same taxi still waiting there by the pavement.

The young cabbie thrust his head through the side window. "Sir," he called.

"Still here, are you?" I said. "Well, that's perfect. Take me back to Shinjuku, will you."

I was just settling into the rear seat when the cabbie thrust a five-hundred-yen note towards me. "You can have this back, sir," he said. "You've got to be joking!"

"Is something the matter?"

"I switched the radio back on, didn't I. And they were talking about you, weren't they. They said you'd been carried off by a rogue taxi driver, who'd deliberately taken you out of your way and squeezed five hundred yen out of you for it! They even mentioned my name!"

Now I understood why I'd been treated so courteously at the client's office.

"I told you, didn't I? We were being followed!"

"Whatever. You can have your five hundred yen back."

"Go on. You keep it."

"No way! Have it back!"

"Well… All right. If that's the way you feel. Anyway, will you take me to Shinjuku now?"

"How could I say no? Next thing they'd say I refused a fare!"

And with that he started off towards Shinjuku.

I was gradually realizing that the plot to drive me out of my mind was unimaginably massive in scale. Apart from anything else, my enemy appeared to have bought off the mass media. Who on earth could it be? And what was his motive? Why would anyone want to do something like this?

All I could do was to follow the flow for now. It would be virtually impossible to uncover the mastermind at the bottom of it. Even if I caught one of my pursuers, he would just be small fry. He wouldn't know who the mastermind was. That was the big cheese – big enough to buy off the media, at least!

"I'm not trying to make excuses, sir," the cabbie said suddenly. "But I did lose that black Nissan. I did, really."

"I'm sure you did," I replied. "But I reckon it's not that simple anyway. They're not just following me in a car. They've probably even bugged this taxi."

Hold on a minute, I thought. How did I know I could trust this driver, anyway? He could be in on it too. Otherwise, how did they know the tip was five hundred yen?

I suddenly noticed a helicopter circling above us. It was flying at dangerously low altitude, almost skimming the tops of the buildings.

"I'm sure I saw that chopper on the way out, sir," said the driver, squinting up at the sky. "Maybe they're the ones that are following you."

There was a thunderous crash, and a blood-coloured flash of light streaked across the sky. I looked up to see fireballs flying in all directions. The helicopter had crashed into the top floor of a multi-storey building. The pilot must have been paying too much attention to events on the ground and lost control.

"Serves him right! Hehehehehehheh!"

The cabbie laughed insanely as he sped away from the scene. He already had the look of a deranged man.

I knew I'd be in danger if I stayed in the taxi any longer. "Ah, I've just remembered something," I said. "Could you let me off here." Actually, I'd remembered there was a small psychiatric clinic nearby.

"Where are you going?" the cabbie asked.

"That's my business," I answered.

"Well, I'm going straight home to sleep," he continued. He looked pale-faced as he took the fare from me. That decided it – he wasn't one of them.

"Good idea," I said as I stepped out into the unbearable heat.

I entered the clinic and sat in the waiting room for about twenty minutes. An apparently hysterical middle-aged woman was followed by an apparently epileptic young man. I was next. I went into the treatment room, where the doctor was looking at a television on a desk by the window. News of the helicopter crash was just coming through.

"Oh dear, oh dear, oh dear. Even the sky's getting congested now," the doctor muttered as he turned to face me. "And of course, there'll be more patients as a result. But they won't come for treatment until it's too late, oh no. Another bad characteristic of people today."

"Yes, you're right," I said with a nod of agreement. I didn't want to seem pushy, but jumped straight in and started to explain my situation anyway. I was supposed to be at work, after all, and didn't have much time. "They suddenly started talking about me on

TV last night. And there were articles about me in this morning's papers. They made an announcement about me at the station. I was even mentioned on the radio. At work, they're all talking about me in whispers. I'm sure they've bugged my house and the taxis I travel in. In fact, I'm being followed. It's a major operation. That helicopter on the news crashed while it was following me!"

The doctor stared at me with a pitiful expression as I continued my story. Finally, however, he made a gesture to signal that he could take no more. "Why didn't you come to me sooner?" he moaned. "But no. You only come when your condition is already too serious! You give me no option but to admit you to hospital immediately — by force if necessary! For there's no doubt about it at all. You are suffering from a persecution complex, a victim complex — in other words, total paranoid delusion. A classic case of schizophrenia. Luckily, there's no loss of personality as yet. I'll admit you to the university hospital right away. Leave it to me."

"Wait a minute!" I said. "I was in a hurry, I didn't explain myself well! I had a feeling you wouldn't believe me. I'm not a good talker, I can't express things logically. But everything I've just said, it's nothing to do with any complex — it's plain fact! Yet I'm just an ordinary office worker — certainly not famous enough to be followed by the media! No, however you look at it, these media people who are tailing me, reporting about me — yes, even someone as ordinary as me — they're the ones who are insane! I just came here to ask your advice, you know, what you think I should do to cope with all this. You've written books about the pathological tendencies of society and the perversion of the media. You've talked about it on TV. That's why I came here. I hoped you could tell me how to adapt to this abnormal environment without losing my sanity!"

The doctor shook his head and picked up the telephone. "Everything you've said merely proves how serious your case is!"

His hand stopped dead as he was dialling. His eyes were now riveted to the picture on his desktop television. It was a picture of me. The doctor opened his eyes wide.

"Some news just in on the Morishita case," said the announcer. "After leaving his client's office in Ginza 2nd Street, Tsutomu Morishita, an employee of Kasumiyama Electric Industries, took another taxi, apparently intending to return to his office in Shinjuku. But he suddenly appeared to change his mind, left the taxi and entered the Takehara Psychiatric Clinic in Yotsuya."

A photograph of the clinic's main entrance appeared on the screen.

"It is not yet known why Morishita entered the Clinic."

The doctor stared at me with glazed eyes, as if in admiration. His mouth was half-open, his tongue dancing about in excitement. "So you must be someone famous, then?"

"No. Not at all." I pointed at the television. "He just said it, didn't he? I'm a company employee. Just an ordinary person. But in spite of that, my every move is being watched and broadcast to the entire nation. What's that, if not abnormal?!"

"Well. You asked me how you could adapt to an abnormal environment without losing your sanity." As he spoke, the doctor slowly got up and moved towards a glass cabinet crammed with bottles of drugs. "But I find your question contradictory. An environment is created by the people who live in it. You, then, are one of the people who are creating your abnormal environment. In other words, if your environment is abnormal, then you must be abnormal too." He opened a brown bottle labelled 'Sedatives' and tipped a quantity of white pills into his hand.

The doctor greedily stuffed the pills into his mouth as he continued to speak. "Therefore, if you persist in asserting your own sanity, it proves, conversely, that your environment is in fact normal, but that you alone are abnormal. If you consider your environment to be abnormal, then by all means lose your mind!" He took a bottle of ink from his desk and gulped down the blue-black liquid until it was empty. Then he collapsed onto the couch beside him and fell asleep.

"On a mad, mad morning in May, two lovers drank dry a bottle of bright blue ink," hummed a nurse as she entered the treatment room, completely naked. In one of her hands she held a huge bottle of ink, from which she took the occasional swig before draping her body over the doctor's on the couch.

So I left the clinic without receiving a satisfactory answer. The sun was going down, but it still felt oppressively hot.

As soon as I was back at my desk, Akiko Mikawa called me from Admin. "Thank you for inviting me out yesterday," she said. "I'm really sorry I couldn't make it."

"That's all right," I replied with undue reserve.

She said nothing for a while. She was waiting for me to ask her out again. She'd obviously noticed that public opinion was starting to shift towards me, and was probably worried that she would now become the butt of media vitriol. She'd called me in the hope of accepting an invitation.

We both remained silent for a few moments.

I sighed before plunging in. "How about today, then?"

"I'd love to."

"All right, I'll see you in the San José after work."

News of our arrangement must have been reported immediately. For, as I walked into the San José, it seemed unusually busy. Normally, it wasn't that kind of place. All the customers were couples, making it impossible to tell which were reporters and which merely curiosity-seekers. But whichever they were, they'd obviously come with one aim in mind – to observe my date with Akiko. While of course feigning a lack of interest, they would give themselves away by glancing over at us every now and again.

Needless to say, for the whole hour that Akiko and I were in the café, we sat in stony silence with our drinks in front of us. For if we'd discussed anything even slightly unusual, it would immediately have been reported in a three-column article with a massive headline.

We parted at Shinjuku Station, and I returned to my apartment. I hesitated for a while, but eventually switched on the television.

In a change to the evening's schedule, they were showing a panel discussion.

"Now, I think we come to a very difficult question at this point," said the presenter. "If events continue to unfold at this pace, when do you think Morishita and Mikawa might be booking into a hotel? Or do you think it might not come to that? Professor Ohara?"

"Well, this Akiko is a bit of a shy filly, if you know what I mean," said Professor Ohara, a racing expert. "It all depends on Morishita's persistence and determination in the saddle."

"It's all in the stars," said a female astrologer, holding up a card. "It'll be towards the end of the month."

Why on earth would we want to go to a hotel, I wondered. If we did, our voices would be recorded and our positions photographed. The whole thing would be reported all over the country, exposing us to universal shame.

Things continued in a similar vein for the next few days.

Then, on my way to work one morning, my heart sank when I saw an ad for a women's magazine inside the packed commuter train.

"READ ALL ABOUT IT – TSUTOMU AND AKIKO'S CAFÉ DATE!"

– it said in large bold letters, next to a photo of my face. And underneath that, in smaller type:

"Morishita masturbated twice that night"

I was boiling with rage and grating my teeth. "Don't I have a right to privacy?" I shouted. "I'll sue for defamation! Who cares how many times I did it?!"

On my arrival at work, I went straight to the Chief Clerk's desk and presented him with a copy of the magazine, which I'd bought at the station. "I'd like permission to leave the office on personal business. I assume you know about this article. I'm going to complain to the company that publishes this magazine."

"Of course, I understand how you feel," the Chief Clerk said in a faltering voice, evidently trying to pacify me. "But there's surely no point in losing your temper, is there? The media are too powerful. Of course, I'd always give you permission to leave the office on personal business. As you know, I'm quite flexible when it comes to that kind of thing. I'm sure you're aware of that. Yes. I'm sure you are. But I'm just concerned for your welfare, you see. I agree, it's pretty disgraceful. This article, yes, it's disgraceful. Yes. I can certainly sympathize with your predicament."

"It really is disgraceful."

"Yes, utterly disgraceful."

A number of my colleagues had come to stand around me and the Chief Clerk. They all started to sympathize with me in unison. Some of the female clerks were actually weeping.

But I wasn't going to be taken in by that. Behind my back, they were all swapping nasty rumours about me and cooperating with the media coverage. Theirs was the inevitable duplicity of those who surround the famous.

Even the company president came over to have his say. So I abandoned the idea of complaining to the publishing company. Now, the strange thing was that, even though I'd ranted and raved like a lunatic, not a word of it was reported in the TV news that day. Nor was it mentioned in the evening paper. So I took a long, hard look at the way in which news about me had been reported over the past few days.

Everything I did in awareness of the media was omitted from the news. For example, the fact that I'd tried to shake off my pursuers, or that I'd lost my temper and shouted about the magazine article. These were either ignored altogether, or reported in a different context. Not only that, but news of the helicopter that crashed into a building while following me was reported as if it were a completely unrelated event. In this respect, the coverage was quite different to that usually given to celebrities. To be more exact, the media were presenting a world in which they themselves didn't exist.

But therein lay the reason why the news about me was gradually growing in scale, why people were taking an interest in this news. I'd become *a nobody who was known by everybody*. One day, for example, the morning paper had an article about me, written with a huge headline straddling six columns on the front page:

"Tsutomu Morishita Eats Eels!
First Time in Sixteen Months"

Occasionally, I'd stumble across people secretly trying to collect information about me. After using the company toilet, I would half-open the door to the next cubicle, only to discover a knot of reporters crammed into it, tape recorders and cameras dangling from their shoulders. Or on my way home, I'd rummage about in the bushes with the tip of my umbrella, only for a female TV announcer holding a microphone to dash out and run away shrieking.

Once, while watching television in my apartment, I suddenly leapt up and slid open the door of my built-in wardrobe. A huddle of four or five journalists (some female) tumbled out of the wardrobe onto the floor. Another time, I pushed up a ceiling panel with a broom handle. A photographer hiding in the attic, in his frantic effort to escape, put his foot through the ceiling and fell to the ground. I even pulled up my *tatami* matting and looked under the floorboards. A melée of reporters and hangers-on crouching in the floorwell hollered and fled in panic.

Of course, none of this was ever reported in the news. The media only ever covered my dull, everyday affairs. These were blown up into major headliners, even surpassing politics, world events, the economy and other more important topics. For example:

"TM Buys a Tailored Suit in Monthly Instalments!"
"Another Date for Tsutomu Morishita"
"Revealed! Tsutomu's Weekly Diet!"
"Who Does Morishita Really Want? Akiko Mikawa – or Someone Else?!"
"TM Slams Co-worker Fujita (25) over Paperwork Error"
"Shock! Mozza's Sex Life!"
"Tsutomu Morishita: Pay Day Today"
"What Will Tsutomu Do with This Month's Pay?"
"Morishita Buys Another Pair of Socks (Blue-grey, 350 Yen)"

In the end, there were even expert analysts who knew everything that could be known about me. I was quite amazed.

One day, I found my photograph on the front of a weekly magazine published by a newspaper company. A colour photograph. Of course, I had no idea when it was taken. It showed me on my way to work among a group of office workers. It was quite a good picture, actually, if I say so myself.

Writing articles about me was one thing. But if they wanted to use me as a model on their cover, I would expect the newspaper company to thank me at the very least. I waited three days, four days after the magazine had been published, but still heard nothing. Finally, I'd had enough. On my way back from a client one day, I paid them a visit.

Normally, I only had to walk down the street for everyone to be turning and gawking at me. But as soon as I entered the newspaper company building, I was treated with total indifference by receptionists and staff alike. It was almost as if they'd never heard of me. I regretted going there at all, as I waited in the reception lounge. Then a man with a sour face appeared and identified himself as the magazine's Assistant Chief Editor.

"Listen, Mr Morishita. We'd prefer it if you didn't come here, you understand."

"I thought so. Because I'm supposed to be a nobody who has no connection with the media?"

"You're not talented or topical. You're not even famous. So you have no business coming here."

"But I am, aren't I? I am famous now!"

"You're merely a nobody whose life was reported in the media. You were supposed to remain anonymous, even when people recognized you. We thought you'd understand that well enough."

"So why did a nobody like me have to be reported on the news?"

The Assistant Chief Editor sighed wearily. "How should I know?! I suppose someone decided you were newsworthy."

"Someone? You mean someone in the media? What idiot had that idea?"

"Idiot, you say? As if there's just one person at the bottom of it? In that case, why are all the media companies falling over each other to follow you? The media don't need to be told. They'll only follow someone if they think he's got news value."

"News value? In the daily life of a nobody?"

"All right then. You tell me. What news items would you consider important?"

"Well... Something about the weather forecast being wrong... A war going on somewhere... A ten-minute power failure... An aeroplane crashes, killing a thousand... The price of apples goes up... Someone's bitten by a dog... A dog is caught shoplifting in a supermarket... The US President is caught shoplifting... Man lands on Mars... An actress gets divorced... The war to end all wars is about to start... A company profits from pollution... Another newspaper company makes a profit..."

The Assistant Chief Editor watched me vacantly as I continued. But now he shook his head with a look of pity. "So those are the things you regard as big news, are they?"

"Aren't they?" I replied in some confusion.

He waved his hand with an air of irritation. "No, no, no, no, no. Of course, they could be *made* into big news. That's why they're duly reported. But at the same time, we report on the life of an ordinary office worker. Anything can become big news if the media report it," he said, nodding. "News value only arises *after* something's been reported. But you, by coming here today, have completely destroyed your own news value."

"That doesn't bother me."

"I see." He slapped his thigh. "Actually, it doesn't bother us either."

I hurried back to the office. From my desk, I immediately phoned through to Admin.

"Akiko," I said loudly. "Will you go to a hotel with me tonight?"

I could hear Akiko catching her breath at the other end of the line.

For a moment, the whole room fell silent. My colleagues and the Chief Clerk gawped at me in amazement.

Eventually she replied. "Yes. Of course," she sobbed.

And so that night, Akiko and I stayed in a hotel. It was the shabbiest, seediest hotel in a street full of tasteless neon signs.

As I'd expected, there was no mention of it in the newspapers. Nor was it reported on the TV news. From that day on, news about me vanished from the media. In my place came a middle-aged office worker, the type that can be found just about everywhere. Thin, short, two children, lives on a suburban estate, a clerk in a shipbuilding company.

I'd once again become a nobody – this time for real.

Some time later, I asked Akiko out again as a test. Would she like to have coffee with me after work? Of course, she refused. But I was satisfied – now I knew what sort of person she was.

A month later, nobody could remember my face. But even then, people would occasionally stop and give me curious looks when they saw me. On my way home one day, two girls were sitting opposite me on the train. One of them gave me that look and started whispering to the other.

"Hey! Haven't I seen him somewhere before?" she said, nudging her friend with her elbow. "What was it he did?"

The other girl looked at me with a bored expression. After a moment, she answered in a tone of utter boredom: "Oh, him. Yeah. He was just a nobody."

Don't Laugh

I had a call from Saita, a bachelor friend of mine, an electric-appliances repair specialist with four technical patents to his name.

"Would you mind coming over?" he said in a tremulous little voice like a mosquito's hum.

"Why? Is something wrong? Has something happened?" I asked.

"Well… You know," he mumbled, then said nothing for a moment. He seemed to be looking for the right words. "Well, I'll tell you when you get here."

It was a diffident voice. Usually, he'd be loudly and forcefully debating with me on subjects like topology, relativity or parallel universes – so much so that I could hardly get a word in edgeways.

"You in a hurry then?"

"Yes. Well, no. It's not particularly urgent. But if you're free… Well, you know. It would help if you came over right away."

His voice sounded even more hesitant now, almost apologetic. But his odd tone had the opposite effect on me – it made me think something really serious must have happened. So I agreed to go over right away.

His shop was on the main street. As I walked in, he greeted me with an "Oh, hi", gazed at me with an expression of utter gratitude, and led me to a small reception area at the back of the shop. There, Saita and I sat facing each other across a table.

"What's up, then? What's happened?" I asked with deliberate nonchalance, taking out a cigarette. He was clearly finding it hard to come to the point.

"Well," he replied, then hesitated again. For a while, he rubbed his palms together, drew circles on the table with his fingertips and stared into space. "Well, it's not such a big deal, really…"

"But you said I should come right away!"

"Yes, that's right." He was cringing with embarrassment, squirming in his seat. Then he glanced up at me with a coy look. "Well, actually," he said, and started to giggle.

It couldn't be anything serious if he could laugh about it. But why on earth was he so embarrassed? I'd never seen him like this before.

Though now quite irritated, I was beginning to catch his giggles.

"What? What's it all about? Tell me, quick!"

His face turned red. "All right. Well, I'll tell you," he said in a throwaway tone, giggling again. He glanced at me briefly before averting his eyes. "I'll tell you. But please. Don't laugh."

"You're laughing, aren't you?!" I said, laughing.

"Am I? Oh. Well, anyway…" This was all quite unlike him.

"What, then?"

"Well, I've invented a time machine," he said.

He clearly didn't know whether to laugh or cry.

I said nothing for a moment. If I'd opened my mouth, I would have exploded with laughter. But I could do nothing about the uncontrollable ripples that were spreading all over my body – bad though I felt about it.

Saita glanced at me sideways and writhed in embarrassment. "D-d-don't laugh. Don't."

In the end, I let out a suppressed snort.

Saita, still with his half-laughing, half-weeping expression, now laughed aloud.

"Wahahahahaha!"

I laughed too.

"Wahahahahaha!"

Saita stopped laughing abruptly. He looked at me rather forlornly as I continued to laugh with no apparent end.

I eventually managed to control myself.

"Sorry," I said, trying my hardest to suppress the chortles. "Tell me again. What have you done?"

As if to contain his embarrassment, Saita rubbed his palms hard over the surface of the desk as he answered.

"Er, invented a t-t-time machine."

"Wahahahahaha!" I gripped my sides.

"Wahahahahaha!" Saita started to laugh like a madman.

We contorted our bodies, bent ourselves double, bent backwards, then contorted our bodies again as we continued to laugh. For a long time we continued to laugh.

At last, our laughter subsided to a point at which we could speak again.

"Have you invented a time machine?" I asked.

"I've invented a time machine," he answered.

We burst into laughter again. We continued to laugh even more insanely than before. For a long time we continued to laugh.

"That's ridiculous," I said in a wheezing voice as I held my aching belly, my face still contorted with laughter. "You've gone and invented a time machine!"

I was virtually laughing my head off. "And where is it, then?" I asked with heaving shoulders.

Still laughing, Saita pointed to the ceiling with his chin. His workshop was on the upper floor, which resembled a loft. He got up and started climbing the stairs to the upper floor. I followed him. In a corner of the workshop was a time machine.

"Is this a time machine?" I asked.

Saita nodded. "Yes. This is a time machine."

We both exploded with laughter at the same time. We pointed at the machine and laughed, pointed at each other's faces and laughed, squatted on the floor, coughed convulsively, and gripped our aching sides as we continued to laugh.

"That's ri-ri-ridiculous!" I said, as wheezing sounds issued from my throat. "How does it work? Go on, tell me!"

Saita, also with shoulders heaving, still managed to climb slowly into the time machine. "Come on in," he said.

"All right," I answered. The laughter had finally subsided, but it was not without the occasional giggle that I got into the time machine and sat next to Saita. "So, are you going to explain?"

"Yes. Well, first of all…" he started in his timid little voice. He scratched his head in embarrassment, and sheepishly pointed to one of the dials with his chubby index finger. "Th-this dial, you see, well, it's for going back in time."

"Wahahahahaha!" I was already gripping my stomach before he could finish.

"Wahahahahaha!" Saita opened his mouth wide and laughed too.

We contorted our bodies and rolled around with laughter as we sat there in the time machine.

Still laughing, Saita casually pointed to another dial. "And this one's for going forwards."

"Wahahahahaha!"

"Wahahahahaha!"

I laughed so much that I thought I would die. Eventually, we stopped and looked at each other's half-crazed faces in the time machine, our face muscles floppy with fatigue from laughing.

"I thought I was going to die," I said.

"So did I," said Saita.

"Just now, when you said you'd invented a time machine," I said with another involuntary snort, "that was b-b-brilliant!"

Saita also let out a snort. We continued to laugh for a while.

"How about going back to see it," I suggested through my giggles, pointing to the dial with my chin. "You can do that, can't you?"

"Yes, I can. Shall we then?" Saita agreed with a giggle of his own.

Still giggling, he turned the dial very slightly, then pressed a button and gave me a nod. "Right. Let's get out."

"All right."

We got out of the time machine, lay flat on the floor, and peered down into the shop below through cracks between the floorboards. I hadn't arrived yet. Saita was on his own, pacing up and down nervously inside the shop.

"Someone's pacing up and down."

"It's me," said Saita.

We were both about to laugh, but hurriedly covered each other's mouths with our hands. Our eyes widened. Only our bodies continued to laugh.

We peered through the cracks again.

I arrived.

"Oh, hi," said Saita.

Saita and I sat facing each other in the reception area at the back of the shop.

"What's up, then? What's happened?" I asked, taking out a cigarette.

"Well…" Saita drew circles on the table top. "Well, it's not such a big deal, really…"

"But you said I should come right away!"

"Yes, that's right. Well, actually," he said, and started to giggle.

"What? What's it all about? Tell me, quick!"

"All right. Well, I'll tell you. I'll tell you. But please. Don't laugh."

"You're laughing, aren't you?!"

"Am I? Oh. Well, anyway…"

"What, then?"

"Well, I've invented a time machine."

"…………………"

"D-d-don't laugh. Don't."

"…………………"

"Wahahahahaha!"

"Wahahahahaha!"

"…………………"

"Sorry. Tell me again. What have you done?"

"Er, invented a t–t–time machine."

"Wahahahahaha!"

"Wahahahahaha!"

"Have you invented a time machine?"

"I've invented a time machine."

"Wahahahahaha!"

"Wahahahahaha!"

"That's ridiculous. You've gone and invented a time machine."

39

"Wahahahahaha!"
"Wahahahahaha!"
We wanted to laugh, but couldn't. So we covered our mouths with our hands and writhed around in contortions on the floor of the upstairs room.

Farmer Airlines

A typhoon started to blow soon after we left the capital. All trains and boats were delayed, forcing us to make unscheduled stops. It was the morning of the third day – the last morning of a three-day trip – when we finally set eyes on our destination: Tit Island.

"Ah. That explains the name." My photographer Hatayama pointed a finger out across the sea. The island had a single, round mountain in its centre. To be more exact, the mountain *was* the island.

We were being ferried across in a fisherman's boat, lurching in all directions with the movement of the waves.

"Is there some legend attached to the island?" I asked as the fisherman rowed on.

"What if there is," he replied with a surly expression. "Look at the shape of it. There's bound to be a story or two. Just like any other island. But we keep them to ourselves. If word got round about our legends, tourists would come pouring in. The place would be wrecked."

So that was one thing less for me to write about. How disappointing.

"What an excellent policy!" said Hatayama with more than a hint of sarcasm. The fisherman grimaced and sniffed loudly. He'd been very reluctant to bring his boat out at all, saying another typhoon was on the way. But we'd managed to persuade him with bribery and a certain amount of grovelling. He was stubborn all the same, as he'd taken an instant dislike to us city types.

"Look! Terraced fields!" cried Hatayama in amazement. He was staring wide-eyed at the foot of the mountain. "I thought it was supposed to be uninhabited!"

"Oh yes! So there are!"

I had every reason to be dismayed. Our magazine had started its 'Uninhabited Islands' series in the previous month's issue. If there were people living on the island, I'd have nothing to write about.

"Daah! No one lives there," said the fisherman. "People from Shiokawa just go across in boats to farm beans and potatoes."

Well, that was a relief.

Shiokawa was a small farming-fishing village on the mainland. We'd stayed there the night before, in the village's single, shabby little inn.

That morning, I'd made a long-distance call from the inn to our Editor-in-Chief in Tokyo. I'd told him we'd be late in reaching the island because of the typhoon, and that our return would also be delayed by a couple of days. For no good reason he'd flown into a rage, accused me of taking it easy when everyone else was working hard, reminded me that 'Uninhabited Islands' was originally my idea, and said that I'd only submitted it because I wanted to skive off work. He'd ordered me to be back in the office by the following morning at the latest. If I wasn't, I'd have my wages docked and the series would be pulled. That had brought me right down. I wondered if we really could return by the following morning. If another typhoon started up, there was no way we'd get back in time. I let out a gloomy sigh when I realized what a disastrous idea it had been.

"The Chief lacks ambition," said Hatayama, intuiting the reason for my sigh. "If he can't see you in front of his nose, he thinks you must be up to no good."

"Yes, but that's understandable for such a small company," I argued.

This Hatayama was even more irresponsible than I am. He used to go around announcing his own grievances as if he'd heard them from someone else. As it happens, the Editor-in-Chief is quite sensitive to people bad-mouthing him. And he disliked me enough already as it was.

42

I did my best to stand up for him. "The Chief doesn't have it easy, you know. If all five of the staff were away, he'd have to man the phones and receive visitors all by himself."

Hatayama looked back towards the stern. "You're sure to come for us after midday, aren't you?" he said with some trepidation.

The old fisherman looked up at the ominously overcast sky. "Well, they say another typhoon's coming."

I had a rush of blood. "Come on! What are we going to do an uninhabited island in the middle of a typhoon?! You've got to come back for us. We'd be in real trouble otherwise. Say you'll come back, for pity's sake!"

"Aah, you'll be all right. There's a hut where you can shelter from the rain. Besides, why else have you brought two lunch boxes each?"

"That's just in case!"

Hatayama and I were on the verge of tears. We threw ourselves before him, our foreheads scraping the bottom of the heaving boat. "Please! Please!!" we begged.

"You like putting your lives at risk, don't you," he said grudgingly. He looked down at us with an expression of astonishment mixed with loathing. "All right, I'll come. Unless something happens, that is."

And that was about the best we could get out of him.

The fisherman headed for the beach opposite Shiokawa, and dropped us there. Then off he rowed briskly, back across the sea, where the waves were starting to swell. I stood with Hatayama at the shore's edge, gazing forlornly at the boat as it receded into the distance.

"Right. Let's give the place a quick once over," I said at length. "We should be able to cover the island in two hours tops."

It took three hours to cover the island. Contrary to our initial impression, it wasn't completely surrounded by sandy beaches. On the far side facing out to sea, the shoreline mostly consisted of sheer precipices. To make matters worse, the wind picked up on our way round and it was starting to rain.

"I can't take any more pictures in this," announced Hatayama as he packed his camera back into its waterproof case.

We returned to the beach soon after midday, the appointed time. Just as we'd feared, there was no sign either of the fisherman or of his boat. The waves were even higher now. On the far shore, the white surf crashing on the rocks seemed to reach up into the ashen grey sky. Judging by the foul weather and the fisherman's tone of voice earlier, there seemed little chance he would come. No, there was no way he would come. He must have heard the weather forecast, saying the typhoon would be severe. When things are going bad, they're just bound to get worse. Or so we decided, as we weighed up our situation with pitiful faces.

"We'll catch cold here," I said, looking up at the terraced fields. "He said there was a hut up there, didn't he. Let's go and find it."

"I've already caught a cold, mate," said Hatayama. He let out an enormous sneeze, hurling nasal matter onto the ground as he did so.

We climbed for a while through fields planted with beans. Then, in the middle of the island's mountainous terrain, we came across a long, thin strip of land that had been levelled over a length of several hundred yards. What was it for? At one end of it stood a tiny shack. Approaching the shack like bedraggled rats, we prised open the door, which was fashioned from logs tied together vertically. Then in we rushed.

There, on a raised platform at the back, we saw two farmers sitting face to face and drinking. One of them, a man in his forties, had horribly sticky eyes. The other was about thirty. The end of his nose was red – probably from an excess of alcohol.

"Sorry to intrude," I said by way of apology. "Does this hut belong to you?"

"Ha! It don't belong to no one," answered the man with sticky eyes. "It's for us folk from Shiokawa who farm the fields on the island. We use it to sleep in, or shelter from the rain." He looked us up and down. "Have you got yourselves wet? Well, there's some firewood over there. Why not light a fire and dry yourselves out."

"Where are you from?" asked the red-nosed man as we made up a fire.

Hatayama and I took turns to tell our tale – that we were a writer and a photographer from an unfashionable monthly magazine for men, that we'd come to the island for a story but had orders to return to our office the next day, that we'd been held up by the typhoon and didn't know what to do, and so on and so forth. Meanwhile, we dried our sodden clothes by the fire.

"It looks as if another typhoon's coming soon. How will you get back to Shiokawa?" I asked. "There's not much chance of a boat coming out for you."

"Ah. You came in Jimbei's boat too, did you?" said the sticky-eyed man. "That's how we usually get across. But sometimes, when the sea's rough like today, the boat don't come and we can't get back. We came over yesterday afternoon, once the typhoon had died down. We're picking beans, see, and stayed the night here. We saw you coming over, when we was in the fields. We've only just finished working, in fact." With his chin, he indicated four big baskets full of beans in a corner of the earthen floor. "And while we wait, we have a drop of this liquor we brought over with us."

So he wouldn't answer my question. That irritated me. "But surely, you don't mean to wait until the typhoon's passed over, do you? Who knows when that'll be?"

"True. Jimbei won't bring his boat out if there's any height to the waves, for safety's sake," mumbled Sticky Eye.

"Are there any other boats?" Hatayama asked expectantly.

Sticky Eye lifted his face and looked at us both in turn. "Do you really want to get back so soon? Are you really in that much trouble?"

"Yes. Of course!" I replied firmly.

Red Nose pulled a face as if to stop him. But he didn't notice and just carried on. "Well, there *is* the aeroplane."

"Aeroplane?!" In his surprise, Hatayama projected a missile of nasal matter onto the earthen floor. "An aeroplane from here to the mainland?"

Sticky Eye gazed at Hatayama's nasal missile with intense interest. "Sheesh!" he cried. "What a trick! This one can blow his nose without using his hands." He turned to Hatayama and laughed. "How do you do that?"

"I don't remember seeing anything about an aeroplane on the timetable," I said. "What airline is it?"

"The company's called Air Shiokawa," answered Red Nose, looking over at me. "They're not on the timetable because they don't do regular flights. They only fly when the weather's bad and boats can't get across, or when people are stuck on the island and want to get back to Shiokawa."

"What? You mean there's a flight just from here to Shiokawa?" exclaimed Hatayama. He bowed his head low. "Thank you very much! When and where will it arrive?"

Red Nose looked at his watch. "Well, if it's coming at all, it'll be any time now. You must have seen the runway outside. That's where it lands."

A bit short for a runway, I thought.

"Yes, but we can't be sure it'll come today," said Sticky Eye. He shook his head with a smile, as if to tease us. "I hear Gorohachi was bitten by a viper yesterday."

"Is Gorohachi the pilot, then?" I asked, overcome by a sense of foreboding. "Doesn't he have a co-pilot?"

Red Nose and Sticky Eye looked at each other.

"Well, I suppose that would be Yoné."

"No, she can't be the co-pilot. You only ever see Goro flying the plane."

"How much does it cost?" asked Hatayama guardedly. He was nothing if not stingy.

"Well, now," answered Sticky Eye, thinking hard. "Us folk from Shiokawa have season tickets, so it's cheaper for us. But when tourists absolutely insist on flying, I think they charge about three thousand yen for the round trip, yes."

"Fifteen hundred yen each way? That's a bit steep." Hatayama wasn't happy. "It must only take about ten minutes from here to Shiokawa."

I poked him in the ribs and intervened quickly. "No, no. If we can get across for fifteen hundred yen it'll be well worth it. But anyway, are you saying this Air Shiokawa only has one aeroplane, and that people who aren't from Shiokawa and don't have season tickets aren't allowed to use it, unless they really insist?"

Sticky Eye was again unforthcoming. "Well. Yes. I suppose so."

In my anxiety, I inadvertently raised my voice. "And does this airline company have a proper business licence?"

Red Nose gave me a sharp look. "Oy. If you want to get back to your office quickly, you'd best not ask that sort of question. And don't go blabbing to others about it. You say you're a writer, and I didn't want you to know about the plane, because you might write about it. I only told you because you said you was desperate."

"I won't tell anyone," I proclaimed loudly, crumbling under the terrifying glare of Red Nose. "I won't tell anyone, and I won't write about it in the magazine." There was no doubt – the aeroplane was privately owned, and operated without a licence.

"Anyway, don't worry," Sticky Eye called over to me with a smile. "Gorohachi's a fine pilot, and he's got a proper licence."

Could anyone fly without a licence?

"All right, shall we take the plane back then?" Hatayama whispered to me with some apprehension.

"Of course we will!" I answered. "We're the ones in a hurry. Something that convenient, we'd be daft not to take it."

I was a bit worried about what sort of plane it would be. But the Chief's temper was more worrying at the moment. I was in no position to be fussy.

"But he was bitten by a viper, was he not," Sticky Eye continued.

"What? I heard he was treated at Shiokawa General. He'll be all right," said Red Nose. "They've got blood there, too."

Now that our clothes were dry, Hatayama and I ate one of the lunch packs we'd brought. Still the plane didn't arrive. The rain had eased somewhat, but the wind merely grew in intensity.

"It won't come," said Hatayama. "I bet it won't." He looked rather relieved at the idea. I could see what he was thinking. Of course he wasn't looking forward to a tongue-lashing from the Chief. But that would be better than dying in a plane crash.

At that moment, there was a faint whirring sound in the distance, mixed with the sound of the wind.

"There he is now." Red Nose and Sticky Eye got up.

We rushed out of the hut in front of them. We wouldn't be happy until we could see this aeroplane with our own eyes.

A light plane, flying at low altitude from the Shiokawa direction, was making a sweeping circle above the bean fields. I didn't know what type it was, but it had a stumpy fuselage with a propeller on each wing.

"Well, it's more or less a proper aeroplane, isn't it. We'll be all right in that. Won't we. Eh." Hatayama was trying to convince himself.

"What else were you expecting, if not a proper aeroplane?" I countered, staring at him. "Don't talk garbage."

Pummelled by the wind, the plane shook violently as it turned and prepared for landing some distance from the runway. Then it came towards us, flapping its wings up and down. The wings weren't flapping in alternation. They flapped up and down *at the same time.*

"Can aeroplanes flap their wings?" asked Hatayama in a frightened little voice.

"Of course they can't," I replied with irritation. "It's just the wind doing that."

"Wait a minute! The runway's too short!" Hatayama shrieked. He stood transfixed as the aeroplane approached, wheels still retracted. How close would it come? Hatayama prepared to run.

When the wheels at last touched the ground, the plane bounced on the runway. I closed my eyes.

"No. It ain't Gorohachi," yelled Sticky Eye, standing behind us. "He's better at it than that."

Who was it, if not Gorohachi? I opened my eyes again to find out. The plane made a thunderous noise as it careered towards us on the runway. It was sure to plough straight into us.

"Nooooo! It's going to hit the hut!" Hatayama was long gone. I followed him, diving headlong into the bean field beside us.

The aeroplane reversed the pitch of its propellers, and screeched to a halt just inches from the hut.

We looked at each other in the bean field. "We nearly died in a plane crash without even getting in!" said Hatayama. In his sheer terror, the pupils of his eyes had contracted to the size of pinheads.

We waited until the propellers had stopped before crawling out of the bean field. As we approached the plane, we saw how close it had come to destroying the farmers' hut.

"Look at that! About five inches," said Hatayama, measuring the gap with his fingers. He turned to me and added sarcastically, "Now that's what I call service!"

I frowned. It was hardly a laughing matter.

Behind the plane lay a parallel trail of deep wheel ruts, two thick ones for the main wheels on either side of a thinner one for the front wheel – like gigantic mole tracks. They must have been made when the pilot had braked on the rain-softened runway.

The door of the plane opened and a wooden ladder was thrust out. Nothing as grand as an 'air stair' for these passengers, then. And onto that wooden ladder stepped a plump middle-aged woman, who clambered down shakily with a baby strapped to her back.

"Hello there, Yoné," Sticky Eye called to her. "I thought it might be you. How's old Goro doing, then?"

"Bah. There ain't nothing wrong with him. Just that the doctor said he weren't to move," she laughed, showing a mouthful of blackened teeth. "Goro knew you was here, and was that worried, saying he'd come and get you, like. But seeing as the doctor told him to lie down, I had to come instead, see."

"Well, it's a long time since we flew with you, Yoné," Red Nose said cheerily. "I see you haven't forgotten how to do it."

"As if I would!" replied the woman, throwing him a flirtatious look as she laughed. She was obviously Gorohachi's wife. "It kept coming back to me as I went along."

Hatayama poked me several times in the backside. "Hey! Hey!"

"What," I groaned. I didn't turn round – I knew what he was going to say.

"Er, you're not planning to get on this plane, are you."

So I did turn round. I looked hard into Hatayama's eyes, which were now completely round with fear. "And why not?"

"You mean you are? You're going to get in a plane flown by a fat farmer's wife who's carrying a baby on her back and hardly knows her wings from her ailerons? An aeroplane you get in and out of using a ladder?"

But he obviously realized that I had no intention at all of changing my mind. A sardonic half-smile came over his face as he continued. "All right, let's do it, then! After all, it'll be a rare experience, won't it, flying in a plane like this in a raging typhoon!"

"Cut the sarcasm, will you? You're getting on my nerves," I said, turning away from him. Actually, I was only pretending to be strong. I needed him to get on that plane with me. But deep down, I was quivering with fear.

Sticky Eye had been talking to Gorohachi's wife and occasionally glancing back at us. Then he nodded and called over to us with a laugh. "Hey, travellers! You're in luck! She says she'll take you!"

"Really?" I approached Gorohachi's wife with a suitably grateful demeanour. We were entrusting our lives to her care, after all. We could do worse than ingratiate ourselves. "Thank you. Thank you very much!"

"It'll cost you though," she said. "Two thousand yen each."

Sticky Eye intervened from the side, rather hurriedly.

"Actually, Yoné, I just told 'em it were fifteen hundred, one way."

"Oh. All right, fifteen hundred then," she said casually, without any sign of discomfort. "Well, come on then. Up you get."

"Gorohachi's wife seems like a good person," I said to Hatayama as we walked across from the hut with our baggage.

He was shivering with fright. "That doesn't mean she can fly a plane, does it," he replied.

I pulled a face. But he just carried on, with his waterproof camera case slung over his shoulder. "Just now, they said this Gorohachi had a proper pilot's licence. I heard them. But they haven't said anything about the wife. Then again, we're in no position to go round asking questions, are we."

"Exactly," I answered in exaggerated agreement. "So don't."

"Yes, well, we're sure to get back to Shiokawa in one piece, aren't we. Yes." Hatayama laughed nervously, nodding to himself several times. "After all, she's had *some* experience as a pilot, hasn't she.

Even if she doesn't have a licence. And even if it *is* a long time since she last flew. Yes. And those two farmers aren't at all nervous about flying with her, are they. Even if they *are* ignorant and totally insensitive to danger. That's all OK, isn't it."

I said nothing. Otherwise, he might have started screaming his head off.

We climbed the ladder into the aircraft. Inside, there were ten half-dilapidated seats, five on either side of an aisle covered with straw matting. There was no partition between the passengers and the pilot; the controls were in full view. Hatayama and I sat in the front two seats, on either side of the aisle.

As soon as we'd sat down, Hatayama started up again. His hawk-like eyes had spotted something in the roof of the cockpit, above the front window.

"Look at that!" he exclaimed. "It's a miniature shrine."

"So it is."

"That's for luck, I suppose."

"So it is."

"So that's why this plane has stayed in one piece so far. Sheer luck!"

"Just shut up." I glared at him again through narrowed eyes.

Hatayama ducked his head apologetically. "Do you have to get so angry at everything I say? Give me a break, will you?!"

The two farmers finished loading their baskets of beans and farming tools onto the plane. Then Gorohachi's wife hoisted up the ladder and closed the door.

"Right then, let's be off!"

She pushed back some loose strands of hair, then parked her sizeable rear on the pilot's seat – all the while trying to calm the wriggling baby on her back. Once in position, she started fiddling with the switches, throttle lever and other controls, displaying a clumsy, heavy-handed touch. Hatayama and I held our breath as we stared in disbelief. The two farmers behind us, meanwhile, were calmly discussing the price of beans.

The aeroplane slowly started to move. It turned until its tail faced the hut, then started to travel along the runway. The plane shook and creaked noisily, making us jump up in our seats.

"We should have sat further back," moaned Hatayama.

Not only were there no seat belts, but because we were sitting at the front, there was nothing for us to hold on to either.

"Be quiet! Or I'll rip your bloody tongue out!" I shouted.

The plane bounced once, then picked up speed. The fuselage shook so violently that it seemed likely to fall apart at any moment. But still it continued to taxi along the runway.

"We can't get off the ground," said Hatayama, cowering in terror. "Oh no! We're not going to make it!"

The runway ended at the top of a cliff looking out to sea. And the end was approaching fast. The plane bounced again, nearly sending us into the roof.

As it flew off the end of the runway, the plane was buffeted by a gust of wind and tilted to one side. We started to plummet towards the sea, the white crests of the waves rushing towards us through the front window. Hatayama let out a feeble cry. "We're done for," he whined. "We're done for. I knew it."

"Come on, you bugger!" Gorohachi's wife cursed as she yanked the control stick upwards. The baby cried loudly.

The nose of the plane lifted, and we gradually returned to a more agreeable angle. Then we started to climb, swaying all the while. Hatayama and I both relaxed our shoulders and let out great sighs of relief at the same time.

"Oy, Yoné," called Sticky Eye. "Is it just me, or were that a bit dangerous back there?"

"A bit's not the word!" answered Gorohachi's wife, cackling hysterically. "Normally, you'd have been saying your prayers!"

"Normally we'd have been saying our prayers," Hatayama repeated to me.

"But I've got willpower, see," she continued. "Not like Gorohachi. So it's a good job I'm flying today."

"She says this plane flies on willpower," Hatayama called over to me in a tearful voice. "Did you hear? Willpower!"

"They're just making fun of you because you're such a baby," I replied.

We were now surrounded by dark clouds. The aeroplane was

creaking and shaking again. Drops of water started to drip down, from a join in the aluminium shell of the roof, onto the straw matting on the floor. Hatayama stared at me. Knowing he was about to start again, I pretended not to notice. So he brought his mouth right up to my ear.

"Er, did you know this plane's leaking. The rain's coming in," he whispered.

"What about it."

"Oh. Nothing."

Suddenly, the plane took a huge dive.

"Oh no!", Hatayama wailed.

My tightly clenched palms were clammy with perspiration and cold sweat ran down my back.

Outside, a seagull was flying beside the aeroplane next to my window.

"That must be Jonathan Livingston," Hatayama said loudly. "He's the only seagull fast enough to keep up with an aeroplane."

"Bah. It's not him that's fast. It's us that's slow," said Gorohachi's wife. "We're flying into the wind, see."

Hatayama was visibly frightened now. "But if we're going that slow, we could stall, couldn't we?!"

She laughed. "Ha! I suppose you mean we could do a nosedive. That hasn't happened at all, recently."

"You mean it happened before?!" Hatayama ejected a nasal projectile onto the floor.

"What a fantastic trick!" Sticky Eye was impressed again. "How do you do it?"

"We should be nearly there now," I said. "Whereabouts are we?"

"Yes, whereabouts are we." Gorohachi's wife tilted her head. "We should have arrived long since. But I can't see the ground for the clouds. I wonder if we've gone off course."

"She wonders if we've gone off course," Hatayama repeated to me with ever-widening eyes.

"Aw, shut your trap," Gorohachi's wife shouted as she hoisted the crying baby further up her back.

Thinking she meant him, Hatayama ducked his head again.

"Could someone take over for a mo? I need to feed the baby," said Gorohachi's wife.

"Right-o," answered Red Nose, standing up nonchalantly.

Hatayama blew his nose again. "Let me out." He started to cry. "I want to get out. Where are the parachutes?"

"There aren't any. But there's a broken old umbrella over there in the corner," answered Sticky Eye, laughing heartily.

Gorohachi's wife handed the controls to Red Nose and squatted down on one of the passenger seats. She opened the front of her overalls, slipped out a breast the size of a softball, and thrust a chocolate-brown nipple into her baby's mouth.

"You'll get mad again if I say anything now, won't you," Hatayama said to me with tears in his eyes.

"Too right," I replied, staring him out before he could go on. "So don't say it."

"I can say what I like, can't I?" He squirmed in his seat. "Why do you have to get so angry at everything I say? You're worried about getting a rollicking from the Chief, aren't you. You're trying to forget your fear by thinking about that. Aren't you." He looked over at me with bloodshot eyes. "But really, you're scared too, aren't you. Just a bit."

"What if I am?" I screeched. "Is that going to change anything?!"

"I'm more scared of losing my life than what the Chief will say. All right?!" he screeched back. "Because me, I'm just a photographer! See? If it came to that, I could earn my living freelance. What do I care if the Chief gets mad and fires me?! But not you. It's not that you love your job, mind. You're just scared of the Chief. You're scared of him because you don't want to lose your job."

"Shut it!" I screamed, standing up. "One more word and I'll punch your face in!"

Trembling under my fearsome gaze, Hatayama put his hand to his crotch.

"I need a wee," he whimpered.

"Loo's at the back," said Gorohachi's wife, still feeding her baby. "But it's full of junk. We use it as a cupboard. So you can't go in there."

"Where can I go, then?!"

Sticky Eye stamped on the straw matting in the aisle. "There's a gap in the floor under here," he said. "Why not do it through that?"

Red Nose looked round from the pilot's seat. "Hold on. We might be going over Fox Hill. You'd better wait. It's bad luck to piss on the Fox."

"I can't hold it any longer!" cried Hatayama. He pulled back the straw matting and, lying face down, hastily thrust his member through a hole measuring a couple of inches in the floor. "Bad luck, Fox," he groaned.

He meant bad luck for you, not the Fox, I thought.

The sound of the engine suddenly dropped. Then the whole plane lurched to one side, making a strange sputtering noise. I looked out of the window. The propeller on the left side had stopped moving.

I pointed to the propeller. "Augh. Augh." No words would come out.

"Aw, has it stopped again?" asked Gorohachi's wife. She'd finished her feeding, and hoisted the sleeping baby up onto her back again. Then she heaved herself out of her seat with a "Hey-oop" and returned to the controls. "Move yourself. I'll take over," she said to Red Nose.

"Has something happened?" asked Hatayama, still squatting there in the aisle.

"One of the propellers has stopped," I replied as if it were nothing.

He started to laugh a dark, demonic laugh. "Heheheh. Hahahah. I told you. Didn't I tell you? I told you." Then he started to sing. "And now, the end is nigh…"

"Shall I thump the wing with that broom handle again?" asked Red Nose. "It worked last time."

"You'd be wasting your breath," answered Gorohachi's wife. "We're almost out of fuel."

Hatayama sang louder. "We're going to die, not in a shy way..."

"Oh, look," said Gorohachi's wife. "The wind's blown the clouds away. I can see the ground now! Look how far we've come!"

South Korea, I wondered.

"Heaven, I hope," muttered Hatayama through his sobbing.

"I must've got me bearings wrong. We've come out by the trunk road at Onuma," said Gorohachi's wife as she pushed the control stick downwards. "We'll have to land there. There's a petrol station down there, anyway."

I jumped up. "You can't land on a national highway! You'll hit the cars!"

"Nah. We'll be all right there," said Sticky Eye. "They're doing road works up at Sejiri, so there won't be many cars. And seeing as there's a typhoon today, nobody'll be on the road anyway."

"How can you possibly know that?" wailed Hatayama. "There's a plane flying up *here*, isn't there?"

"In any case, we've no choice. We'll have to land here. There's too many trees in the primary school yard," said Gorohachi's wife, turning the plane wildly.

The aeroplane made a loud creaking noise and appeared about to break up. The cabin shook violently. Hatayama cried aloud. The inside of my mouth was parched.

Then the grey asphalt of the highway appeared right beneath us. Just before the plane touched down, a car raced towards us from the opposite direction. It sped under our right wing, missing us by inches. The plane hit the ground, bounced, and bounced again.

Through the front window I could see a dump truck heading straight for us.

"We're going to crash!" I yelled, bracing myself.

"Oh, he'll swerve all right," said Sticky Eye.

The truck driver panicked and careered into a vegetable field next to the road.

The plane came to a halt right in front of the petrol station. *Maybe Gorohachi's wife is actually an expert pilot*, I thought for the briefest of moments.

As soon as we'd stopped, Hatayama made a bolt for the exit and opened the door. Ignoring the ladder, he jumped straight out onto the asphalt, where he lay face down for several seconds. Just as I was wondering how long he'd stay there, I noticed that he was actually kissing the ground in utter delirium.

I followed Gorohachi's wife down the ladder. The road skirted the foot of a mountain, which rose abruptly behind the petrol station. On the other side of the road, I could see nothing but vegetable fields.

"We've run out of petrol!" Gorohachi's wife called out laughing to the young pump attendant, who looked at us with eyes agog. "Fill her up, will you? We need to get to Shiokawa."

"I've never filled an aeroplane before," the attendant said as he pumped petrol into the fuel inlet on the wing, under instructions from Gorohachi's wife.

Sticky Eye and Red Nose climbed down after us. "Ready for another ride?" asked Red Nose. They laughed contemptuously.

I looked at the map on my timetable. Onuma was about twenty miles east of Shiokawa.

"Not me," replied Hatayama, glowering at me as he came back out of the plane with his camera case.

"But there isn't a railway station near here," I said sinuously. "How else can we get to Shiokawa? Even if someone gives us a lift, we'll never be there in time for the train."

Hatayama widened his eyes in disbelief again. "You mean you're planning to get back in *that*?" he raged. "You're out of your mind! You're just doing it for pride! Well, if you want to die so much, go and die on your own! Leave me out! I'm waiting here till the typhoon passes!" He nodded vigorously in determination. "All right? I'm staying here!"

I gave up trying to persuade him. Actually, I wasn't that keen on getting back in myself. But considering how things would be if I lost my job, I had to accept a certain amount of risk. "Please yourself. I'll take the plane. I'll be back in the office by tomorrow morning."

"Or maybe you won't," said Hatayama with a trace of a smile.

I was on the verge of hitting him.

"I will," I said. "I'll get back. You'll see."

"We don't need that," Gorohachi's wife announced to the pump attendant. He'd finished filling the tank and was clambering onto the nose of the plane to wipe the front window. "We'd better be off. I'd be in real trouble if the law found me parked here."

"I hear the typhoon's approaching southwest of here," said the attendant with a look of concern.

Gorohachi's wife laughed it off. "Don't worry. We'll be all right," she said breezily.

Rain started to pour in torrents. I climbed back into the plane with the farmers, leaving Hatayama standing alone outside.

We started to taxi along the highway. As we did, several cars swerved into the vegetable field to avoid us. Soon we were airborne once more, and turned westwards.

It wasn't until the following morning, during the Chief's tirade on my return to the office, that I heard what had happened. Just after we'd taken off, the side of the mountain had collapsed, burying the petrol station and killing Hatayama along with the pump attendant.

"Why the hell didn't you get the film off him first?!" bellowed the Chief.

Bear's Wood Main Line

We were just a few minutes from Boar's Wood Station.

"Where are you headed?" asked a thickly bearded man sitting opposite me.

"Four Bends," I replied.

I'd heard they made good buckwheat noodles in the little town of Four Bends. So I planned to go there and eat my fill, then buy as much as I could to take home with me. That's why I was travelling on the Hairybeast Line. You see, I'm quite mad about buckwheat noodles. If I hear of a place that's famous for them, I have to go there and try some for myself – no matter how remote it is.

"What, you mean you're going to stay on this train, all the way round Hairybeast, till you get to Four Bends?"

The bearded man looked at me with eyes agog. With his close-cropped hair and a towel hanging from his belt, he looked like some kind of mountain lumberjack.

"Why, yes," I replied. "That's the only way, isn't it?"

"Ah well, you could get off at Boar's Wood and change onto a train going to Deer's Wood from there. That's only one stop from Four Bends," said the bearded man. "At Boar's Wood, you change onto the Bear's Wood Main Line. It's only a single track, mind. But it'll get you to Four Bends four hours quicker than going all the way round Hairybeast."

"Oh, really? I didn't know that!" I said, staring at him in surprise. "I really didn't know that."

"I'm going to Bear's Wood myself," said the bearded man, looking out at the night sky.

A clear, star-filled sky stretched out over the forest on either side of the tracks. It was already half-past eleven. There weren't many passengers on this train as it journeyed deep into the mountains. In our carriage there were only twelve or thirteen, including the bearded man and myself.

"I get it. It's called the Bear's Wood Main Line because it goes through Bear's Wood, right? Yes, of course. But if it's only a single track and it's so short, why's it called a main line?" I asked. I took out some cigarettes and offered one to the bearded man. He pulled a strip of matches from his shirt pocket and lit up, took a deep puff and slowly started to explain.

"In olden times, the Bear's Wood Main Line was the only railway in these parts. That was before Hairybeast got so big. In those days, this line we're on now was also part of the Bear's Wood Main Line. It went up into the mountains from Boar's Wood, passed through Bear's Wood and Deer's Wood, and ended up in Four Bends. When was it, now? Well, when the railway to Hairybeast was built, going the long way round to Four Bends, people began to think of that as the main line. So they started calling this the Hairybeast Line. But us people who live round here, we still call it the Bear's Wood Main Line. Just the bit between Boar's Wood and Deer's Wood, mind. The Main Line, we call it."

Yes, I vaguely remembered reading about it in a magazine some years back. The local railway line that runs through the mountains to Deer's Wood.

"Right, I'll change onto that then," I said.

The bearded man nodded vigorously. "That'd be best," he said.

Boar's Wood was a tiny station in the middle of the forest. Only two passengers got out – me and the bearded man.

At the end of the platform was another, smaller platform set at right angles to it. It was the terminus of the Bear's Wood Main Line. A train was already waiting there. Actually, it was more a single carriage than a train. I'd imagined the train would be pulled by a branch-line locomotive, but there was nothing of the sort. It just moved by itself. A single-carriage, self-powered train.

As we got in, I noticed that the carriage had rows of double seats facing the front, on one side only. There were no other passengers — just me and the bearded man.

"Here you are at last!" said a voice. It was the driver, coming up beside us. He looked exactly the same as the bearded man. *They must be brothers,* I thought, *or cousins.*

"It was so sudden, I was that shocked. I came back as soon as I got the letter," the bearded man said to the driver. Then he pointed to me. "This gent wants to get from Deer's Wood to Four Bends," he said.

"Well, we'd best get going, then," said the driver, returning to his seat.

The train started its gentle climb up the mountain, into the gloomy depths of the forest. Chilly mountain air flowed around the carriage through an open window.

"By the way, what about the connection at Deer's Wood?" I asked the bearded man, who seemed lost in thought.

He blinked. "Connection? What connection?"

"I mean, how long will I have to wait for the train to Four Bends?"

"Ah. Well, at this time of night…" He looked at his watch and thought for a moment. Then he suddenly slapped his thigh. "What a great fool am I! I've done you wrong, I have. Truth is, you'll have to wait four hours and a bit at Deer's Wood."

"What?! Four hours?" I said in astonishment. "What do you mean?"

"That's right. You'll have to wait for that train we just got off. How much of a fool am I? I wasn't thinking straight. I thought you'd be able to catch the one before it."

I forced a smile as he continued to apologize.

"No, no, it's fine," I said. "After all, I got the chance to ride in this most unusual train, didn't I."

The bearded man grinned as I looked the carriage up and down. "Yes, it is unusual, isn't it," he said. "Soon you'll see why it is, too."

"And the driver, is he your brother?"

"Well, how shall I put it?" He thought hard, but then seemed to give up. "Let's just say we're related," he concluded.

I imagined his whole family living with him there in Bear's Wood. And just as I thought that, the bearded man started to explain – as if he'd been reading my mind.

"Yes, come to think of it, nearly everyone who lives in Bear's Wood is a relative of mine. And this morning, one of them passed away. I was working in the mountains, and I only heard the news this afternoon. So I'm going back for the wake tonight."

"Oh dear. I am sorry to hear about that."

For the next few minutes, I looked out of the windows on either side of the carriage. "This is quite a long stretch, isn't it," I said at length. "Are there any other stations on this line, besides Bear's Wood?"

"No," replied the bearded man. "Boar's Wood at one end. Deer's Wood at the other. And Bear's Wood in between."

"Really? So this train is more or less exclusively used by your family, is it?"

"Well, yes, I suppose it is," he replied, quite earnestly. "In olden days, there were three hamlets in these parts – Boar's Wood, Bear's Wood and Deer's Wood. The senior member of my clan, in Bear's Wood, used to be the Village Elder of all three hamlets. These days, Boar's Wood and Deer's Wood have been opened up, like. So the only hamlet that's still unspoilt is Bear's Wood. The Village Elder in Bear's Wood is much respected by everyone round here. If ever anything happens, people get in this train and come up to Bear's Wood for advice. Yes, that must be why we call it the Main Line."

The train slowed and came to a gentle halt.

"Oh! We've stopped," I said, poking my head out of the window to survey the scene. "Is this Bear's Wood?"

The bearded man shook his head. "No, this isn't Bear's Wood. We're still at the bottom of Bear's Wood Mountain. The station's at the top."

We were still surrounded by mountains. All I could see around us was dense forest and undergrowth. And a little hut standing beside the track. Looking down, I noticed we'd been joined by a second track running alongside us. The rails shone brightly in the moonlight.

"It's a double track here," I said vacantly.

"That's right. From here, the train changes into a cable car. That's why it's a double track."

"You mean – this is a cable car?!" I was surprised again. But now I understood the strange appearance of the carriage.

The driver got out and went into the little hut. Through the open door, I could just see something that looked like electrical equipment inside. Eventually, he emerged from the hut and, after doing something at the front of the train for about ten minutes, returned to his seat. He'd probably been attaching the carriage to a cable.

The little hut began to vibrate, making a loud humming noise like a motor. With that, the cable car slowly started to climb the steep incline of the mountain. I supposed there must be some kind of winch at the top of the mountain, which could also be operated from the bottom.

I gazed out of the window as my body was forced back into the seat. Suddenly, I remembered the whole of the article I'd read in that magazine a few years back. I jumped up. "That's it! Now I remember!"

"What is it you remember?" The bearded man, sitting next to me, gave me a sideways look.

I hesitated for a moment, wondering if should I go on. But then I turned to him and let it out: "Didn't they close this line down four years ago, because it was too expensive to run and there weren't enough passengers?"

The bearded man seemed unperturbed, and just smiled. "You do have a good memory! That is absolutely right," he answered slowly. I sat there dumbfounded as he continued. "But, you see, if they closed this line down, we in Bear's Wood would be in trouble. People in the other hamlets would be in trouble, too. Not only would they be unable to get to Bear's Wood any more, but people in Boar's Wood would have to go all the way round Hairybeast just to get to Deer's Wood. And take four hours and a bit doing it, too. So we got the railway company to sell us the line. On condition that the Bear's Wood residents take care of the operation and maintenance, mind. As you saw, my relative from Bear's Wood works full-time as the driver. But only when there are passengers wanting to use it."

"Is that right," I said with a sigh.

The other carriage passed us silently on its way down the mountain. The train must have been operating on a counterweight system, with no stops in between. The other carriage had no lights on, and was completely dark inside. Of course, there was nobody in it.

"We have to balance out the weights, you see. So we fill that one with buckets of water," the bearded man explained.

A few more minutes went by.

"So all the people in Bear's Wood must be quite rich, then?" I asked casually.

The bearded man said nothing.

"After all," I argued, "you'd have to be pretty well-off to buy a whole railway line. And it would cost a lot to maintain, too."

He smiled meaningfully.

So that was it − they hadn't bought the line at all. The railway company thought they'd closed the line down, but all the people living in the area had colluded to keep using the carriages, and the electricity − which they were using illegally − as well as all the other equipment and what have you, without the permission of the railway company. That must be it. The station staff at Boar's Wood and Deer's Wood were related to the people in Bear's Wood, so they turned a blind eye to it all. And the money they needed to maintain the line was being raised through some kind of subterfuge. After all, where would people in a poor mountain hamlet find the money to buy up a whole branch line? It just wouldn't happen.

The incline grew steeper as we approached the top of the mountain. I put my head out of the window and looked at the summit. There, I could see a very large thatched house. The cables and rails were heading straight towards the ground floor.

"That's where the Bear's Wood clan lives," said the bearded man.

There was nothing else resembling a house anywhere near the top of the mountain. So I guessed the whole clan must live in that massive house.

Eventually, our carriage moved into the ground floor of the house, as if being sucked into it. The rails continued into an earth-floored room on the ground floor, and there the cable car terminated. On our right was a cooking area, including a hearth, water jugs, pails and other requisites. On the left was a raised wooden floor that must have measured about forty square yards. As the cable car came to a halt, the far end of this wooden floor formed a kind of platform.

On the wooden floor, about thirty people, including elders and children, had gathered to hold a wake. They knelt on floor cushions, eating, drinking and talking as others paid their respects.

The cable-winching machinery was fixed high in the ceiling of the earth-floored room. Looking up, I could see two large pulley wheels wound with cables. The wheels were attached to thick beams and crossbeams, from which families of bats were hanging. The ceiling over the earth-floored room was so high and dark that I couldn't even see it.

A man of about fifty, his face red from drinking, got up and climbed into our carriage through the open door.

"Well, that were quick, Sasuke," he said.

"Yea, I came back as soon as I got the letter," the bearded man said, then pointed to me. "This gentleman wanted to go to Four Bends, so I advised him to take the Main Line," he explained to the red-faced man.

The red-faced man stared at me in wonderment. "What? But if he goes to Deer's Wood now, he'll be waiting four hours and a bit before the train to Four Bends arrives!"

"I know, I know," said the bearded man apologetically. "I just weren't thinking straight. I thought he'd be able to catch the one before it. What a great fool I am."

"Well, seeing as you're here now, why not join us for a while?" the red-faced man said to me. "You must have a drink before you go."

"Oh no, I couldn't!" I replied, shaking my head. "I'd be disturbing the wake."

"Nonsense. You'd be welcome. You've four hours to kill, haven't you? We'll make sure the driver gets you to Deer's Wood in time for your train."

Now the bearded man joined him in coaxing me out of the cable car. I could hardly refuse their kindness, so I got out of the carriage and took my place on the wooden floor.

"Have you brought someone from your travels?" asked a white-whiskered old man sitting in the place of honour at the head of the coffin. I assumed he must be the Village Elder.

"This gentleman was going to Four Bends, so I advised him to take the Main Line," explained the bearded man.

"That's good," answered the old man with a smile.

I followed the bearded man as he proceeded to the coffin, which was covered with a white cloth. After lighting some incense, I returned to my space on the floor.

"Come on, girls! The guest is waiting for a drink!" the red-faced man called in a sonorous voice.

The noise was enough to wake a girl of about seventeen or eighteen who was sleeping with a group of children in a corner of the room. Sitting up abruptly, she rubbed her eyes and looked at me with a dazed expression. Her face was white and perfectly beautiful.

"We are but rustic folk, we haven't much to offer," said a middle-aged woman who closely resembled the girl. She placed a dish full of cooked wild vegetables in front of me, and poured me some liquor from a small earthen bottle.

"Thank you," I said, taking a sip. The liquor was thick and dry, and tasted exceedingly good.

"By the way, who was it that passed away?" I asked the middle-aged woman.

"My uncle it was."

"Your uncle? Oh, I'm sorry to hear that."

People in this village seemed to live long. Besides the Village Elder, there were four other men and about seven women who must have been well over eighty. The men all had thick beards and large round eyes, and the women must all have been beauties in their time.

The men started talking amongst themselves. The return of the bearded man seemed to have brought a new buzz to the proceedings. Even the sleeping children were starting to sit up. The beautiful girl who'd been sleeping with them was now serving food and drink, together with the other women. Everyone called her Luna. There were three other girls of around her age, and they were all pretty. But none of them could match Luna's beauty.

The red-faced man seemed especially partial to drink, and kept coming over to pour me another. When I returned the compliment by filling his cup, he would drink it down in one and proffer his cup again.

"What's up? Do you not like drinking?" he asked.

"No, it's not that. This liquor really is delicious."

"Yes! It's a local brew called 'Morning Monkey'."

An hour passed, and then another. The gathering grew more raucous by the minute. By now, I'd been given about three earthen bottles of "Morning Monkey" and was beginning to feel quite drunk.

"Come on, drink up!" said the red-faced man as he came to pour me another cupful.

"Sorry, I'm feeling a bit woozy," I said. "If I have a drop more, I'll be under the table. And then I won't be able to continue my journey. Could I possibly have a glass of water?" I asked.

The red-faced man looked around him. "Oy! The guest would like a cold drink!"

"I'll get it!"

Luna, who happened to be nearby, hopped down onto the earthen floor, stepped over the cable-car rails and crossed to the kitchen area. There, she opened a huge refrigerator and took out a bottle of Coca-Cola, which she brought over to me.

"Will you leave this village when you get married?" I asked her after taking a swig.

Luna looked at me blankly, with no sign of embarrassment. "Why, yes. Most of the women here marry men from Boar's Wood or Deer's Wood. Sometimes the husbands come to live here, and sometimes people from Bear's Wood even marry each other."

Someone called her, so she left me and started serving liquor again. The other women were all dressed in rustic garments. Only Luna was wearing jeans and a sweater.

As the night wore on, the women found themselves with less to do, and started taking turns snoozing with the children in the corner. Two young girls slept with their feet facing me. Each time they turned in their sleep, I was presented with the sight of their milky white thighs. I hardly knew where to look.

The men started clapping a beat.

"Come on, then! Who's ready to sing?" called the Village Elder, beaming.

"Who's ready to dance?" said the bearded man.

"All right then, I am!" The red-faced man got up and moved to the centre of the floor.

Everyone started laughing. He was obviously very popular.

The red-faced man glanced over at me. "Well, seeing that we have a guest, let us now sing the Song of Bear's Wood!" he said loudly.

With that, the whole place erupted. Luna and the others knelt down on the wooden floor, clutched their trays to their stomachs and laughed aloud. *This must be a funny song*, I thought. I started clapping my hands in time with the others.

The red-faced man now started to dance a very curious sort of dance. As he did, he sang in a clear, penetrating voice:

Nanjoray Kumanocky!
Kanjoray Eenocky!
Nockay Nottaraka,
Hockay Hottaraka,
Tockay To-to-to-to-to!

The men and women were rolling across the floor with laughter. Even the girls and children sleeping in the corner had woken up.

The red-faced man returned to his seat amid tumultuous applause. Now everyone started clapping hands in time.

"Who's next?"

"Let us have more!"

It seemed they would continue the Song of Bear's Wood.

The bearded man moved to the centre of the room.

"Yea! It's me now!"

That alone was enough to set off eddies of laughter.

The bearded man started to dance in a way that differed just slightly from the red-faced man's effort. In a rich, deep voice he sang:

Nanjoray Kumanocky!
Kanjoray Eenocky!
Yockay Yottaraka,
Ockay Ottaraka,
Kockay Ko-ko-ko-ko-ko!

Well, this was so funny that even I was gripping my belly. The men, and even the women, were bent double with laughter, tears streaming down their cheeks. The children were upturned on the floor, feet shaking uncontrollably in the air. Not only was the song out of tune and utterly nonsensical, but the dance was so completely absurd as to be from another world. Whoever sang or danced it, guffaws of laughter would surely ensue.

With the opening "*Nanjoray Kumanocky!*", the dancer would arch his upper body to the right, as if to depict a great mountain. Then, with "*Kanjoray Eenocky!*", he would depict a mountain to the left. Then he would hop to the right and adopt a pose, then hop to the left and adopt the same pose in reverse. Finally, he would lift one leg, screw up his face, and hop along like a chicken.

"Who's next? Who's next?"

At last the laughter died down, and the clapping started again. They all seemed to be in some kind of frenzy. I began to feel carried along with it myself.

A lightly built, affable old man moved to the centre of the room. He resembled the Village Elder, though not such an imposing figure.

Everyone burst into laughter again. The women and children shrieked with merriment as they clapped to the rhythm. The old man must have been particularly popular with them. Baring his gnarled old arms and legs, he danced with great skill and sang in a husky voice:

Nanjoray Kumanocky!
Kanjoray Eenocky!
Sockay Sottaraka,
Mockay Mottaraka,
Dockay Do-do-do-do-do!

Some laughed so much they were gasping for breath, clutching their chests. Others were in convulsions, still others had collapsed on the floor. The din was so loud that the house seemed ready to burst. I had tears of mirth in my eyes, and my head was starting to feel numb.

The clapping started again.

"Who's next, who's next?!"

"Let us do the whole hog!"

"All do it in turns, all in turns!"

The driver of the train danced out from his place in the corner to the centre of the wooden-floored room. The mere sight of that was so comical that the women were already laughing hysterically. He was obviously an accomplished buffoon. As I reeled with laughter, a thought flitted dimly across the back of my mind. If this funny man were to dance the same dance as the others, I might just die laughing, or failing that, go stark raving mad.

The train driver started to dance, singing in a crazy high-pitched voice:

Nanjoray Kumanocky!
Kanjoray Eenocky!
Kuckay Kuttaraka,
Zockay Zottaraka,
Pockay Po-po-po-po-po!

I was pole-axed, laughing so much I could hardly breathe. Some of the women just couldn't bear it any longer. They ran across the wooden floor, jumped down to the earthen floor, crossed to the hearthplace and crouched down there for comfort.

Next, the young man sitting next to the driver was urged out by the clapping, and moved to the centre with a sheepish look. It really seemed that everyone would have to sing and dance in turn. As I clapped time with the others, I wondered if I would have to join in as well. Because if that were the case, I would be next in line.

The young man started to dance, singing in a woeful voice:

Nanjoray Kumanocky!
Kanjoray Eenocky!
Sickay Sittaraka,
Gockay Gottaraka,
Kackay Ka-ka-ka-ka-ka!

By now, they'd repeated the song so many times that even I knew more or less how it went. As long as you started with "*Nanjoray Kumanocky! Kanjoray Eenocky!*", you could change the second part as you felt fit.

The young man returned to his seat, accompanied by a thunderous ovation. Now they all started clapping the beat again, and smiled over at me. I hesitated for a moment. Perhaps it would seem a bit impertinent of me, a stranger, to sing and dance in front of these people. But they were evidently expecting just that. And besides, I'd been so generously wined and dined. It would have been rude not to dance for them.

As I dithered, the Village Elder, still clapping to the beat, suggested: "Well. P'raps our dance is a bit too hard for the guest."

That got me up on my feet. "No, no. I'll do the dance!" I said.

Everyone applauded. "The guest will do the dance!" they exclaimed.

"Good old guest, good old guest!"

Luna and the other women now came closer, and watched with looks of expectation.

This dance was funny, whoever danced it. So the same should be true for me. First, I moved to the middle of the room. Then, after swaying two or three times in rhythm with the clapping, I started to sing the song and dance the dance.

Nanjoray Kumanocky!
Kanjoray Eenocky!
Buckay Buttaraka,
Yackay Yattaraka,
Bockay Bo-bo-bo-bo-bo!

I finished the song, I finished the dance. Laughing aloud at my own foolishness, I waited for the plaudits. And then I noticed.

Not a single person was laughing.

All of them – the Village Elder and the other seniors, the bearded man, the women – they'd all stopped clapping, and now cast their heads down with uneasy looks. The red-faced man and the train driver, visibly paler now, examined the bottoms of their liquor cups and scratched their heads in embarrassment. Even Luna, standing there on the earthen floor, looked down awkwardly at her feet.

I knew I shouldn't have done it, I thought as I flopped down onto the floor. I, a stranger, had danced the dance badly and ruined the wake.

With trepidation, I turned to the Village Elder to apologize. "I really am very sorry," I said. "I, a stranger, have danced your dance badly and ruined your wake."

"No, no. That's not the problem." The Village Elder lifted his face and looked at me with pity, shaking his head. "You sang and danced most well. Almost too well, in fact, for an outsider."

"Oh?" I said. Maybe I was wrong to dance too well! "In that case, why did no one laugh as they did before?"

"The words you sang were not good."

I looked at him in disbelief. "The words? But all I did was sing nonsense, like everyone else!"

"That's true," the Village Elder replied. "The others all sang nonsense because they were trying not to sing the real words. But you, intending to sing nonsense, accidentally sang the real words."

"The real words?!" I said, aghast. "You mean, what I sang was the real Song of Bear's Wood? That Bockay Bo-bo-bo-bo-bo?"

The very sound drew gasps and moans from the villagers as they squirmed in their seats.

"Why?" I asked the Village Elder as if to cross-examine him. "What is wrong with singing the real words?"

The Village Elder started to explain. "The Song of Bear's Wood, it's taboo. We're forbidden to sing it. It's been passed down since olden days here in Bear's Wood, but we're not allowed to sing it out loud in front of folk. For if we sing it out loud, something terrible will surely happen to this country of ours."

"Oh?" I said with mounting incredulity. "You mean this whole country we're living in?"

"That's right."

Superstitious nonsense! I just wanted to laugh it off. They'd all ganged up to make a fool of me. But as I looked around again, it didn't seem like a joke at all. They all wore genuinely gloomy expressions and looked quite crestfallen.

I felt a shudder. Then I turned again to the Village Elder. "Please don't make fun of me!" I begged. "I'm quite superstitious, you know, for my age!"

"There's nothing superstitious about it," said the Village Elder, looking at me sternly for the first time. "Whenever someone from this hamlet accidentally sings the song, something terrible happens to this country of ours. So we take special care to tell everyone, adults and children, not to sing it. But every now and then, some parent, through lack of care or attention, lets a child sing it, for whatever reason. And every time that happens, some awful disaster or misfortune afflicts this country. Well, until now, it's only been children, so the punishment has not been too bad. It's never been so bad that the whole country has gone to ruin. But tonight, a fine young man like yourself has come, and has sung the song, so loudly, so well. The punishment will surely be severe."

"I just didn't know." An involuntary cry of anguish issued from my throat. "All I did was sing nonsense. I didn't know what it meant! Will there be punishment even for that?"

"There will," the Village Elder replied with horrible certainty.

I buried my head in my hands. "Why did you let me do the dance?" I cried. "If the song is so taboo and dangerous, why did everyone urge me to sing it? You're all responsible too, you know!

And anyway, why did you start singing the Song of Bear's Wood in the middle of a wake?! Didn't you think someone might just sing the real words by mistake?"

"It's true. We're partly to blame as well," said the red-faced man, who'd been the first to dance. He spoke with true remorse, and shifted uneasily in his seat.

"Yes. We'd be wrong to put all the blame on you," echoed the Village Elder, looking at me with sorrowful eyes. "The reason why we do so enjoy singing the Song of Bear's Wood is that, one day, someone might just sing the real words by accident. It's so miraculously funny, because the singer puts us all in a state of nervous excitement. And deeper down, there's a feeling of pride that our clan holds the key to this country's fate. That makes the song even funnier. On top of that, we all got a bit carried away tonight. When you said you would do the dance, I had a bit of a foreboding. I'll wager the others did too. But none of us could ever have imagined, not even in our wildest dreams, that you would go and sing the real and proper words, sound for sound, without a single mistake from beginning to end. We were all just enjoying the thrill, the sense of danger. And now it has ended in this."

I was almost crying. "Is there no way of purging it?" I asked.

They all shook their heads as one.

"No. There's no way," the Village Elder replied. "Well, what's done is done. Let us not think too much about what might happen to our country now."

"Yes, let us not think about it," echoed the others, doing their best to console me.

"There's no point tormenting yourself, thinking what might happen."

"Put it out of your mind."

"Do not concern yourself."

Could I help concerning myself, I wondered.

The driver stood up. "Right, then," he said. "Had we better be on our way? It's half-past three."

"Yes. You send the guest off, will you," said the Village Elder.

"Goodbye then," I said.

I got up with a heavy heart and bowed to them all.

The men and women all bowed back in silence. Luna, half hiding behind the middle-aged woman who looked remarkably like her, nodded to me from the earth-floored room.

I climbed back into the cable car. The young driver took me back down to the foot of the mountain, and from there to the little station at Deer's Wood.

Just as he was leaving, the driver turned to me. "Would you kindly not say anything to anyone about this Bear's Wood Main Line, or our Bear's Wood clan, or the song just now?" he asked.

"Of course," I replied. "I have no intention of telling anyone at all."

Two days later, I finally returned home. And ever since then, I've been waiting, nervously waiting, wondering every day what terrible catastrophe will befall our nation. So far, to the best of my knowledge, nothing seems to have happened at all. Sometimes I think they were just making fun of me after all. But maybe, just maybe, something awful might just be about to happen. Or perhaps it already has happened, and I'm the only one not to know about it. Perhaps something really, really terrible is happening to our country at this very moment...

The Very Edge of Happiness

As I returned home from work one day, my wife looked up from her woman's weekly magazine, opened her mouth until it was almost as big as her face, and started to scream at me.

"What a fool I was to marry you!"

"What?! What are you talking about?"

She smacked the open page of her magazine with the back of her hand. It was yet another ludicrous article – this time, 'Measure your husband's sex rating'.

"It says here your erection is the size of an eleven-year-old's. Your staying power is no better than a chicken's, and your technique is Grade C average. You do it as often as a fifty-year-old, yet you're still in your thirties and I'm only in my twenties! What are you going to do about it?! You've been deceiving me until now, haven't you! What a fool I've been!"

"Don't be so bloody stupid! It's just a lot of sex-obsessed nonsense!" I pulled the magazine from her hands and tossed it away. "Sex, is that all you've got left to think about? Shame on you! It was my payday today, and I've come straight home just to bring you the money. Well, I'm not going to buy you anything now. You can think what you like!"

She gasped, and a look of regret flitted across her face. Then, with a coquettish smile, she apologized most submissively.

"I'm sorry, dear. I had no right to say such things. Did I, dear?"

"No, you didn't. You had no right to say such things," I replied. "You've never wanted for food, nor ever had to cry because you've nothing to wear. We have everything that most other families have.

And all provided by me. You should be happy. That's it! You're so happy that you're desperately trying to find a reason to be *unhappy*. So you try to find fault with your husband. Isn't that right?"

"Yes, dear. I apologize," she said, gazing at me with eyes full of expectation.

Faced with such unconditional submission, most husbands would lighten up, give a big smile and hand over the pay packet. But not me. I hate that sugar-sweet family sitcom behaviour. No, I'm not ready to sink into such phoney pre-fabricated happiness. If I suggested I was happy, I'd be falling into a TV drama stereotype of a husband, as other husbands do.

I was getting changed in the bedroom when my sixty-five-year-old mother came in from the kitchen.

"It was payday today, wasn't it son," she said, sidling up to me suggestively. "Go on, give us a bit of cash. Shigenobu keeps asking for a pedal car. Let me buy one for him!"

"No!" I shouted. Filial affection was not for me, either. "Go and get the dinner ready. Go on, you stupid cow! Before I kick you out!"

But still she stood there grumbling. So I kicked her out, and she shuffled off to the kitchen crying. Served her right.

I went back to the living room.

"Could you give Shigenobu his bath, dear?" said my wife.

Our son, nearly two, was sprawled across the floor watching a soap opera on TV. *How much does he understand*, I wondered. Ignoring his moans, I got him out of his clothes and carried him off to the bathroom. Shigenobu still spoke in a baby voice, and it was sometimes hard to know what he was on about. But I found that really loveable. So loveable, in fact, that I hated myself. I hated myself for finding my own child loveable. Partly out of embarrassment, I would even ill-treat him sometimes – telling myself, all the while, that boys are best treated rough.

As I opened the bathroom door, white plumes of steam wafted up from the bath tub. I lifted Shigenobu and plunged him in up to the waist. To check the temperature, you understand.

It was scalding hot. Shigenobu issued a loud scream and started to cry. When I lifted him out of the water, his lower body was lobster-coloured.

"Shigenobu!"

"Whatever's the matter?!"

My wife and my mother came rushing up and peered at me through the open doorway.

"It's nothing," I pretended, laughing casually. "Just testing the water, you know."

"How could you do such a thing?!" said my wife, picking the boy up. "There, there. Poor little thing. Look how red he is!"

"Mummy! Mummy!"

My wife hugged him tightly as he continued to cry. "Couldn't you have tested the water yourself?!" she said, glaring at me with tear-laden eyes.

"Shut up! It's a wife's job to test the water before her husband has his bath. Fool!" I slapped her full on the side of her face. "Do you want me to sit naked in cold water so I can catch my death of cold?!"

My wife started to cry. My mother started crying too, and desperately tried to calm me as I stood there shouting and raving like a madman.

Luckily, Shigenobu wasn't burnt. An ointment was enough to ease the pain. I got angry again at my own sense of relief. I was angry all the way through dinner. And the cause of my anger was obvious. It was this "phoney little happiness" of ours.

After dinner, Shigenobu and my mother went to sleep in the next room. Our apartment consists of three rooms, plus kitchen and bathroom, on the 17th floor of Block 46 in a massive housing estate. The rooms are all small. One of them is our bedroom, one is used by my mother and the other is our living room. Each room is filled with the most fashionable furniture. In fact, with a massive colour TV and a coffee table in the middle, there's hardly any room at all in our living room.

I sat at the coffee table and peeled a tangerine as I watched a foreign film on TV. My wife sat next to me, sewing some clothes for Shigenobu.

"You know," said my wife as I made for my sixteenth tangerine. "We could do with a new television, couldn't we dear."

"What – again?!" I said, looking at her aghast. "We've only had this one six months!"

"It's the latest flat-screen type. I'm sure you'll like it. It shows foreign films dubbed or undubbed at the flick of a switch."

"Wow!" I said, opening my eyes wide. "That's good. I've never liked these dubbed films. Let's go for it!"

"Well, would you go to the bank tomorrow and complete the debit forms? Twenty-four monthly payments, five thousand yen a month."

I couldn't stand the thought of so much money leaving my account every month. But then, if there were other things we wanted, we could always buy them in instalments too. Most of the furniture in our apartment was bought in instalments, and we're still paying for nearly all of it. We rarely need large sums in one go. As in many other homes, most of my salary is used up on monthly payments. If my mother suddenly kicked the bucket, we could even pay the funeral costs in instalments these days.

Rampant inflation of land and house prices has made it increasingly hard for people to buy their own homes – not just first-time buyers, but even people with a bit of money. Though actually, that isn't such a bad thing. You work like a dog in the hope of buying your own home, all the while wondering whether house prices are going up faster than you can save. But in fact, you're merely holding on to cash that's gradually losing value with inflation. Forget it! It makes much more sense to use your whole income on monthly instalments – even with the interest payments. Salaries are going up all the time. If you can just forget how cramped your home is, you can eat good food and live a rich life, surrounded by high-class goods as well as the latest furniture and electrical appliances. Personally, I don't completely agree with this trend. I realize that it merely accelerates inflation. But I've no doubt that it's far more sensible to spend money than to keep it – and therefore, not to own a home. So I have no option but to follow the trend.

I sipped some tea my wife had made for me. It was finest Uji tea, ordered direct from the store in Kyoto.

The grandfather clock struck ten. The clock was an expensive handcrafted piece. Paid for in monthly instalments, of course.

My wife started knitting.

I drank my tea as I watched TV.

It was a contented family scene.

My wife suddenly shuddered, lifted her head and looked at me. "Darling, I'm so happy," she said in a self-demeaning voice. There was even a hint of a tear in her eye.

I couldn't hold back the anger, the loathing, the sheer abhorrence of it. I kicked the coffee table and got up. "You bloody fool!" I shouted. "You stupid bloody fool!" I opened my mouth so wide it seemed likely to split, and bellowed with all the air in my lungs. "What do you mean, happy?! You're not even slightly happy! Now I know why they call you cows! You think happiness just means being satisfied! You call yourself human?! You think you're alive? Well, I wish you were dead! Dead, dead, dead!!"

I punched and kicked her wildly. She keeled over and tumbled onto the linoleum floor of the kitchen, where she crawled about in confusion.

"I'm sorry, dear! I'm really sorry!" she wailed.

"What do you mean, you're sorry?! You don't even know why I'm angry! How can you possibly be sorry?!"

I was boiling with rage. I grabbed hold of her hair and slapped her on the cheek perhaps ten, twenty times.

Startled, my mother and Shigenobu rushed out of the next room. They knelt on either side of my wife on the floor, apologizing to me as they wept.

As always, I went off to the bedroom in a fit of pique, leapt into bed and pulled the sheets over my head.

There was nothing unusual about this. I have an outburst like that about once a month, on average. For my family, who don't understand why I'm so angry, it must seem like some kind of natural disaster. But by the next day, it's all forgotten, and they try to smother me once more with their sickening phoney happiness.

That utterly repulsive, *extraordinarily ordinary* blinkered happiness, so false it saps my energy, so tepid it makes me want to vomit. A kind of happiness in which a minor dissatisfaction might surface every now and again, or a small disagreement might occasionally flare up, but we pretend to make up almost immediately.

Just after lunch the next day, I went to the bank near my office. I wanted to deposit my wages and complete the direct debit forms for the television. The bank was heaving with other office workers like myself, taking advantage of their lunch break, as well as salespeople from the nearby shopping centre. Expecting a long wait, I sat on a bench near the window and lit a cigarette.

While I was waiting for my number to be called, a gaunt young woman with narrow slanting eyes came and sat on the bench in front of me. She was accompanied by a boy of about the same age as Shigenobu, a mischievous-looking brat who just couldn't keep still. Before long, he started knocking over ashtray stands and grabbing handfuls of leaflets, which he scattered all over the floor.

"Yoshikazu! Stop that!" shouted the boy's mother. "What do you think you're doing? Stop it, I said! You naughty boy! Keep still! Yoshikazu! Where are you going?"

Ignoring his mother's incessant scolding, the boy continued to wander around, until he eventually knocked over the entire leaflet stand.

"YOSHIKAZU!"

The boy's mother stood up, grabbed the brass pipe of an ashtray stand and, brandishing it high above her head, brought the solid metal base down onto his head.

There was a dull, sickening sound, like that of a wooden post being driven into the ground by a mallet. The child cowered on the floor, his eyeballs turning white. With the look of a woman possessed, the mother continued to beat the boy over the head with the ashtray stand. He was sprawled belly-down on the floor, but I could still see his face. White matter was coming out of his nose. His mouth was gaping open, and it too was full of white matter. His pummelled brains were oozing out through his nose and filling his mouth. The tips of his fingers twitched convulsively at first, but then stretched out limply. The mother staggered out of the bank with the same empty look in her eyes, leaving the boy's body on the floor behind her. And still the aftersound of the incident continued to echo in the vaulted ceiling of the bank.

Two or three of us stood up slowly. After checking the expressions of those around him, a middle-aged man in a business suit went up to a security guard and whispered to him. The guard nodded gravely, went over to the body and peered at the boy's face. Then he went to a nearby telephone, picked up the receiver and calmly started dialling.

Eventually, the police arrived. They questioned two or three people, then turned to me.

"Did you see it all from the beginning?" they asked.

"Yes," I replied.

"Could you be sure it was the child's mother? The woman who killed him?"

"Yes, I think it was."

"Why do you think she did it?"

I said nothing. How could I possibly know? But I could immediately picture the headline in the newspaper that evening:

"Half-crazed Mum Beats Child to Death
in Front of Bank Customers"

But until she picked up the ashtray stand, there was nothing to suggest she was "half-crazed" at all. And although there were other people in the bank, she wasn't really "in front of" us. It was absolutely certain that the people who read the article would never see the incident as I'd seen it just moments ago – vividly, with horrible reality.

Everyone in the bank had displayed a kind of indifference when the incident happened. I wondered if all the incidents we read about in our newspapers were actually reported in the same way – with a casual concern akin to indifference. To be sure, a kind of peace was maintained in the process. But I wondered if, perhaps, something really awful might be happening. Or perhaps this incident was just the start of something else.

Why did you just sit and watch so passively? – I asked myself.

It's not that I was indifferent, I protested in reply. No, I was merely stunned by it all. I'm not like the others. I'm sure I'm not.

As the days went by, abnormal incidents started to happen all over the place. So much, at least, could be gleaned from the newspapers – which, as always, satisfied themselves with nonchalant concern and smug explanations.

"HYSTERICAL NURSE TORCHES HOSPITAL – SIXTY-SEVEN MENTAL PATIENTS BURNT ALIVE"

"UNBALANCED OFFICE WORKER STABS PASSERS-BY IN BROAD DAYLIGHT"

Despite the use of phrases like "random killing", most of the perpetrators were paradoxically described as "hysterical" or "unbalanced". When neither of these applied, mental conditions that are more or less universal – such as "agitation" or "irritation" – were cited as the cause. But you only had to open your eyes just a little wider to realize that these episodes couldn't be explained so easily.

Meanwhile, our sham family happiness continued as before. The pretence was merely encouraged when my salary was increased to three hundred and twenty thousand yen a month.

Then, in June, I was given an extra day off per week. Other employers were increasingly changing to a four-day week, some even to just three days.

On the last weekend in July, I decided to drive my family to the seaside. I wasn't all that keen, to be honest, as the holiday season had only just started and the roads were bound to be congested. But I was getting pretty fed up of lounging around at home for three whole days every week. So I resigned myself to the coming "leisure hell" and decided to go. Of course, the others were all delighted.

As we moved out of the city centre, we had little more than light congestion to contend with. But when we turned onto the trunk road leading down to the coast, it was jammed solid with traffic. Each car was packed with family members. We'd remain stationary for several minutes at a time, sometimes up to an hour. When at last we'd start moving, we'd travel for a few hundred yards before stopping again. There was no room to manoeuvre, and it was already too late to turn back. Trains on the line running alongside the road were packed to the rafters. Passengers were piled high on the roofs of the carriages, while others clung onto doors, windows and couplings.

We'd left home in the early hours, but were only halfway to the coast when it began to get dark.

"Shigenobu! Where are you? It's dinner time!"

He was playing tag with children from another family in the spaces between stationary cars. My wife brought him back to our car, where we enjoyed a truly bland meal.

Expecting the worst, we'd brought blankets with us. The others went to sleep. But I had to drive on through the night. If I thought we'd be stationary for a while, I'd rest my head on the steering wheel and take a nap. Then, when the traffic started moving again, I'd be woken by the driver behind me blowing his horn. With so much congestion, at least there was no fear of causing a major accident. Everyone was falling asleep at the wheel; the worst that could happen was a minor bump from behind.

The following afternoon, we crawled into a small town about two miles from the coast. We had to abandon our car on the town's main road. Vehicles had been abandoned on all roads worthy of the name, including back streets no more than two yards wide. Continuing the journey by car was quite impossible. The town had ceased to function altogether – simply because it was near the coast.

We changed into our beachwear in the car, then started to walk along the pavement. It was already full of families like us, and nearly everyone was in swimwear. We had no choice but to join the flow of people and keep shuffling forwards with them. The sky was clear and the sun shone a bright shade of purple. I was immediately covered in sweat. The back of the man in front of me also glistened with drops of perspiration. Beads of sweat dripped from the tip of my nose. The whole surface of the pavement was moist and slippery with human sweat.

As we moved out of the town and onto a rough country road, clouds of dust blew up around us. Our bodies turned black as we continued to walk. People's faces became dappled with sweat and dust. My mother and my wife were no exception. Shigenobu and the other children had faces like raccoons, caused by wiping their eyes with the backs of their hands. Where did people get this extraordinary power of endurance, just in order to have a good time? I asked myself, and tried to guess the mental state of others around me. But I couldn't find any reason. Perhaps it would be clear when we got to the beach...

We negotiated a level crossing, and the commotion grew more intense. People arriving by train had joined the throng. Already, cries of "Don't push!" could be heard here and there. In one hand I held a basket, in the other the hand of my child, who was gripping mine ever so tightly. We were already walking on sand. And even the sand was soaked with sweat.

We entered a pine wood, and the numbers increased again. Everywhere around us was packed with people, the air rank with the smell of humanity. Some, crushed against tree trunks and unable to move, were calling out for help. Then there was the astonishing spectacle of countless items of clothing hanging from the branches of pine trees, like colonies of multicoloured bats. Young women as well as men, now indifferent to the gaze of strangers, had climbed the trees to take off their clothes and change into swimsuits.

We passed through the pine wood and came out onto the beach. Even then, all I could see was the horizon in the far distance. The sea of human heads made it impossible to know where the beach ended and the water started. To my right and to my left, behind and in front of me, all I could see were waves of people, people, people, people. Their heads stretched as far as the eye could see. The sweat on their bodies was evaporating and curling up into the air.

"Hey! Stick tight together!" I barked loudly in my wife's direction. "Stay close to me! Hold mother's hand!"

The sun was beating down on our faces. Sweat ran off my body like a waterfall. We were being pushed from behind, jostled by bodies that were slippery with sweat and could only move forwards. We, in turn, had no option but to press our bodies into the sweaty backs of the people walking in front of us. It was worse, much worse than a packed commuter train.

Shigenobu started to cry. "I'm hot! I'm thirsty!" he whined.

"We can't go back. You'll have to put up with it!" I shouted. "The water will be nice and cool, you'll see."

But as it stood, I had no way of knowing whether the sea would be cool or not. Perhaps it was already more than half made up of human sweat, all warm and slimy.

Every year, they used to build makeshift changing rooms around this area, with walls made of reed matting. But I couldn't see them, however hard I looked. They must have been pushed over and trampled underfoot by the wave of humans. Yes, maybe the reed matting we just waded through was, in fact, the remains of the changing rooms.

It reminded me of an advancing herd of elephants that flattened everything in its path. Or perhaps a swarm of locusts, leaving nothing standing behind it. *These people aren't human*, I thought, as I surveyed the half-witted smiles of those around me. *They're leisure animals.*

"Please keep moving. Please keep moving," screamed a voice through a loudspeaker at the top of an observation tower. But of course – we had no alternative. If we'd stopped moving, we'd have been pushed over and trampled to death. So we all just kept moving forwards in silence. Only the tearful cries of children could be heard here and there.

As I was relentlessly pushed from behind, my sweat-soaked chest and stomach were now wedged into the tattooed back of the man in front of me. I'd long since lost sight of my mother and my wife. For all I knew, they could have drifted off anywhere in the human tide.

At last, I felt sea water swirling around my feet. But the human congestion remained the same, and I continued to be pushed from behind. I looked down to see the water glistening slimily with human fat. It was grey-brown in colour, like liquid mud.

Soon I was up to my waist in muddy water, sickened by the unpleasantly lukewarm sensation of it. It was only then that I first realized the danger we might face if we kept being pushed forwards like this. Once the water came above our heads, with the mass of humanity around us as it was now, we might not even be able to tread water. Then what would happen?

Shigenobu, already out of his depth, started clinging to my waist. I hastily threw away the basket I'd held in my hand and lifted him up in both arms.

The water now came up to my chest. I shuddered on noticing the sensation under my feet. I'd been so preoccupied with the lukewarm feeling of the water that I'd failed to notice. For some time now, it was clear that we weren't stepping on pebbles any more, but something soft.

It was the bodies of drowned people. I was sure of it. The drowned bodies of children who'd become separated from their parents and had gone under the water.

I took another good look at the faces around me. No one was calling out or making any noise. I could hear nothing but an eerie silence. That and the dimly roaring echo of the clamour from the beach.

Everyone was smiling, as if demented with euphoria. They simply stared ahead with vacant eyes and a look of longing. Sometimes, as if wanting others to recognize their joy, they would look around, face each other, then give another smile of satisfaction. Perhaps even I, unknown to myself, might also be smiling that smile.

The water was up to my neck now. A woman near me started to drown. I thought it might be my wife – but it wasn't. Even so, both she and my mother must now be drowning, somewhere. As she started to go under, the woman suddenly seemed overcome, for the first time, by the fear of dying. With eyes opened wide, she desperately tried to keep the water away from her nose and mouth, and kept splashing against the surface of the water. Soon, people who were shorter than me started drowning on both sides.

The sensation of soft meat on the soles of my feet remained as strong as ever. Drowned bodies must be piling up on the sea bed. *If it weren't for them*, I thought, *I would have gone under long since.*

The number of people advancing had decreased somewhat, and

my field of vision was slightly broader. But I could still see no facial expressions on the procession of watermelon-heads that now floated, now sank to right and left ahead of me, as far as the eye could see. The water came up to just below my nose. My nostrils were tickled by the sickly sweet smell of sweat, rising with vapour from the water.

The body of a drowned woman wrapped its hair around my neck. I pushed the floating corpse away and at the same moment let go of my son. He tried to cling to my chest, but I thrust him away and let him drown. Because from here on, swimming was the only way forwards. He sent air bubbles floating to the surface as he struggled, but quickly sank out of sight.

My mind was blank through lack of sleep, and the heat. The only thought in my head, a hazy notion of unknown origin, was that I just had to keep going forwards. When they fall to their deaths at the end of their march, lemmings have no noble intention of restoring the balance of nature by keeping their numbers down. In the same way, I entertained no feeling of introspection over the abnormal wealth, the abnormal peace, or the abnormal happiness of the human race.

There was just enough room for me to start swimming now. But, perhaps due to lack of sleep, I started to tire immediately. I looked down the line of watermelon-heads. They were thinning out now, but still stretched to the point where the sky merged with the sea. I wondered if I could really swim that far. Still I continued to move my arms and legs... automatically... automatically...

Commuter Army

"Huh. Now they're recruiting day soldiers for the army! I wonder when that started?"

An ad in the *Galibian People's Daily* made me sit up that morning.

"Conscription makes the government unpopular. But there aren't enough volunteers. So, as a last resort, they've started placing recruitment ads in the newspapers. 'Commuters Welcome,' it says here."

The current Galibian government seized power following a successful coup last year. Now, they're bending over backwards to win public support.

"Really? That must attract a lot of people," said my wife as she buttered some toast. "There are a lot of jobless homeowners nowadays, aren't there. Even the unemployed have their own homes these days. So if they can commute from home instead of staying in the barracks, I should think a lot of people would be interested in signing up. I mean, instead of getting posted to the front, they can go home every night, can't they."

"People get *sent* to the front, not *posted*." I took a gulp of coffee. "But yes, it would be easy to commute to the front from here. It's only ninety minutes by train."

"An hour on the fast train."

Galibia is currently embroiled in a border conflict with its neighbour, the People's Republic of Gabat. The dispute revolves around a small Galibian town called Gayan, at the end of the railway line.

"What kind of terms are they offering?" asked my wife. She can't read a word of Galibian.

"Pretty good ones," I replied, glancing through the ad. "The basic salary is 120,000 Galibian dollars. Then there's an outfit allowance of 25,000 dollars, paid on signing up. Pay rises and bonuses are given twice a year when winning the war, once when losing. There's also 5,000 dollars in 'fight money' for each battle you take part in. They even give prizes for fighting spirit. Sickness benefits and health insurance are covered. Well, that goes without saying. There's no unemployment insurance, of course. I mean, what would everyone do if the war ended?! Oh and look. They even pay travel expenses. In full. Lunch is provided. Hey! And you get two days off per week! Even paid holidays. Part-timers welcome, it says."

"Goodness!" My wife sighed, her eyes growing steadily wider. "So you could get much more than you do now. What qualifications would you need?"

"Hold on! You're not asking me to sign up, are you?!" I said with a laugh. I looked back at the ad. "All ages welcome, no experience required, it says. Oh. Applicants with a driving licence get priority treatment. Other particulars to be arranged by personal interview. In other words, the more qualifications you have, the more pay you get."

"Well, I'm sure you'd do very well there, honey. After all, you're an expert on guns, aren't you."

"Yes, I suppose I am," I said, forcing a smile. "But if they're recruiting so many soldiers, they're sure to need more guns, aren't they. Then the Army Ministry will order more from our company. So rather than actually going to war myself, it would be much easier to wait here for those orders, wouldn't it."

"Well, yes, I suppose that would be easier. For you." A familiar look came over my wife's face. I braced myself for the usual onslaught. "Thankfully, things are cheap here, so we can just get by on your salary, plus the overseas allowance."

By "things are cheap", what she really meant was that there weren't any luxury goods for her to buy.

The customary moans were now imminent – when could we go home, when could we have children without worrying, and so on. I quickly left the table.

"Right. I'm off to work."

"Work" is actually a five-minute walk away. From our one-room rented apartment, along the main road, to the office building that houses the Galibian Branch of Sanko Industries. I'm the Branch Manager. My staff consists of a single secretary, a local man called Purasarto.

As I walked in, Purasarto came up to me with a memo. "I've just had a call from the Army Ministry," he said. "It's about the five hundred rifles we delivered recently. They say they don't work properly."

I stopped dead in front of my desk. "What, all five hundred?"

"It seems so. But they only realized they were faulty when they tried to use them at Gayan. As a result, we're losing the war."

"Oh my God." I slumped down at the desk and put my head in my hands. "So the General must be pretty mad, then?"

"Hopping! He wants to see you right away."

I got up with a groan from the chair I'd just occupied. "There's nothing for it. I'll go now."

"Er…" Purasarto added nervously. "There's something else."

"What?"

"I want to quit. They've been advertising for day soldiers in the newspaper, and I'd like to apply."

"Well, I can understand that. You've got your own home, and three children to feed. I'm sure you could do with the money. But you can't leave just like that. I'm sorry. What, I suppose it's the idea of commuting that attracts you, is it?"

"Yes. And the pay would be much higher than what I'm getting here."

"But if you go to war, you might die. Have you thought of that?"

"I have," Purasarto answered with a smile. "But we all have to die some time."

The Galibians' lack of concern for human life was rather worrying.

"You can't quit now. Wait till I find a replacement."

If most Galibian men were signing up as day soldiers, only the women would be left. *So maybe I could hire a beautiful young female secretary next*, I thought as I left the office.

I hopped into one of those tricycle-taxis, like the ones found all over Southeast Asia. Just three blocks along the main road stood the Galibian Army Ministry. Wiping the sweat from my brow, I showed my pass at Reception and went through to the General's office. He was bellowing into the telephone, his face resembling some kind of mad fiend. When he saw me, he replaced the receiver neatly and stood up, ready to sink his teeth in.

"Thanks to your rifles, three battalions have been wiped out! What are you going to do about it?! Give us our money back!"

"Calm down, please!" I called out in desperation. "I'm sure those rifles were checked most rigorously before being shipped out. What exactly is wrong with them?"

"What *isn't* wrong with them?!" the General yelled, spitting everywhere. "We've only had them three days, and now they jam after the first shot. So they can't be fired consecutively. You know what that means? We use them when charging the enemy. So we fire the first shot, then rush at them. But the second shot won't fire. It's a bloody massacre! How do you intend to account for this? If I don't get good service from you, I'm going to complain to your government. We might even declare war!"

"Please don't joke. If you do that, my company will go bankrupt and I'll be out on the street," I shrieked. "Anyway, could you show me one of these faulty rifles?"

"Here's one. It's just come back from Gayan." The General plucked a rifle from his desk and angrily tossed it towards me.

I dismantled the rifle and carefully examined the faulty part. "Ah. Well, this will be easy to repair," I said with some relief. "The screw in the trigger spring axle has come loose. That means that, even though gas is released when the first shot is fired, the bolt doesn't return automatically. All we have to do is tighten the screw."

"So that screw was loose on all five hundred rifles?" the General asked, rather more calmly.

"Yes, I'm really sorry. You'll have to recall all five hundred."

"IMPOSSIBLE!!!" the General roared once more. "We're at war, for God's sake! Those rifles are being used in fighting as we speak! Call it what you like! If we can't shoot consecutively, we'll lose the war!"

"So, well, what do you want me to do about it?" I asked timidly.

"Go to Gayan," the General replied, with a look of menace. "Wait at the battle zone, and when a rifle stops working, repair it on the spot!"

A shiver went through me. "I'm J-J-Japanese! I can't go to a w-war zone. If I did, I'd be a combatant – I'd be taking part in the war!"

The General pursed his lips. "You're already taking part in the war, aren't you? You're supplying weapons to our country. What bigger part could you be taking?"

"But what if I get hit by a bullet and die?" I whined. "You'd have forced a Japanese citizen to die in a war. It could spark an international crisis."

"Our governments would hush it up. Don't worry. We'll send your remains home."

"Remains?! That's what I'm worried about!!"

"Oh? You mean you're scared of war?" The General stared me in the face, as if surprised. "Haven't the Japanese always been war animals, even after the last one ended? I thought you were always ready to give up your lives for your Emperor, or your company, with your famous *kamikaze* spirit!" He sighed. "Well, never mind. If that's the way you feel, we'll order our guns from another company in future. They'll be more expensive, but that can't be helped. Then we'll lodge a formal protest with the Japanese government and, depending on the answer, we'll declare war."

"W-w-wait a minute! I'm only a company employee. I can't just go doing as I please. I'll telephone Head Office in Tokyo and see what they say." Surely Head Office wouldn't make me go to the war zone!

"By all means," answered the General with an air of smugness. "Of course, they'll tell you to go to the war zone." He laughed. "Actually, I just called them myself."

"What?!"

"They said that if the fault can be repaired on the spot, we can enlist you in our army and send you to the front on a daily basis, as a commuting conscript." The General nodded approvingly. "Your superior gave the OK."

"The *bastard*!" I held my head. "It's jealousy. That's what it is. He fancies my wife and envies me because of her. It's a trick to get his hands on my wife!"

The General smiled. "No. I'm afraid the order came from your President."

An order from the President? What could I do?

My shoulders sank. "Even so, there's no need for me to join your army, is there?" I asked, expecting the worst.

He pulled a stern face. "What do you mean? You can't go wandering around the battle zone in civilian clothes. It's bad for discipline. You'll be drafted to the Third Platoon of the Second Infantry Battalion. You start tomorrow. Report to Position 23 in the suburbs of Gayan at nine o'clock sharp."

"You mean… it's already been decided?" I groaned pathetically.

"Come on, don't look so disappointed," he said, suddenly changing his expression to an amiable smile. "After all, you'll get paid, won't you? And since you're a rifle expert, you'll get a special allowance as well."

"You're going to pay me?" I blinked. I didn't know whether to laugh or cry. "Actually, my wife was just talking about that this morning."

"Your wife? What about her?"

"No, well… I mean…" I was wavering. "Well, anyway, I'll have to check it with her… You know…"

"Oh, come now!" The General sounded confident again. "When she hears how much you're getting, she'll be pushing you out of the door!"

She probably will, I thought. She'd led such a pampered life that she was completely oblivious to the horrors of war.

"I'll have your things ready by this evening – ID tag, uniform, equipment, all that. Come back later," he said casually, then returned to the telephone. "Get me General Staff Headquarters," he barked. "Is that you, Colonel? Well, the rifle business is sorted. One of their chaps will join the Second Infantry Battalion tomorrow. He'll be reporting to the front every day. Oh, and about those women for the officers. There'll be six of them coming on the fast train at 19.00 hours tonight. What's that? You don't need that many? Oh, go on. You can have four or five to yourself!"

I left the room in utter devastation, the General's laughter still ringing out behind me. Try as I might, I couldn't see any way out of it. Of course, I could just quit my job. But I didn't have the guts to do that. Because, if anything, being out of a job scared me even more than going to war.

On my return to the office, I found Purasarto talking to a local woman in the reception lounge. She was fair of skin and voluptuous of body, a woman of striking beauty.

Purasarto stood and introduced her. "Sir. This lady has come about the vacancy. She's an acquaintance of mine, actually. She comes from a good family, and has just graduated from university." He must have been desperate to leave – he'd already found his own replacement!

The woman also stood, and introduced herself with a warm, winsome smile. The demon of amorous adventure began to stir within me. But I patted him down and shook my head. This was no time to be getting amorous with any secretary.

"There is no vacancy," I said, then sat at my desk and picked up the phone. "This is not the time for that."

Purasarto shrugged. The woman struck a coquettish pose. "What a pity," she said. "I would love to have worked here."

"I would love to have had you, believe me," I replied with total sincerity.

I dialled Head Office in Tokyo. It was the Department Manager, my boss, who answered.

"Well, hello there!" he said, laughing.

"This is no laughing matter!" I countered. "It's not my fault those rifles are defective! So why do I have to go to the front to repair them? More to the point, why weren't they checked properly before being shipped out?" I knew it was useless saying anything now. But I just had to have my halfpennyworth.

"Apparently, there was an oversight at the factory," he replied nonchalantly. "It seems they let some part-timers do the final assembly."

"In that case, send an engineer from the factory! Let him go to the war zone! That's what anybody else would do!"

"Yes, maybe. But I'm afraid it's not possible. We're understaffed as it is, you see. And anyway, if we sent someone from here, he wouldn't arrive in time. All the Branch Offices send their staff out for simple repairs, after all."

"If I go to the war zone, there won't be anyone left *in* the Branch Office!"

"That's too bad. The Army Ministry is our biggest client there. The others can wait."

"What if I get hit and die?"

"I've already had a word with the President. You'll get special danger money, don't worry." He sounded as if he expected me to thank him. "And if the worst should come to the worst, you've nothing to worry about. I'll take care of everything." By which he presumably meant my wife. "In return, if you do a good job, I'll recommend you for Head of Sales when you're next transferred."

I gave up. I'd only earn myself a bad name in the company if I kept complaining – especially when they were offering so much.

"The army say they'll pay me too. What should I do?"

"Hmm. I'd just take it, if I were you. We'll keep sending your pay every month, anyway. You'll be getting two salaries, but, well… Considering the danger you'll be in, it sounds fair. Of course, you'll be under the command of the army until you get all five hundred rifles fixed, however long that takes. That's the agreement between us and the Galibian Army Ministry. And I expect you to honour it. All right? From now on, you're to take orders from them." Suddenly his voice changed to one of gentle coaxing. "After all, it *is* for the sake of the company. OK?"

"I suppose I have no choice." I put the phone down in resignation.

I gave Purasarto his back pay and dismissed him. Then I locked the office door. I had no way of knowing when I'd return, or indeed if I'd ever return again. My only consolation was the double salary, and the promise of promotion. But what use would they be if I died?

I returned to the Army Ministry, where I completed the procedure for signing up. I was given my outfit allowance and travel expenses, my uniform and equipment, and directions to Position 23, where I was to report the following day. It was on a hill in the suburbs of Gayan.

"There are two big bodhi trees at the bottom of the hill," explained the issuing officer. "A hundred yards west of them, you'll find the time recorder. Here's your time card. Don't lose it. Got that? Don't be late. Otherwise you'll be penalized. All right?"

I left the Army Ministry and took a taxi to the railway station. There, I bought a forces discount season ticket, checked the timetable, and finally went home to our apartment.

"It's turned out just as you said this morning. I've got to commute to the battle zone from tomorrow onwards."

I explained the whole story to my wife.

When she heard the details, her eyes glistened with excitement – as I'd expected. "My! You'll get two salaries! And promotion to Head of Sales when we go home!"

"Unless I die first."

"Of course you won't die, honey! All you're doing is repairing rifles, isn't it?"

"There'll be bullets flying all over the place."

"So just avoid them, then!"

She was completely and utterly unconcerned. I tried to explain the awful realities of war, but soon gave up. Because I didn't even understand them myself.

"Well, I'd better get your things ready for tomorrow," said my wife, in exactly the same tone as when I went on a business trip. She started picking over the uniform and equipment I'd been given. "Gosh, is this your identification tag?" she mused. "Wow. And hey, what's this?"

"Don't touch that!" I yelled. "It's a hand grenade!"

In her surprise and panic, she hurled the grenade to the far corner of the room, ran to the opposite corner and buried her head in her arms. After a moment, she turned around with a sheepish look. "Oh. Was it a dud?"

She obviously thought it would explode if you just threw it.

She glared at me as I laughed heartily. "Honey! How could you bring such a dangerous thing home?!"

"What can I do?! They don't have lockers in the battle zone! I have to bring it all back with me every day. The other soldiers take their guns home, you know. Some of them even have bazookas! That's right. The other day, a child was playing around with a machine gun her father had brought home, and ended up massacring six people!"

My wife stood speechless for a moment. Suddenly, she slapped the table with her hand. "Oh yes! You'll need a packed lunch, won't you."

"Meals are supplied."

She laughed. "What? Proper meals? I doubt it, honey!"

Of course she was right. Galibian food tastes like horse feed. One of the country's most renowned restaurants is quite near my office. But I can never quite bring myself to eat there, and always go home for lunch instead. It stood to reason that the food dished up at the front would be even worse.

My wife pulled out a recipe feature she'd found in a woman's magazine: "One Hundred Tasty Picnic Lunches". "Let's see," she said as she leafed through it. "I've got some chicken. Shall I fry it?"

That night, we were due for some "marital activity". Normally, once we start, we're at it for about an hour and twenty minutes. But I didn't want to tire myself out for my first duty the next day. So, as soon as we'd finished dinner, I jumped straight into bed and went to sleep. Well, after all. It would be a shame to die because I'd had too much sex the night before and couldn't run away quickly enough.

My wife shook me awake at just past seven the next morning. "You'd better get up, honey," she said. "You don't want to be late at the front."

"You're right," I said, hurrying out of bed.

She'd prepared a stupendous breakfast of deep-fried prawns in breadcrumbs, bacon and eggs with pancakes, vegetable juice and coffee with milk.

"It's to give you energy," she explained with a smile. What did she have to be so happy about? "Do your best to win that prize for fighting spirit, won't you!" she added, as if she were sending her child off to the school sports day.

I read the morning paper over breakfast. The 'War News' column had taken on particular significance now – seeing as my life depended on it. Things didn't look good. The Galibian army was in retreat. I read the 'War Zone Weather Report': mostly fair, with a southerly wind. 'Yesterday's Casualties': 18 infantry, 1 petty officer. 'Places To Avoid Today – Fierce Fighting Expected': Position 16, Position 19, Position 23. I felt sick.

While I was still immersed in the newspaper, I suddenly noticed the time. The fast train would be leaving soon. I got up in a panic, hurriedly donned my uniform, and fastened my helmet onto my back.

"Don't forget anything, honey. What about your lunch box? And your hand grenade?"

"In my bag."

"Handkerchief? Wallet?"

"Wallet? I shouldn't think I'll need money. All right, I'll take it anyway."

"Come straight home when you've finished, honey. No dropping in anywhere!"

"Am I likely to?!"

I left the apartment, seen off by my wife's smiling farewell. In the main street, now bathed in morning sunlight, Galibians were making their way towards the station in streams. *They must be commuter soldiers too*, I thought. I joined them as they walked along. I suddenly had the strange feeling that I'd lost my identity. All the others were carrying guns; I was the only one holding nothing. What was I doing here? Why was I going to the front? My mind started to wander. Then I came to my senses with a start.

I'd forgotten my toolbox! How could I repair those rifles without a screwdriver? I did an about-turn and started running.

"Oy! Where are you going?"

"You'll miss the train!"

"You'll be late!"

I ignored the warnings of the others as I passed them, and just kept running until I reached our apartment. There, I picked up my toolbox before dashing out again and re-entering the main street. The stream of commuter soldiers was now a mere trickle.

By the time I reached the station, my fast train to Gayan had already left. The next departure was at 07.50. I would arrive in Gayan an hour after that. I'd have to run to Position 23 in only ten minutes to reach it by nine o'clock.

The platform was full of soldiers waiting for the next fast train. When it finally arrived, it was packed to the rafters. The doors opened and we all piled in.

"It's the same every morning. That's the worst thing about it," said a little man standing by the opposite door inside the train. His face became wedged in my chest as the crowd behind me surged forwards. "We're all exhausted by the time we get to the front. They ought to let us go flexi-time. Especially as it's war."

"I disagree," said another soldier with bulbous eyes who was standing beside us. "It's having to get there during the rush-hour that makes it like proper commuting! After all, we're not like them namby-pamby part-timers or night workers. You should be proud of that!" *A funny thing to be proud of*, I thought.

"What position are you going to?" the little man asked me.

"Position 23," I answered in broken Galibian. "It's a bit far, so I'm worried about being late."

The little man opened his eyes wide. "You'll never get there by nine!" he exclaimed. "That's right on the front! Everyone on this train works at the rear!"

The man with bulbous eyes had been eyeing me suspiciously. Suddenly, he called out to the others. "Hey! This one's not Galibian! He talks funny!"

The soldiers around us started to grow restless.

"A spy!"

"Yeah! Like that KCIA rat the other day!"

"Get him!"

"I'm not a spy! I'm Japanese!" I shouted in sheer panic.

"Why are you wearing our uniform then?"

"He must be a spy!"

"I've come to fix your rifles," I explained falteringly. "I work for the company that makes your rifles!"

"Eh? So you're the one that sold us all those duds?!"

They started getting boisterous again.

"I nearly had it yesterday!" The man with bulbous eyes lifted his rifle above his head and started badgering me. "This thing only fires once! I was nearly done for!"

"A lot of men have died!"

"What are you going to do about it?!"

"The bastard! Let's kill him!"

"It's not my fault! The company made a mistake!" I cried. "You've got to believe me!"

"Oy, you lot! Pack it in! You're upsetting the other passengers!" yelled a man a little way down the train, craning his neck over the throng. I assumed he must be an officer. "And leave that man alone! We know all about him."

The man with bulbous eyes reluctantly released his grip on my lapels and moved away, cursing. "All right then. Fix this rifle now!"

"I can't do it in a moving train. And anyway, I'm not on duty yet."

"Huh! As if it's none of your concern!"

Having aroused so much hostility, I shrank into a corner. The train passed through some paddy fields before at last pulling into Gayan Station. On the platform was another mêlée of soldiers, evidently waiting to go home. They were squatting and sprawled all over the platform in utter exhaustion. Some were wounded.

"That's the night shift," explained the little man. "Actually, they get better pay. I wanted to be on the night shift, but as luck would have it, I'm night-blind."

We parted just before the ticket gate.

"Well, let's do our best to stay alive," I said. "I'm not interested in the pros and cons of the war. I'm just going to look after Number One."

"Yes. That's the best way."

As I left the station, I could already see the black smoke of battle rising silently behind a hill on the far side of town. Muffled sounds of gunfire and shelling could be heard in the distance. I was going to be late anyway, but I had no idea what the penalty would be. So I ran through the little town – a virtual ruin due to repeated shelling – and sped towards the hill as fast as I could.

Panting, I raced up the slope of the hill. When I reached the top, I was presented with a sight that took my breath away. The entire landscape stretched out in front of me was one vast battlefield. Virtually the whole area – from the tops of the hills in the foreground to the mountains in the middle distance – was occupied by troops of the People's Republic of Gabat. The fighting was taking place in lowland woods and forests that spread out to right and left of the foreground. Troops from both sides were locked in battle like the teeth of two combs. Minor skirmishes here and there broke up the shape of the combs, as each side tested the other's endurance. Both Galibia and Gabat are poor countries, and they only appeared to have two or three tanks each. What's more, being such precious commodities, these tanks weren't taken too far forwards, but were being kept in the rear on both sides. The offensive was being maintained by the more expendable infantry.

I tried to forget my fear as I raced down the hill, towards what I thought was Position 23. But when I got there, the time recorder was nowhere to be seen.

"Er, I'm sorry to bother you," I said to a pair of soldiers who were operating a bazooka in a crater. "Do you know a place near here where there are two big bodhi trees?"

"They were right here till a minute ago," answered the one who had the barrel of the bazooka on his shoulder. "But they were blown up by a shell just now. This is the crater it left."

"This area used to be the rearguard," said the other soldier. "Now we're retreating so fast, it'll soon be the front line!"

I really hoped it wasn't just because the rifles were faulty. I poked my head out of the crater and looked over to the west. A hundred yards away, I could see the burnt-out wreckage of a truck, with the time recorder in its shadow.

"There it is!"

I ran towards the truck, keeping my body low, as bullets skimmed and whizzed past my helmet from all directions.

Heeeeeeeeeeeeeeeeeuuuuuuuuuuuuuuuuuuu!!!...

I heard a ghastly whining sound as a shell hurtled towards me. Suddenly there was a dazzling flash of light, and a deafening roar as the shell exploded. I was thrown into the air and hurled onto the ground. When I eventually lifted my mud-caked face, I could see no trace of the wrecked truck, nor of the time recorder.

"My God! No time recorder!" If I'd arrived just moments earlier, I'd have been blown to bits along with it.

I looked at my watch. It was 09.13. There was no denying it – I was late. But now there was nothing to prove it. I felt slightly relieved. Now I could say there'd been no time recorder, and might even get away without a penalty.

That last shell had sparked off a salvo of firing, and shells were falling all around me. I ran to take shelter in a nearby wood. There, scores of soldiers were crouching amid dense undergrowth at the foot of the trees.

"Er, excuse me," I said, approaching one who wore the stripes of a platoon leader. "Could you tell me where the Third Platoon of the Second Infantry Battalion is? I've been seconded to them, you see."

"Ha! You're late," he replied with a smile. "We're in the same Battalion. The Third Platoon was ordered to attack first thing this morning. They've just been wiped out."

"W-wiped out?" I stood speechless for a moment. Then I quickly shook my head. "It's not because I'm late that I survived. I'm a non-combatant. I work for a Japanese company, and I've just come to fix the rifles."

"Oh, it's you, is it? The chap who's come to fix the rifles? In that case, you're in the right place." He pointed to a pile of rifles lying in the undergrowth. "They're the ones that went wrong last night and this morning. Fix them immediately. I'm transferring you to our Platoon as from now. I'll inform HQ of the change later."

"All right."

I immediately opened my toolbox and started repairing the rifles. No bullets or shells would penetrate these woods. I was safe here.

An orderly came with instructions from General Staff Headquarters. The Platoon Leader and all the men were to leave the wood immediately and charge the enemy. I was left alone in the wood, where I continued my work.

Things didn't go well. It took me the whole morning just to fix four rifles. As soon as I'd fixed one, it was immediately taken off by a soldier. Other soldiers, meanwhile, kept bringing more faulty rifles back in with them. And so, the pile of rifles next to me just kept growing higher.

Noon approached. I was beginning to feel hungry, and decided it was time to open my lunch box. Just then, a platoon of soldiers came into the wood. They passed beside me, chatting noisily. One of them, tall and bearded, followed a little behind the rest. He stopped and stood in front of me.

"What are you doing here?" he asked.

"What do you think? I'm having my lunch," I replied, removing the lid from the box.

"Really. Lucky you. Bring your own lunch, do you. Looks good, that." He swallowed with a gulp. "Army catering's shite. We can't fight on that. You got a fag, then?"

I took a pack of cigarettes from my top pocket and passed it to him.

"I haven't seen this brand before," he said. "Hold on. These are Galibian cigarettes!"

I looked up in surprise.

The bearded soldier took a step backwards. "You — you're Galibian!"

I leapt up with a yell and started to run. I'd been so immersed in my work that I hadn't noticed. The Galibian army had retreated and I was now surrounded by the enemy.

"Stop!" he called out behind me. "Stop, or I'll fire!"

My legs turned to jelly. I raised my arms and turned around. The Gabati soldier had picked one of the rifles from the pile and was pointing it at me.

"Let me go. I'm a non-combatant!"

The bearded Gabati shook his head. "No. I'm going to shoot you."

"Sh-shoot me?" I said, shaking with fear. "I don't want to die! Can't you just take me prisoner?"

"We'd have nothing to feed you with. There's no food. So we've been ordered to take no prisoners. All Galibians are to be shot!" He checked that the rifle was loaded before aiming the barrel at me once more.

"Say your prayers, mate!"

"Don't shoot me!" I cried. "I'll give you my lunch box!"

The bearded Gabati looked down at the lunch box and thought for a moment. Then he shook his head again. "No, no. My superior officer is a right greedy bastard. If he knew I'd let an enemy get away for such a tasty looking lunch box..." He shuddered. "He'd have me shot."

"I've got a wife waiting at home," I pleaded. "I don't want to die!"

"I'll make sure it doesn't hurt," the bearded Gabati said apologetically. "I'll shoot you straight through the heart. I've got a good aim."

"Really?" I had an idea. I took a fountain pen from my breast pocket and placed it on my shoulder. "Show me. Shoot the cap off this pen."

"All right." He aimed the rifle at the pen and blew the cap off as if it were nothing.

I took the hand grenade out of my bag and pulled the pin.

"What are you doing?!"

"Running away!" I turned my back on him and fled.

"Shit!" I heard the bearded Gabati cursing behind me. "Bloody thing doesn't work! The bugger's tricked me!"

As I'd expected, the rifle had jammed after the first shot.

I turned and hurled the grenade. Then I continued to run for dear life through the wood. My feet hardly touched the ground.

Douff.

There was a dull explosion, and the bearded Gabati's voice could be heard no more. As I continued to run, I couldn't help feeling sorry for him. He wasn't all that bad. He probably had a wife and children, too. If only he'd accepted my offer of the lunch box, he would still be alive.

As I emerged from the wood, I could see no sign of friend or foe. Abandoned vehicles and trucks, empty ammunition boxes and other remnants were scattered all over the plain as far as the eye could see. I assumed that both sides had withdrawn from the front line to have their lunch. It was a lunchtime ceasefire.

I made my way back to the foot of the hill I'd raced down that morning. There, men from the catering corps were dishing out lunch, and soldiers were grouped together around large soup pots. I'd blown up my lunch box with the hand grenade, so I had no option but to join them, however disgusting the food might be. I joined a queue of soldiers lining up for their rations.

As luck would have it, the soldier in front of me was the little man I'd met on the train.

"Hey! So you survived?" he said by way of a greeting.

"Yeah, just. I was about to be shot by a Gabati just now." I explained the whole story to the little man.

"I had a similar experience myself, once," he replied. "It was just after I'd signed up. I was queuing up for my lunch, just like we are now. But when I looked around me, I didn't recognize any of the other blokes. I thought I'd gone back to my own lot, but they were actually the enemy. I was going to eat lunch with the Gabatis! When I realized that, I could hardly stand upright. I actually wet myself. Oh dear. Why did I have to tell you that?"

"What happened, anyway?"

"Well, I knew the game would be up if I ran for it. So I collected my ration as normal, then I gulped it down as fast as I could and slipped away quietly."

After eating a tasteless lunch, we had to listen to instructions from our officers. Army officers and company presidents have that much in common – they keep wanting to make speeches.

An officer sporting a colonel's stripes stood on a low mound and started spouting forth. "As you all know, there's going to be some serious fighting in this area tomorrow," he said. "But as soon as that was announced, a lot of you wanted to claim your paid leave tomorrow. Shame on you!" His face turned a shade of beetroot. "What do you think war is all about?! Have you never given a thought for your country? Bloody home-loving rabble!"

I felt rather deflated. He was no better than some ogre of an office superior, shouting at his staff for refusing to work overtime. My respect for army officers plummeted.

"No one will be allowed paid leave tomorrow. You'll all be charging the enemy. And I hope you all die in the process. Hahahahaha!" In his raging fury, the Colonel started to look slightly deranged.

The afternoon's fighting was about to start. I sought out the officer who was now my superior and gave him a piece of my mind.

"Platoon Leader! Why did you evacuate like that without telling me? I was surrounded by the enemy and almost got killed!"

"Oh. Awfully sorry. No need to be so angry!" He smiled and patted me on the shoulder. "To make up for it, you can work here this afternoon if you like. It's safe. Look. There's already a pile of faulty rifles waiting for you."

"I've lost my tools."

"I'll order some more from HQ."

"And you're sure this won't be the front line next?"

"We won't retreat any more than this. I shouldn't think."

I worked all afternoon with the new tools, but only managed to repair six rifles. It looked as if I'd be commuting to the front for some time yet. The war itself had been going on for more than four months now, with no sign of ending. Both sides had refused offers of support from the superpowers, while the United Nations, faced with appeals from both sides, couldn't decide which stance to adopt. There were more pressing matters for it to be concerned with, anyway. Safe to say that such minor conflicts between neighbouring mini-states, like family feuds, were simply ignored. Whatever the case, this conflict looked likely to continue for several months to come.

It was nearly time to go home, so I started putting my tools away. The Platoon Leader appeared again, smiling as usual. "You were late this morning, weren't you," he said. "So I'm going to invoke the penalty clause."

I looked at him in dismay. "P-penalty clause?"

"You'll be on sentry duty tonight."

"What?! You can't make me do that!" I rammed the screwdriver into the ground. "That's a combatant's job!"

He made a hand gesture as if to placate me. "Calm down. Sentry duty's easy. All you have to do is carry on working here, then go over to check the ammo that's hidden behind that rock once every hour. There's not much fighting round here at night. The enemy won't try to steal the ammo, either."

"How do you know that?!"

"Because the Gabatis all have vitamin A deficiency. They're all night-blind." He nodded. "You'll be relieved at two in the morning. You can sleep at General Staff Headquarters after that. And don't forget – you'll get paid time and a half for night work."

"I'd rather go home. My wife will be worried."

"I'll explain it to her on the telephone. And anyway, look how few rifles you've repaired!" Gradually, his tone had changed to that of someone mollifying a child. He wasn't at all like army officers in the old war films. His behaviour was quite odd, in fact, considering we were supposed to be superior and subordinate.

I decided to test him out. "And what if I refuse your order?"

"Refuse? Would you?" He kept his smile, but lowered his voice in a menacing way. "Look, I know all about you. Your company ordered you to come under our command. So you should look on me as one of your company's directors. Do you want me to send them a performance assessment?"

"I understand," I replied with a sigh. "I'll stand guard."

"Ha! No need to stand. Just sit down and get on with your

work." Suddenly his relaxed, light-hearted tone had returned. He gave me a patronizing smile. "I'll make sure you get your dinner," he said, then started humming to himself as he walked away.

I got up and had a stretch. The sound of gunfire was far off now, and there were few soldiers to be seen. An evening breeze wafted over the area. The slope of the hill was soon awash with the glow of sunset. Soldiers passed me in twos and threes on their way home, chatting cheerfully. Their faces bore expressions of relief that the day's work was over. In their minds, they were already back home.

I squatted down again, and got back to work repairing the rifles. I was getting used to it now, and could carry on working even in the gathering gloom. After finishing the next rifle, I carried it with me to check the ammunition that was hidden behind a rock some three hundred yards away. The ammunition had been carefully placed in six different piles, with several boxes to each pile. Everything was in order.

Far to the east, over in the paddy field area, fighting between the night troops was already starting up. I could hear the sound of shelling, gunfire, screams, and the rest. Just as in the daytime, it seemed to be a war of minor skirmishes between combat units, a kind of guerrilla warfare in and around the forests. Exploding shells lit up the darkening sky, silhouetting the slopes of hills in the distance.

At last the sun sank below the horizon. I stopped working and stretched myself out on the side of the hill. The moon appeared in the night sky, casting light over the whole area. A breeze blew over from the direction of the mountains occupied by the Gabatis. As I waited for my night rations, I took out a cigarette and lit up. It was already past eight o'clock; dinner should have arrived long ago. I started to wonder if the Platoon Leader had forgotten to order it.

Then I heard my wife's voice.

"Where are you, honey?"

I got up. "Over here," I called.

My wife, carrying a basket over her arm, was struggling down the hill towards me.

"What are you doing here?"

She squatted down beside me. "They said you were doing the night shift, so I've brought your dinner."

The Platoon Leader had actually telephoned her.

"That's good of you. How did you know where to find me? Did you come by train?"

"That's right." She laid a plastic sheet on the ground and started to arrange the food from the basket on it. "I thought I'd join you, so I've brought enough for both of us. And some wine."

"That's grand!"

We started eating on a slope near the foot of the hill.

"It's nice and cool here, isn't it. Where's the fighting now?" she asked.

"Over there. Can you see the gunfire? And there's a forest burning over there."

"Really? Isn't that beautiful. Oh, I can hear screaming. Has someone just died?"

"Probably. Could I have some wine?"

"Here you are, honey. By the way, how did your work go today?"

"Well. Not so bad." I didn't tell her I'd nearly been killed. I'm the type who prefers not to take work home.

"Wow. These fish goujons are fantastic," I said. "And I haven't had konjak noodles for a long time. Hey! You've dropped some pork skin over there."

"Funny. I didn't bring any pork skin."

I picked it up from the ground. It wasn't pork skin — it was a human ear. The ear of some poor wretch who'd been blown apart by a shell. I quickly hurled it into the distance.

After finishing a whole bottle of wine, I was feeling rather tipsy. I stood up lazily, rifle in hand.

"Where are you going, honey?" asked my wife.

"Time to check the ammo," I said as I set off towards the rock. "Back in a minute."

"Mind how you go!"

That's what she always said when I left the house. But here, there were no cars to run me over, no roadworks or manholes to fall into. There was no danger overhead or under foot. Of course, I had to be careful about the enemy. But I wasn't worried, as I'd been told the enemy wouldn't come at night. With that comforting thought in mind, I reached the rock in good spirits. Then something hit me really hard on the back of the head. I saw a dazzling display of fireworks dancing at the back of my eyeballs before I lost consciousness.

When I came to, I found myself tied to one of the ammunition boxes, bound with something that felt like wire. A man was laying fuses to each of the six piles of ammunition, connecting them all to a detonator he'd placed about a hundred yards away. He was obviously a saboteur from the Gabati army. He was planning to blow up all the ammunition, and me with it. I was going to shout out for help. But I stopped myself in time. If I called out now, my wife would come. Then the man would capture her too, and we'd both be blown up together. She didn't deserve that.

Even so, I didn't want to die. The man came towards me, so I decided to plead for my life. "Help me! Please! I don't want to die! I'm a non-combatant. I'm just here to repair rifles. Don't kill me!!"

"Sorry. I can't let you go," said the man. In the moonlight, I could see him clearly now – a goofy-looking, weasel-faced man with glasses. "You won't suffer. It'll be over in a split second."

"No, but really, I'm not a soldier at all. I'm Japanese!" I urinated with such force that my trousers swelled up like a balloon. "I'm a Japanese company employee. I'm just a day soldier!"

"You mean – you're Japanese too?!" He spoke in Japanese as he came towards me. "I work for a pharmaceuticals company that makes explosives," he whispered in my ear. Then he grinned and nodded. "But that's OK. I'm just a day soldier, too."

Hello, Hello, Hello!

"Could I buy some new clothes, dear?" said my wife. "I've had these for two years now."

"True," I replied with a frown.

I needed a new suit myself. Being a company man, my clothes should have been more important than my wife's, from a practical point of view. But if I'd said *that*, we'd only have ended up having another row. Of course we would. And the result would have been an overwhelming victory for my wife, as always. She'd have pointed out that I didn't earn enough money. That, even after five years of marriage, we couldn't afford to have children and were still living in rented accommodation. I would have been denounced for my incompetence and left without a leg to stand on.

Just as I was wondering how to respond, the apartment door opened and a middle-aged man appeared.

"Hello, hello, hello! Here I am, here I am, here I am! Tanaka, Tanaka, Tanaka's the name!"

The man walked straight into our apartment, came up to the kitchen table where we sat and continued to speak as we looked on in amazement. "New clothes, is it? Out of the question. You mustn't buy new clothes. Must she, sir? You mustn't buy new clothes, madam. Just look at your husband's suit. It's nearly worn out. Your husband's clothes are more important than yours are. Aren't they, madam? But even then, it's too soon to have a new suit made. You can still use your old one, sir. This is where you must both persevere. You really must. If not, you'll never save any money. Am I wrong?"

For a while, I gaped open-mouthed at his sparsely moustached face as he continued to speak. My wife looked on wide-eyed, staring up and down at his neatly trimmed hair – parted on one side – and his carefully brushed suit.

After a moment, I turned to my wife. "Come on then," I said. "Introduce us. Who is he?"

She gave me a confused look. "What? Isn't he one of your friends?"

"You mean you don't know him?!" I said, half standing in surprise.

My wife also rose, and turned to the moustache man. "Er... May I ask what you, er, what you..."

"Have no fear, have no fear," he said loudly, "Tanaka, Tanaka, Tanaka's the name!"

As I stood there stunned, he took my hand, squeezed it tightly and shook it vigorously. "I see. I see. You didn't know me. I see." He sat on a chair and started to introduce himself.

"Tanaka's the name, Tanaka, Household Economy Consultant, sent to your apartment block by six local banks, Tanaka's the name!"

"Did you ask for someone to come?" I asked my wife.

"No," she replied with a shake of her head.

"Tanaka, Tanaka, Tanaka's the name!!" The moustache man rose and knelt on the chair with an air of urgency. "With respect, madam, with respect, you must have ticked the box on the questionnaire from your bank, asking if you needed a free Household Economy Consultant?"

"Oh... yes," my wife replied vaguely. "Well, I thought, if it's free..."

"Tanaka, Tanaka, Tanaka's the name!!" repeated the moustache man, shaking my wife's hand triumphantly. "Here I am. Here I am!" He suddenly knotted his eyebrows. "Madam. I cannot agree with you buying clothes in your current financial straits. Your clothes are perfectly good. Of course, I understand what you mean. You've been wearing the same clothes for so many years, they don't look good, they're out of fashion. But you'd have nothing to gain by buying new ones, madam. After all, you're still young. You're beautiful. You could wear whatever you liked. God gives young people health and beauty to encourage frugality. Go and buy your clothes then. And you won't be able to make this month's saving towards your home. Or would you rather have just one meal a day this month? Could you do that? Could you?"

"You're right. Of course, you're right," said my wife, hanging her head low in dejection. "I can do without new clothes."

I laughed in the pit of my stomach. If I'd said it, she'd have been fuming. But now that an *expert* had said it, she couldn't help but agree. I looked at my wife, marvelling at the power mere names and positions of authority have over women.

"Come on, then. Make the guest some tea!" I said, cheerily shaking hands with the moustache man. "You came at just the right time. Just the right time! Hahaha!"

"Yes, I'll make some tea."

But as my wife was about to stand up, the moustache man banged his fist hard on the table. "Out of the question! You have nothing to gain by offering me tea. Tea must only be offered to the most exceptional of guests. Even tea's expensive these days. If you're thirsty, drink water. You're both too young to appreciate the taste of tea. Water's perfectly good for you."

"Yes, you're absolutely right," said my wife with moistened eyes.

In that case, I thought somewhat vacantly, *it would also be rather wasteful to bring my friends home.*

"Well, seeing as you're here now, I wonder if you could look at our household accounts," said my wife.

The moustache man stood up in a hurry. "No. That I cannot do, madam. After all, I'm looking after all fourteen households in this block. I've enough on my plate just seeing you all. Besides, in your case, I can more or less guess your accounts without even seeing them." So saying, he moved to the hallway and slipped his shoes back on. Then, as he opened the door, he turned to face us. "Whatever you do, avoid being wasteful. Though of course, if ever you're about to be wasteful, I'll be sure to come and warn you. Hahahaha!" And with that, he left.

"If he's a Household Economy Consultant, you'd expect him at least to look at our accounts!" my wife said with some dissatisfaction.

"I'd say that shows what a professional he is," I replied. "He just takes one look around a house and understands everything without seeing the accounts. And anyway, all the houses in this block have about the same income and the same family composition. I bet all the household accounts are the same too."

"Well. Experts are experts, after all," said my wife, nodding solemnly in appreciation.

From that time on, the moustache man started appearing before us on a regular basis. Not only in our apartment, but when my wife was out shopping in the local supermarket, too. Once he even turned up in a restaurant near my work.

"Hello, hello, hello! Here I am, here I am! Tanaka's the name!!" He looked at the set lunch I was about to eat, and said loudly, without regard for privacy, "Just as I thought. As if eating out weren't beyond your means already! But no, you have to eat an expensive meal in a high-class restaurant!"

I put my knife and fork down. "Sorry," I said, bowing my head.

"From tomorrow, get your wife to make you a lunch box. I'll tell her myself if you like."

"No, no. I'll do that."

"Well, you've already ordered, so it can't be helped. You'd better eat it now," he said over his shoulder with some annoyance, as he returned to his seat at the back of the restaurant. I finished my lunch with no pleasure at all. As I got up to leave, I craned my neck to look across at the moustache man's table. He was sitting by himself and eating a steak. There was no doubt about it – it was the prime steak lunch.

"Mr Tanaka turned up at the supermarket again today," my wife said with a hint of irritation as we ate our dinner at home that night. "I was going to buy some meat, but he said I should buy potato croquets instead. He said it out loud in front of all our neighbours. I was so embarrassed!"

"By the way," I started hesitantly. "It's my school reunion

tomorrow night. Two thousand yen a head. I didn't go last year, and if I miss this one, who knows what they'll say about me? They'll say I can't show my face because I've gone down in the world. They're sure to. People can't bear going to class reunions when they're down on their luck."

"Yes, your class reunion," said my wife with a smile. "I wonder what Mr Tanaka would say about that!"

"Well, it's already eight o'clock. He's not going to know about it, is he. And even if he did, I've locked the door, so he can't get in, can he."

"Hello, hello, hello! Here I am, here I am, here I am! Tanaka, Tanaka, Tanaka's the name!" The moustache man slid open the French windows and came in from the veranda.

I gave a silent groan.

"What's that you say, sir? What's that you say? A class reunion?" He came up and sat beside us at the kitchen table. "Out of the question! Will your life end if you miss your class reunion, sir? Does it matter what they say behind your back? Everyone has things said behind their back! Weren't you just talking about me too?!" He wiggled his moustache.

"No, it was just that…"

"Anyway, never mind, that's not important. Do you think your financial status will allow you to attend your class reunion? Of course not. But you still want to go. That is pure vanity, sir. Vanity is the greatest enemy of thrift. Some people have sufficient financial status to afford a modicum of vanity. But you don't even have that."

I thought I'd try standing up to him this time. "It's all right to indulge myself a little, isn't it?"

The moustache man shook his head resolutely. "No, sir. It would not be indulging yourself. Yes, you'd have a drink or two. But drinking at a class reunion would not be indulging yourself. All you'd gain is fatigue. When you saw how well your classmates are doing, you'd be full of anger and resentment. And that would only make you drink more to drown your sorrows. Am I wrong, sir?"

Yes, that's exactly what would happen. I hung my head abjectly. "I understand. I won't attend the class reunion," I said. I felt so miserable that I could have wept.

My wife couldn't hide her relief.

"Oh dear, oh dear, oh dear. More needless luxury," the moustache man said, looking in dismay at our kitchen table. "Not just potato croquets, but no fewer than three bottled condiments, too. I'm not saying they're excessive in themselves. The problem is this: not only do they lack nutritional value, but they also encourage you to eat more of the main dish. And as you know, overeating is bad for your health. Well there! Just as I thought. Look how much rice you've made!" he cried as he took the lid off the rice-cooker.

My wife blushed and hung her head. "I'm sorry. I only wanted to make our humble meal look a little grander," she said. A single tear rolled down her cheek.

My feeling of misery was beyond description. I put my chopsticks down and turned to the moustache man. "You make us sound like paupers," I said with some sarcasm. "I'm not sure if I like that!"

But he didn't take it as sarcasm. "What's that, sir?" he said. "I make you sound like paupers?" He rose from his seat and knelt on it again. "You mean you don't see yourselves as paupers? How wrong you are. You *are* paupers. It's an undeniable fact that salaried workers today are the lowest class of all in this country. People selling bananas at late-night markets, tradesmen with special skills, they all earn more than salaried workers do. They may not save much, but even beggars are better off than you. You're just going to have to accept it. Salaried workers often fail in life. Why? Because they're weighed down by their superiority complex. The successful ones are those who quickly discard their sense of superiority. Prudent salaried workers are the ones who, though not actually saying it, know they're all paupers."

"How wretched we are," my wife said, starting to sob.

"What makes you think you're wretched, madam? You mustn't," the moustache man continued. "Because you see, being paupers also proves that you have no vices. All you're doing as salaried workers is using your meagre income to save for your own home, pay for your children's education, and contribute to pensions for your old age. In that way, you're helping the national economy and maintaining the healthy state of the country. There's nothing to be ashamed of at all, madam."

I'd been staring sideways at the moustache man as he cheerfully launched into his lecture. "How can you possibly understand how miserable we're feeling?" I countered. "After all, you can afford the prime steak lunch, can't you."

His eyes widened. "How could you say that, sir? How could you?! Oh, that you should be so petty in mind! Spying on others while they're eating, envying them! When did you succumb to such sordid thoughts? They bring far more shame on you than poverty ever will. How sad. How truly sad." He looked up to the ceiling as tears fell from his eyes. "How poverty dulleth the wit. Well fed, well bred, 'tis true. Alas, alas. Doth a life of poverty corrupt a man's heart so?"

Starting to loathe myself, I felt so utterly full of remorse that I too burst into tears.

"I didn't mean to say that," I pleaded. "I had no intention at all of saying that. Oh God! I feel so ashamed!" I slumped down on the kitchen table, held my head in my hands and cried uncontrollably.

"Darling! Darling!" My wife rushed up and held me from behind, weeping aloud herself.

The moustache man, who'd continued to weep and wail like a baby, now stopped abruptly and fixed his bloodshot eyes on me. "Please, cooperate with me. I'm trying my very hardest for you. No – for everyone in this block. The others are being most cooperative. Some of them are being much more frugal. For example, your neighbours the Hamaguchis. They haven't bought a new TV, they haven't bought a new washing machine. They've just persevered and persevered, and now they've saved fifteen million yen – nearly enough to buy a brand new home!"

"What? Fifteen million yen?!" My wife's eyes were gleaming.

"That's right, madam. With just a little more effort, they'll reach their target saving. What's more, they're both only forty-eight. What a truly wonderful couple. And it's all because they cooperated with me. They were as frugal as frugal could be, and saved up the money. So. You should try your hardest too!" The moustache man slapped us both on the shoulder with each of his hands.

"Yes," we both answered meekly, nodding like schoolchildren.

"When things are getting hard, when you're feeling low, I'll come and share your tears with you," he said. Then he pulled out a pure white handkerchief and wiped his cheeks.

"Thank you," we said in unison. "We'll be even thriftier than before. We'll try hard to save."

From that day on, the moustache man visited us with increasing frequency. Sometimes, I might feel like eating something special, and I'd come home with some sea-bream *sashimi*, for example. Then he'd invariably appear at our kitchen table, and glare at me through narrowed eyes. Sometimes he'd even take the food away with him, or beat me hard on the back with a length of washing-machine hose. What's more, he would always, always appear, however carefully we locked the front door or the French windows on our veranda.

"Hello, hello, hello! Here I am, here I am, here I am! Tanaka, Tanaka, Tanaka's the name!"

Sometimes he'd enter the kitchen from the next room, which has no other means of access. If we were in our bedroom, he'd emerge from the built-in wardrobe. I thought he must be getting in through the ceiling. All the apartments in our block share a communal loft space – he must have been using that. So I nailed up the ceiling panels above the wardrobe. Then he appeared in the toilet.

On the train in to work one morning, I met my neighbour Mr Hamaguchi. I just had to ask him when he was planning to buy his brand new home.

"Well, however hard we save, house prices just keep going up faster," he replied in a tone that suggested he was on the brink. "It might be all right if my salary kept going up too. But Mr Tanaka keeps telling us to be frugal, so I can't buy drinks for my staff any more, even though I'm the Chief Clerk. It's affecting my work. My superiors don't like me because I never give seasonal gifts. So

I'm not likely to get promoted. I don't know what we're saving for any more."

Actually, I'd been starting to feel the same way myself. If house prices were going up faster than we could save, what on earth were we saving for?!

One night, my wife looked at me reproachfully in bed. "You don't do anything for me these days," she said.

"Sorry. I'm really sorry," I said – and meant it. "I don't eat well enough. I'm always too tired."

"No. That's not it. You've changed." She started sobbing again. "When we were students, when we lived together, you used to love me then." Ours was a student romance. "We didn't have any money in those days. All we ate was junk food. But you still made love to me nearly every night. You don't love me any more. It's because I'm old and ugly, isn't it. That's why you don't make love to me any more."

"No, it's not that, really it isn't," I protested, and went to hold her. "You're still attractive. You're still beautiful."

She clung to me tightly. "Say it again! Say it again!"

"You're still attractive. You're still beautiful."

"Oh darling. Darling!"

"Hello, hello, hello! Here I am, here I am, here I am! Tanaka, Tanaka, Tanaka's the name!"

The moustache man came down through the ceiling panels just as we were starting to make love. I groaned on top of my wife. My wife heaved a sigh of desperation under me.

"Oh dear, oh dear. What's all this then, what's all this? Oh dear, oh dear. Look how close you are together." He squatted beside our bed and peered under my belly. "You mustn't, madam. Absolutely not. Your husband's tired. You should let him go to sleep. It's all right for a lady, but for a man, intercourse is very hard work. It's equivalent to a two-mile run, madam. What's more, one to six cubic centimetres of semen in a single ejaculation contains a huge amount of nutrition, namely protein, calcium, and glucose. Don't you care if your husband uses that much energy when he's had hardly anything to eat all day? Madam! Oh dear, oh dear, oh dear.

Look how he's sweating. What a waste. What a waste. This will really interfere with his work tomorrow. Don't forget, he has to put up with the packed rush-hour train as well. Madam, are you not aware how much strength he needs to endure that? Oh dear, oh dear, oh dear. You're still clinging so tightly to each other. Sir. Please remove yourself from your wife's body as soon as possible, sir. Sex is like a poison for the lower classes. You should both abstain from such wasteful pleasures. Oh dear. You're still so close. Come on. Quickly, now, quickly. Disengage, please. Disengage."

My wife began to wail uncontrollably.

Until now, I'd remained still with my head bowed as I lay there on top of my wife. But now I could take it no longer. I got up and started yelling at the moustache man. "WHO THE HELL DO YOU THINK YOU ARE, YOU SLIMY LITTLE PERVERT?!" I screamed.

But the next words wouldn't come out. My brain wasn't working properly, due to fatigue and malnutrition – though being so angry didn't help. I felt so abjectly worthless that large tears started to fall from my eyes. "Or, or do you mean to rob us paupers of our last remaining pleasure?" I added pathetically.

The moustache man had jumped back at first, startled by the ferocity of my tone. But now he knelt on the floor, stared at me through eyes that were red with tears, and said in a perfectly restrained voice: "Please cooperate with me."

"Cooperate? With you?! A vile peeping pervert like you?! Who asked you to come and spy on us in bed? I'll bloody kill you!" And I tried to grab hold of him.

"Just a minute. T-Tanaka, Tanaka, Tanaka's the name!" he said, resisting me passively with hands behind his back.

As he repeated his mantra, his voice had a hypnotic effect on me. Strength instantly drained from my limbs, and I flopped down onto the floor where I stood.

"If it means we have to feel this miserable," I said, "I'd rather not save money at all. I'd rather just spend every penny of it. After all, however much we save we'll never keep up with the rise in house prices."

At that, the moustache man jumped back to his feet with a cry. "You mustn't say that, sir!" he said. "I knew you'd say it sooner or later. That's what makes prices go up – half-desperate people who give up, thinking they'll never buy a house! They squander their meagre incomes hunting for the latest fashionable goods – and it's their consumer lifestyles that push prices up and cause big corporations to pollute! The root of all evil is the indiscriminate luxury, the desperate lust for merchandise, the beggar-like vanity of all these salaried workers! Do you want to demean yourself to their level?"

He sounds like a government official, I thought somewhat abstractedly. But I couldn't find the vigour to contradict him. My body quite lacked the energy to defy him now. I didn't even have the strength to listen to him any more.

"Well, it's late now," the moustache man said at length, having berated me continuously for a full half hour. "Just go to sleep now, ready for work tomorrow. You mustn't think about anything else. All right, sir?"

My wife, who'd been sitting in bed listening to the moustache man's lecture, had already fallen asleep and was snoring away without a care.

The moustache man went back up through the ceiling panels. I imagined him crawling around the communal loft space, peering down into other apartments and spying on other couples as they were having sex.

As if she'd learnt her lesson, my wife never again tried to arouse me at night. From that day on, she just went to sleep tamely on her own. Perhaps she wasn't actually suppressing her desires but had found some other method of satisfying them. Because, far from being hysterical, she always had a glint of pure satisfaction in her eyes. She was probably being satisfied by someone else. It may have been an illusion, because I was hungry and my vision was blurred. But two or three times, when I returned home from work unannounced, I saw my wife and the moustache man hurriedly moving away from each other. Maybe she was having an affair with him. But I didn't feel like questioning her about it. And anyway, even if I did discover she was having an affair with him – or with a different man altogether – I no longer had the strength to get angry about it. I would have no option but to pretend I hadn't noticed. In fact, vitality was slipping away from my body day by day, as I wasn't eating properly. Even my capacity to think straight, to grasp situations and work out how they would develop, was quickly starting to disappear.

"But hey," I thought incoherently, idly inside my feeble head. "He's satisfying my wife on my behalf, since I don't have the energy to. Because of him, I'm released from my wife's demands. I can go to work without collapsing, so I can carry on working. That's good, isn't it? If anything, I ought to thank him!"

But one day, the moustache man suddenly stopped visiting us. Not only did he stop visiting us, but he suddenly vanished from our apartment block, from our entire neighbourhood.

It was just a few days later that I realized he'd withdrawn almost our entire savings from our bank account before he vanished. And we weren't the only victims. All fourteen households in our block had suffered the same fate. All had believed, nay, never doubted that the moustache man had been sent from their bank. They'd entrusted him with their passbooks, and had handed him money and name seals to let him deposit their salaries into their accounts. In other words, they saw him as a kind of roving bank employee. And he disappeared the day after payday.

But at least he was human – at least he had some sort of conscience. For he'd been kind enough to leave the small sum of five thousand yen in each account to tide us over. That made me feel better. It was about the same amount as we spent on food each month. Yes! That was all we needed to keep us going until the next payday.

You see, our hard-earned savings are always going to be taken from us by *someone* – whether we have any or not.

The World Is Tilting

Marine City started tilting at the end of a particularly blustery autumn one year. A typhoon in September sent waves of almost tsunami-like proportions into the bay, where the City rested on an artificial island. The waves breached one of the bulkheads on the ballast tanks used to stabilize Marine City, causing its centre of gravity to shift south-southwestwards.

The entrance to the bay was on the south-southwest, and just after the middle of October, Marine City gradually started tilting towards the Pacific Ocean. But the angle could have been no more than about two degrees, and nobody noticed it at the time. Nor did it cause any inconvenience. Rod Le Mesurier first became aware of the tilt when an old university professor, Proven McLogick, spoke to him at a bus stop. They were both waiting for a bus to take them over Marine Bridge into the metropolis.

"Look you there, Master Le Mesurier," said the Professor. "Look at the northeastern wall of yon North No. 2 Block. The wall is supposed to be vertical, is it not. But try lining up the perpendicular of the corner with the perpendicular of the wall on that thirty-six-storey building – oh, what is it called? Yes, the Notatall Building, over there in the distance. Do you not see? Their tops are askew of one another."

Unlike the City's women, Rod was always most deferential to Professor McLogick, and perhaps because of this the Professor often spoke to him. Rod looked out in the direction indicated by the old man's leaden-grey, spindly finger, and saw that the top of the multi-storey building across the water in the metropolis was indeed tilting by about half an inch to the right, as his eye saw it, from the fifth floor of an apartment block on the northern edge of the City.

"So it is. It's sticking out a bit, isn't it. The Notatall Building must be tilting to the northeast."

"No, young man. The North No. 2 Block is tilting to the southwest. Look from over here. It's parallel to the perpendicular of North No. 1 Block, is it not."

Their conversation, which concluded somewhat sonorously that the whole of Marine City must therefore be tilting to the southwest, was overheard by Miss Loyalty, an office worker with proper and orderly features, who happened to be waiting at the same bus stop. Later that morning, she used her office telephone to report the conversation to the Mayor. The Mayor of Marine City, still in her first year of office, was a fifty-eight-year-old woman named Fedora Last. She'd always been on bad terms with Professor McLogick anyway. It was she who'd called for the creation of a "marine city" in the first place, and this distinction had led to her being elected the City's first Mayor. She loved Marine City to an almost obscene degree.

Fedora Last took the call from Miss Loyalty in her private office. She'd never entertained any particular opinion or feeling about Le Mesurier, though she knew him to be a salaried worker, since she was acquainted with his wife Caprice, an employee of the City. But she reacted quite strongly when she heard the name of Professor McLogick.

The Mayor ordered Rory O'Storm, the Chief of Police, to investigate the Professor, on the grounds that his observation was an uncivil act designed to spread malicious rumours, based on his spiteful intent to cause anxiety among the citizens. Later that day, Professor McLogick was called to the telephone in his university laboratory, and answered it with calm composure.

"Another order from Old Fat Arse," he said with a chuckle. Old Fat Arse was his nickname for Fedora Last, that being an anagram of her name. He was certainly fond of annoying her.

Marine City had an official news journal as befitting any large town, and at the beginning of April six prominent citizens, including the Mayor, had gathered in the Community Hall for an editorial round-table discussion. During the discussion, there was a heated confrontation between Fedora Last and Professor McLogick. Asked what Marine City needed most of all at the present time, the Mayor answered "A narrative". The other five interpreted this "narrative" as they wished, and so voiced their agreement. In fact, Fedora Last was thinking of a "Marine City Creation Story" in which her own name would go down in legend, along the lines of Joan of Arc. Professor McLogick, on the other hand, took the "narrative" to be a modern concept. The "narrative" as a postmodern term dates way back to 1979, when Jean-François Lyotard used it in his book *La Condition Postmoderne*. Here, "narrative" as a modern concept was used for the first time, for example in the sense that "the narrative of democracy is over". But then people started using the term to mean just what they wanted it to mean. Very few people interpreted the word correctly and used it in its original sense, as Professor McLogick did. So it would be fair to say that Fedora Last and Professor McLogick stood at opposite ends of the spectrum in their interpretation of the word "narrative". And it was therefore inevitable that they would not see eye to eye.

"Who will create this 'narrative', Mayor?"

"All of us, of course."

"Who do you mean by 'us'? Someone first has to create an ideology for the narrative, do they not?"

"A narrative is not an ideology. Do you mean to deny our democratic principles?"

"So your intention is not to create a narrative that will replace democracy?"

"My intention is to create a narrative."

"What are you talking about?"

"What are you talking about?"

Professor McLogick, exasperated at the Mayor's utter lack of comprehension, could hold back no more. "Alas, I fear it's true. By nature, women are in all respects inferior to men."

"I could have you arrested for that," the Mayor retorted. "Women will respond to the physical violence of men with the violence of language. Sometimes, women's linguistic violence will spark physical violence by men. Therefore, linguistic violence should also be punished. It was a man who said that. But now, men's linguistic violence is a penal offence, while that of women is not. It was me who proposed this law and pushed it through. You know that very well."

"Yes, I know. But it wasn't me who said what I said. It was Schopenhauer."

"Shoppinghour?! Bring him here. Where is the man with such a ridiculous name?"

"He died about 180 years ago," answered the Professor.

Fedora Last was speechless. As she later divulged to her subordinate Caprice Le Mesurier, she'd been momentarily stunned by the thought that, if he knew someone who'd died about 180 years ago, Professor McLogick must himself be more than 200 years old.

Also at the meeting were the entrepreneur Kapital Interest, the poetess Stille Hungova, and the writer Justa Plagiarist. The round-table meeting was somehow brought to a conclusion through their mediation. But from that time on, Fedora Last remained wary of Professor McLogick. This argument was followed by a series of trifling incidents between the pair, which would be quite risible to record in detail – for example, the incident concerning the assessment of municipal tax, the quarrel in the French restaurant "Le Château" that had to be broken up by a waiter, the students who were incited to set off fireworks and use abusive language in front of the Mayor's official residence – and so on, and so on.

On returning home from work that day, Rod Le Mesurier was surprised to find his wife Caprice at home before him. She immediately began to attack him.

"You started the rumour that Marine City's tilting, didn't you."

"It's not a rumour, it's true."

Rod made abundant use of voice impressions, hand gestures and other signals to explain his conversation with Professor McLogick at the bus stop that morning, along with their various observations and conclusions.

"Look, you can see it from here. All the blocks in that estate are tilting, but not the Notatall Building."

Caprice made no attempt at all to look across to the dusk-smothered metropolis to which Rod pointed from their 11th floor window. Instead, she spat out with venom: "You're a fool."

"Am I?"

Rod's eyes widened. He fixed a stare on his wife, who stood there in her negligée with arms folded.

"Didn't you think it might just be the Notatall Building that's tilting to the north-northeast? That's why I say you're a fool."

"Actually, that's what I thought at first."

"You were completely taken in by that old goat. How many times must I tell you not to talk to idiots like him?"

Rod Le Mesurier found himself struck lightly on the head with a bottle opener, fashioned from a kangaroo's paw, that lay on the dining table. He calculated the pain level at 3.6 kiltago. "I'm a fool, yes I am," he said in utter dejection.

"Yes, you're a fool. Come over here, then."

Miss Loyalty arrived home at about the same time. Noting that the angle of the Chagall print on her wall was wrong, she adjusted the frame with an abnormal degree of precision that amply explained why she was still single. Despite her realization that this was already the third time she'd corrected the angle, she failed to make the connection between this and the conversation she'd reported earlier in the day.

The next day, Professor McLogick proceeded to the police station with drawings showing the tilt of Marine City, which he'd ordered a student in the Engineering Department to survey the previous afternoon. To the detective who came to take his statement he roared, "This is a serious matter, you won't do, get me the Chief of Police!" He showed the drawings to Rory O'Storm when the Chief at last came out, and explained that the tilt of Marine City was neither false rumour nor malicious gossip, but was, in fact, fact.

"And what do you think is the cause of the tilt?" asked O'Storm as if seeking guidance, unable to contradict the proof he'd been shown.

"The typhoon in September, and the fact that the ballast is unstable, I should say."

By "the ballast is unstable", he meant that it was made of pachinko balls.

"But what about the bulkheads?"

"One of them has been breached. And it's possible that others might also be breached in future, by way of a chain reaction."

"So you're saying the tilt could get worse?"

"That's right. I'm glad you're so quick to understand." Professor McLogick smiled. "It's a good job the Chief of Police isn't a woman, at least."

Rory O'Storm thought he might just go ahead and commission the university to do a detailed survey for the police. He could report it to the Mayor later. It was not beyond him to understand that Fedora Last would never trust the drawings and other data that Professor McLogick had brought with him. If he reported them heedlessly, she might turn her anger on the Chief of Police himself.

That night, a magnitude 4 earthquake awoke Fedora Last as she slept in her private room at the Mayor's official residence. She herself had proudly proclaimed that Marine City could never be struck by an earthquake, as it rested on a floating artificial island. But she'd recently learnt that violent upheavals of sea water could also shake the island to a perceptible degree. Fedora couldn't sleep. Was it just her imagination, or had she heard the faint sound of thousands of pachinko balls rolling coarsely along the bottom of the city's foundations just a moment ago? It was a sound that held such loathsome memories for Fedora Last, who somewhat regretted using these, of all things, as ballast for an artificial island.

Though it was now thirty-five years ago, Fedora Last's husband, who used to work in a paper factory, had been an avid gambler. He would waste his whole monthly salary on pachinko, a pinball game that used hundreds of metal balls. As if that weren't enough, he mounted up debts as well. Losing a small amount on pachinko in one day would turn into a monumental loss over the year. And though he might win a small sum every few days, he would merely spend the winnings on drink, and the cash would vanish before he got home. With no spending money and a child to care for, Fedora was unable to find a side job. So, when her husband was sacked for skipping work and taking excessive advances on his salary, Fedora took the opportunity to divorce him, and from that time on devoted all her energy to a women's group in the lower echelons of a political party.

Due to the ensuing tsunami rather than the earthquake itself, Marine City was tilting just over three degrees to the south-southwest by the following morning. The poetess Stille Hungova awoke with a terrific headache that day. At first, she thought she must be still hungover, but her head failed to clear by lunchtime, and in the afternoon she decided to go to the nearby Toximere Clinic. In the Clinic's waiting room she found many other women with the same complaint. Her conversations with them merely told her that many of their husbands also had the same headache, that all of them were also suffering from vertigo, and so on. They did not inform her, however, that they'd all slept with their heads turned to the south the previous night and that none of them had slept facing north, which was generally considered unlucky.

The first to confirm the tilt in Marine City's elevation, now more than three degrees, was Stubber Nasamule, head of the public works contractor Nasamule Engineering. He was in the process of putting up a sales kiosk in Marineland Park, under commission from the Parks Department. At first, on surveying the half-completed kiosk with a spirit level and finding that the floor was tilting by three degrees, he started to panic, thinking he'd botched the job. But when he placed his spirit level at various points inside and outside the park just to be sure, he discovered that every point he surveyed was tilting a little more than three degrees to the south-southwest. He went to City Hall to report this fact, and was received there by Caprice Le Mesurier. She disliked his old-fashioned, chauvinistic tone of voice, started to argue with him in the middle of his report, and handed him over to security when he began to shout back. To make matters worse, she deliberately omitted to pass the report to Fedora Last. This was partly because she was afraid of further aggravating the Mayor, who, for some reason, had been in a bad mood since the morning. But it was also because she had a premonition that the tilt in Marine City's elevation would have inauspicious consequences for her.

There were a number of casualties in Marine City that day.

Many resulted from falls on stairs, sloping roads, sloping entrances to buildings, and so on. Some women and elderly citizens were in critical condition after suffering blows to the head as they fell. Several infants playing on a south-facing slide at a nursery school suffered broken teeth and other injuries when they collided with the ground after sliding down at abnormally high speed. As luck would have it, those with the most serious injuries were all taken to different hospitals, where they were assumed to have sustained their injuries through carelessness. As a result, no one was able to grasp the unusually large scale of casualties in the City as a whole.

Meanwhile, many others who lived in Marine City but worked in the metropolis started to complain of headaches, ringing ears, and dizziness caused by abnormality in the semicircular canals of their inner ears soon after they started work, and sought treatment at clinics near their respective workplaces. Rod Le Mesurier also had a headache, again. Calculating the pain level as 5.2 kiltago, he took himself to a clinic near his office during the lunch break. In all cases, the symptoms soon disappeared when the functions of locomotive analysis in three-dimensional space returned to normal. But when evening came, the sufferers all returned to Marine City, which was of course tilting at an angle of more than three degrees, and this restored the abnormality in their semicircular canals.

"You know, it's just as I thought – the whole island's tilting!" Rod Le Mesurier felt compelled to announce that evening, knowing only too well how his wife would react.

Caprice Le Mesurier glared at her husband with eyes glinting yellow, like a leopard's. "You're going to start on about that again, are you. Well, you know that if the rumour spreads, they'll all say it's your fault. Then I'll be sacked, and we'll have to leave Marine City."

"Haven't you got a headache? Well anyway, you know those things builders use, spirit levels? I'm going to try and bring one home tomorrow, you see." It was the first time Rod hadn't been silenced merely by the look on his wife's face. He worked for a company that made nothing but measuring instruments for stationery, construction tools, medical instruments and the like. He belonged to the Development Division in the company's laboratory.

To her credit, Caprice gave it a moment's thought. After all, there'd also been the altercation with Stubber Nasamule earlier in the day. Of course, the central thrust of her "thought" was self-protection and self-advancement, as always. "If I'm the first to discover that Marine City is tilting and report it to the Mayor, I could get promoted. But what if it's all a pack of lies?"

"Actually, it was Professor McLogick who first discovered it."

"No," and she glared at him again. "Once the tilt has become undeniable, I will be the first to discover it and report it to the Mayor – officially, not as a malicious rumour. Do you understand?"

Unable to follow his wife's logic, Rod changed the subject. "The North No. 2 Block was tilting a bit more when I looked this morning. Well, I'm going to get our company to make a lot of spirit levels and distribute them to stationers all over Marine City. We'll make a lot of money when everyone starts noticing the tilt, I should think."

Caprice smiled wryly. "That's about the best you can come up with, isn't it. Look what happened last time, when you thought of that, what was it called, that funny thing. You made yourself a laughing stock."

"You mean the painometer. There was nothing funny about it. The Director merely said it would be difficult to commercialize." When it came to matters technological, Rod had no thoughts for anything else. "I figured they might need them in hospitals and the like. That's why I worked out the units of pain. Look!" He slapped himself hard on the cheek. "Whenever you do that to me, the pain level is one kiltago. Of course, pain thresholds differ from person to person. It's like the average body temperature. The painometer calculates the degree of pain based on the heat emitted from the affected area, the sensation in the tactile region of the brain, the pulse and so on. The first models will be very primitive, but they'll gradually increase in precision, and then I think everyone will be interested and want to buy one."

Caprice stared blankly at Rod as he continued his discourse. Not that she was listening to a word he said. No, she was thinking, "Oh dear. Why did I have to marry this man? He's so brainless, unrefined and cack-handed, slow on the uptake, so dull that he can only think of one thing. But, well… maybe he's just right for me."

At around the same time, the pianist Histe Rica was giving a recital in Marine City Hall, a 200-seater venue. Soon after she started performing Bartók's *Improvisations for Piano*, her grand piano started to edge, little by little, across the stage towards the auditorium. The first to notice this was a young lighting technician whose job was to train the fresnel lens spotlight on the artiste. Ms Rica herself failed to notice the movement, as her chair was shifting along with the piano. Moreover, since the purpose of a fresnel lens is to soften the edges of the light, the piano's right leg was only a few inches from the edge of the stage when the lighting technician realized what was happening. As he was desperately wondering how to inform the artiste, the piano plunged into the auditorium with a deafening roar, performed a half-turn with its three legs pointing upwards, then described another half turn that broke its legs and pedals, hurling them into the air, scattering the hammers and keys, and causing the strings to fly out. The momentum sent Histe Rica sprawling, exposing her fleshy white thighs and lemon-yellow underwear, and leaving her upside down at the foot of the stage. Three women in the front row were either struck by the lid of the piano or crushed under it. They suffered ruptured organs, skull fractures, and smashed faces, and all died instantly. Another woman was decapitated by a snapped piano wire, while twelve others nearby suffered non-fatal injuries of varying degrees. Panic broke out in the Hall, which was virtually full for this recital. After all, Histe Rica had a music school in Marine City, and a large number of protégés. The Hall was soon surrounded by police cars and ambulances, and it wasn't until the following morning that the situation was brought under control.

At first, the families of the victims rushed to point the finger at Histe Rica's over-enthusiastic performance as the cause of the accident, but it was quickly discovered that this was not the case. For the results of the university survey had already reached Rory O'Storm, and it was immediately proved that the southwest-facing stage was tilting at an angle of three degrees – even before Stubber

Nasamule, who lived near the Hall and heard the commotion, could race up with spirit level in hand as if to say "I told you so!"

Fedora Last first heard of the incident when Rory O'Storm called her at seven o'clock the following morning. She immediately considered sacking both O'Storm and Caprice Le Mesurier, he for withholding his report on the conversation with Professor McLogick, she for turning Nasamule away. But then she had better thoughts, realizing that the incident was ultimately due to the spiteful vengeance of pachinko balls. Instead, she turned her anger partly towards self-reproach, partly towards her former husband.

As she had consolidated her position inside the party, so Fedora Last's anti-pachinko movement had gathered momentum, until finally, after twenty years of struggle, the Pachinko Parlour Prohibition Bill that she herself had proposed was passed by the National Assembly. Of course, that wasn't her only achievement. If it had been, it would merely have been disregarded as "an idiotic Bill proposed by a silly old cow who hates pachinko". No, by this time the concept of Marine City as a feminist paradise had already started to take shape, more or less through the single-minded determination of Fedora Last alone.

As a result of the new law, some 10,102 pachinko parlours across the country had been closed down and 2,926,461 pachinko consoles destroyed. As these figures were taken from a survey of police stations and tax offices in 2019, they may not have been strictly accurate. But since 4,000 pachinko balls had been used for each pachinko console, this would suggest the astronomical quantity of 11,705,844,000 pachinko balls. The next problem had been how to dispose of them. Fedora Last, who had assumed personal responsibility for this undertaking, had the idea of using them as ballast for her Marine City. The Construction Ministry had not approved the plan, pointing out that pachinko balls were too unstable to be used for this purpose. But Fedora Last, now the party's leading woman, already had a large number of supporters. A member of her self-styled Brain Trust, partly out of an uncon- scious desire to flatter, had proposed that bulkheads be built in chessboard formation to contain the ballast balls. Fedora had jumped at this proposal and insisted on it to the end.

Work had started on building the foundations of Marine City. Well, "foundations" might not be the word, since the City was floating on sea water. But work had started on installing the ballast tanks that would be equivalent to its foundations. There had been some corruption at this point, a case of bribery that also involved Caprice Le Mesurier. The construction company had falsified the bulkhead specifications to increase the amount of the bribe, but had used bulkheads made of slightly thinner walls and offering lower resistance than those stated in the specifications or drawings.

Since it was now clear that the tilt in Marine City was due to some abnormality in the ballast tanks, three surveyors were sent down a manhole into the City's sewers on the afternoon after the incident with the piano. From there they descended further, through an opening used for repair work, into the ballast tanks at the bottom of Marine City. The surveyors walked across the tops of the bulkheads that divided the blocks into their chessboard formation, each block containing a fixed weight of pachinko balls, and eventually located the damage. A hole had formed in one of the bulkhead walls, and the pachinko balls that should have been in the block to the northeast of it had all flowed into the block to the southwest, disturbing the general equilibrium. Considering the overall tilt of Marine City, it seemed unlikely that this would be the only breach point. Nevertheless, the surveyors climbed down the bulkhead wall along a rope ladder, quickly reaching the bottom of the block some three metres below, where they started to survey the state of the damage.

As luck would have it, another earthquake struck a little more than twenty minutes after the survey started. Pachinko balls flooded back into the northeastern block and trapped one of the surveyors there before returning to the southwestern block. The impetus breached another bulkhead, through which the balls flowed into the next block on the southwestern side. Unable to rescue their colleague owing to the obvious danger, the other two surveyors hurried back to the surface, where they called for help from the police and fire services.

With this, a great commotion broke out. Nearly all police and fire service personnel were mobilized, and Rory O'Storm even had to ask for support from the metropolis, since there weren't enough personnel in Marine City alone. The trapped surveyor was rescued but was in a critical condition, with bruises all over his body. An aftershock during the rescue operation caused further damage to the bulkheads, seriously injuring two of the rescuers and lightly injuring three more, while another died of asphyxiation when his bronchial tubes were filled with pachinko balls.

It wasn't until the following morning – when Caprice Le Mesurier, learning of the commotion in a memo from the City offices but not thinking for a moment that an investigation into the corruption would start that very same day, was in the middle of berating her husband for not hitting on his spirit-level idea a day earlier – that it was discovered that there were more than a hundred breach points in the bulkhead walls, and that the walls used for the bulkheads were thinner than specified on the design drawings.

The angle of tilt in the city's elevation was now four degrees. Readers may like to equip themselves with protractors from this point on. At an angle of four degrees, danger is imminent, and in fact, this was when serious accidents started occurring all over the City.

The roads of Marine City were mostly made of concrete, laid horizontally. That morning, Justa Plagiarist went out for a stroll and, as usual, saw a boy going to school on his skateboard. Justa was still unaware of the tilt and, astonished by the unusually high speed at which the boy was travelling, inadvertently called out:

"Oy! You'll have an accident! Stop!"

The boy turned to look at him. "I can't!" he cried.

Justa closed his eyes. A lorry approached from the opposite direction. When he looked again, he could see the boy disappearing under the lorry, still squatting on his skateboard. *Thank goodness it was a high-floored vehicle*, thought a relieved Justa, before turning back to have another look. The boy, who'd now emerged from under the lorry and was sliding into the distance on his skateboard, was headless. He'd been cleanly decapitated by something protruding under the lorry's chassis.

With the sirens of police cars and ambulances wailing from early evening until well into the night, most people in Marine City had by now realized that something was afoot. In spite of this, Mayor

Fedora Last ordered that the true situation should not be announced until the end of an Emergency Meeting, which started in the early morning. As a result, life went on as usual in various parts of the City, and this led to numerous accidents.

The supermarket operated by Kapital Interest opened for business at ten o'clock. Customers who'd been enticed by newspaper advertisements rushed onto escalators to reach the bargain sale counters. The south-facing escalators, originally inclined at an angle of thirty degrees, had now tilted to thirty-four degrees, while the steps themselves were inclined at four degrees. An obese middle-aged woman at the head of the throng, stepping off the upwards escalator on the first floor, slipped on the grooved cleat and fell flat on her backside. This set off a landslide, as two shoppers on each step behind her toppled backwards in a domino effect. Shrieking like exotic birds, scores of women became piled up in clumps at various points of the escalator, which continued to travel upwards. As it did, the women on top of each pile were hurled over the handrails and down onto the ground floor below. Some fell into glass showcases. Store personnel managed to stop the escalator, but the impetus of this set off another collapse among the clumps of shoppers, leaving scores of them with major injuries on the ground floor. It was a disaster.

Reports of accidents came flying in as the Emergency Meeting continued. Besides the escalator catastrophe, there were two incidents in which runaway wheelchairs rolled down the slope in front of a hospital and were hit by moving cars on the road outside, and nine incidents in which people collided with each other after slipping and falling from stairs, resulting in contusions, fractures, badly bitten tongues, and other injuries. Some were drowned and others went missing when six anglers, including children and seniors, slid into the sea from a seafront angling arena. And so on, and so on, and so on.

The meeting continued until late afternoon. At one point, Fedora Last – at the stern insistence of Rory O'Storm – reluctantly issued an order prohibiting the use of escalators. However, she forcibly deferred measures designed to prevent other kinds of accidents, saying it was "too early to tell". The meeting ended with the following resolutions.

1. All residents of Marine City will sooner or later come to know of the City's tilt. As such, no special steps shall be taken to report it.

2. As for accidents caused by the tilt, measures shall only be taken in serious cases. The others shall be ignored as they are too insignificant.

3. Until the damage at the bottom of Marine City is repaired, City employees shall not officially admit to the existence of the tilt in word or deed.

4. Marine City employees shall not be permitted to move home or evacuate outside the City.

5. City employee Caprice Le Mesurier, currently under police investigation on suspicion of corruption, is to be released immediately, since her services are needed in responding to this emergency.

At the conclusion of the meeting, Rory O'Storm – the only man to attend it – was utterly enraged and announced his resignation.

On the same day, Rod Le Mesurier toured stationery shops and builders' merchants in the City to accept their many orders for spirit levels, protractors, set squares, T-squares, and other sundry instruments, then returned to his office to order them from the company warehouse. One week later, the warehouse had no stock left at all. By the time the City's residents knew of the tilt and were falling over themselves to buy these items because they needed to stop their furniture moving – as a result of which the products were soon sold out – the tilt had already become so severe that such measuring instruments were utterly useless. Even without earthquakes or tidal waves, the weight of the pachinko balls leaning to the southwest was enough to set off a chain reaction of breaches in the bulkhead walls. It was far too dangerous to even attempt repair work. With no contractors willing to accept the work, the progressive destruction of the ballast tanks was allowed to continue. The angle of inclination increased to eleven degrees. There was a series of accidents involving overturned vehicles, and the number of cars crossing from the metropolis decreased. But Mayor Fedora Last took no measures to cope with these accidents. Her reasoning was that it was perfectly normal to have sloping roads.

It was the punctilious Miss Loyalty who was most annoyed by the tilt in her home, which put her in a state of nervous exhaustion. Though not actually an employee of the City, she was a member of the women's group, and had pledged allegiance to Fedora Last as an external member of the Mayor's Brain Trust. As such, she wouldn't even dream of leaving Marine City. She fastened down all her furniture like a woman possessed, adjusted her picture frames, and fixed them at an angle to match the overall tilt of her apartment. Then she started walking with her body inclined at an angle of precisely eleven degrees to the southwest, or, to be more exact, to the south-southwest-by-west, ensuring that she remained perpendicular to the ground. The same was true when she stood still. In this way, Miss Loyalty could demonstrate that Marine City was not tilting, as she was still standing perpendicular to the ground, enabling her also to confirm her loyalty to Fedora Last. What's more, she maintained this eleven-degree inclination when she commuted into the metropolis to work every day. Thus she was able to assert that it was not Marine City that was tilting, but the rest of the world.

Soon, others who worked in the metropolis started to copy Miss Loyalty, and tried to find spiritual balance by tilting their bodies. As a result, many people could now be seen in the metropolis walking with their bodies tilted eleven degrees to the southwest. Not only did this mark them out as residents of Marine City, but the direction in which they tilted was also a useful aid to judging compass bearings.

Early on Sunday – the day the tilt increased from eleven to twelve degrees – Professor McLogick prepared to move out of the City. He didn't keep many books at home anyway, and his furniture easily fitted into a single removal van. He'd nearly finished loading the furniture, with the help of two removal men and two of his students, when they were spotted by some local housewives who'd just got up and now came to surround them. Most of them were sympathizers of the Mayor, and had already tried various tricks to stop people escaping. This time, however, their adversary was Professor McLogick. They knew that their persuasion would be to no avail, that the tables would only be turned and he'd start lecturing them, and that, if anything, they'd end up wishing he would just leave. So all they did, at first, was to surround the truck from a distance and loudly hurl abuse.

"So you're running away then!"

"Coward! Call yourself a man?!"

"Frightened of a little slope, are we?"

But Professor McLogick wouldn't be Professor McLogick if he didn't have his say at this point. "Ladies," he called out loudly. "You'd better leave quickly too. The buildings will start falling soon. After all, it stands to reason that they haven't been built properly, with all this bribery and corruption."

From among the housewives stepped one woman. She strode forwards, stopped in front of the Professor, and slapped him hard on the face.

It was Miss Loyalty. The sound of the slap rang out through the fresh morning air.

"What do you think you're doing?!" screamed one of the students, full of youthful vigour. He ran straight up to Miss Loyalty and punched her to the ground.

All hell broke loose. The house was in the middle of an estate. One look from their upper floor balconies told the other residents what was happening right away. Housewives came swarming in like wasps from all directions.

The Professor jumped onto the loading platform at the back of the van. "Get in quick! Get in quick!" he yelled at the students, who were fighting with the women over some boxes that hadn't been loaded yet. "I don't need those. Get in quick. If we're caught by the police, we'll all be executed!"

"Jesus!"

"Move it!"

The removal men, shaken at the thought of execution, started up the van in a panic. The students managed to free themselves from the women, and jumped onto the platform in the nick of time. The housewives, being women, declined to chase the van in a bid to stop it leaving. And so, Professor McLogick made his escape from Marine City.

The following morning, the poetess Stille Hungova awoke at six o'clock, still hungover, and went to get a drink of tap water. "Urghhh!" she exclaimed as she spat it out. It was sea water.

The water pipes from the mainland had burst. They'd been designed with sufficient tolerance for movement, bearing in mind that Marine City was built on an artificial island. But now the pipes had been crushed on the seabed. The water supply to Marine City was cut. The gas supply was also turned off, in view of the obvious danger. That day, Mayor Fedora Last asked the Waterworks Bureau for a supply of water to Marine City using tank trucks. Meanwhile, shoppers fought tooth and nail over mineral water in supermarkets and propane gas in hardware stores; dozens of housewives were seriously injured.

Caprice Le Mesurier, appointed Chief of Police to succeed Rory O'Storm, suddenly started to assume a more friendly attitude towards her husband Rod. This was partly because she saw him in a different light now that he'd been promoted to Head of Sales. But it was also because she'd been compelled to vow even greater allegiance to Fedora Last, like it or not, in view of the tremendous debt she now owed her. She'd be in dire straits if Rod said he wanted to move out. On that day, as it happened, the Transport Bureau gave notice that the bus service between the metropolis and the City would terminate the following day. Now Caprice would have to buy Rod the car he'd always wanted.

Prompted by the loss of water and the termination of the bus service, more citizens now tried to escape to the mainland, resulting in scores of skirmishes with people trying to stop them. The writer Justa Plagiarist realized there was no way he could carry all his household effects off, so he simply boarded the last bus to the metropolis with nothing but the clothes on his back. Supermarket owner Kapital Interest and his young wife were about to sneak away in their car, taking only their art works and other belongings of value, when they were discovered by the neighbourhood housewives, who immediately destroyed the car and the art works in it. For good measure they also pulled the clothes off the backs of the fleeing pair, leaving them to run for their lives, half-naked, across Marine Bridge.

THE WORLD IS TILTING

Children and students who attended schools and colleges in the metropolis gradually fled across the bridge to safety, some with their parents, some on their own as their parents insisted on staying, some after violent rows with their mothers. At least the housewives didn't prevent *them* from leaving. They also turned a blind eye to parents who left with their children. This was because there'd been a series of accidents in which infants had fallen to their deaths from tilting stairs or balconies in their homes, fallen on roads and suffered serious harm, and so on. But men who tried to leave on grounds of greater convenience for commuting were stopped and forced to commute from Marine City by car. Rod Le Mesurier did so every day, taking five others with him. Often, husbands who worked in the metropolis would fail to return home in the evening, leaving their abandoned wives to be pilloried and vilified by their neighbours.

The national government issued an order for all residents of Marine City to leave the island. Furious, Fedora Last declared her intention to disobey the order. It was "tyrannical interference in the affairs of a local authority" and a "serious challenge to feminism". "I will not obey the order. **Marine City is not tilting**."

The tilt worsened with each passing day. On Wednesday it was eighteen degrees, on Thursday it was twenty. Soon, the power had failed and telephone links were broken. On Thursday evening, Marine Bridge collapsed into the sea with a great reverberating boom. With that, the road connection to the metropolis was lost.

Professor McLogick's prediction that buildings would collapse was, in fact, inaccurate. The only building to fall was Marine City Hall, which was built of brick. Most steel-reinforced concrete buildings had upright metal sections welded to the steel base of the City, replacing the usual pile-driven foundations. But now those buildings were starting to become warped. Of course, lifts stopped working. Doors would not open once closed, nor close once opened. So, for fear of being trapped inside their homes, residents started to leave their doors open. Even so, the buildings somehow stayed upright. But the shift in their centre of gravity only served to accelerate the tilt in Marine City. On Friday, the angle reached twenty-three degrees. At such an acute angle, even pavements that were originally flat could no longer be walked on. Well, "walk" was hardly the word anyway – people would be sliding and falling as they crept along the roads. They also had to be wary of objects falling from above. Children's toys, shoes, kitchenware, and sundry household goods falling from verandas were one thing. But sometimes even dogs or people would come tumbling down, or pianos would crash through iron railings and plummet to the ground. Which was not such a laughing matter. Soon, it was normal to see housewives, who'd popped out for a spot of shopping, returning home with bloody injuries and their clothing in shreds.

Several buildings along the coast at the southwestern end of Marine City – including a children's amusement centre, the Toximere Clinic, and a poodle parlour – were soon submerged. A nearby road that ran from north to south sloped diagonally into the sea. Sometimes cars or people would slide sideways off the camber of the road and simply disappear under the water. For this reason, the area came to be constantly patrolled by police boats. As well as saving people who came sliding down the road, they also had the admirable task of rescuing desperate Marine City residents who tried to escape the City secretly at night and ferrying them over to the mainland. Helicopters circled above the City during the day, urging residents to leave and telling them where the police boats were waiting.

"Damn. It could at least have collapsed while I was at work. Then I needn't have come home!"

Caprice Le Mesurier dragged Rod, still grumbling thus as he gazed out through the window of their apartment – which now leant at an angle of twenty-six degrees – at the straits into which Marine Bridge had collapsed, back into bed on Saturday morning.

"What are you moaning about? Come here, I said."

"But it's every morning these days!"

"What about it?! You haven't anything better to do, have you?!"

The Le Mesurier residence was on the northeastern side of the building, at the far end of an open walkway on the eleventh floor. As the couple entered the throes of ecstasy, the nails that fastened the legs of their bed to the floor came loose, causing the bed to slide out of the bedroom with considerable force. It travelled across the living room and out through the front door (which had of course been left open) onto the walkway, where it struck a woman and hurled her high over the railings, before finally colliding with the iron railings at the southwestern end. The railings stopped the bed, but the momentum sent Rod and Caprice, still in their coital embrace, flying naked through the air.

Miss Loyalty, who could no longer get to work, was appointed Chief of Police to replace the late Caprice Le Mesurier. Nothing could have suited her better. Since the only remaining police staff were two female deskworkers, she donned the uniform herself, correctly tilted her body at an angle of twenty-six degrees to the south-southwest, and ran around Marine City investigating incidents and accidents as if considerations such as gravity were not an issue. If she spotted anyone trying to leave the City, she would take out her pistol and fire shots at them. She remained active even at night, when she would be involved in spectacular gunfights with the police boats as she tried to stop them carrying escapees to the mainland. With this, those left on the island lost their last remaining means of escape.

The alcohol requirement of the poetess Stille Hungova increased. If anything, the drink took effect more quickly now that she was living in a tilting world; she was more or less in a permanent state of inebriation. One day, she went out in search of more alcohol, and started to negotiate the southwest-facing stairs of her apartment building. As the stairs were originally inclined at forty-two degrees, the angle was now more than seventy degrees. She immediately fell, hit the road, bounced twice on its surface, then started sliding along it. Wearing an Oriental gown, she continued to slide along in her wholly unseemly state, then, after sinking six metres into the sea on the already submerged road, gently floated back to the surface. The crew of a tourist pleasureboat, carrying fifty-six passengers who callously wanted to see the tilting Marine City for themselves, threw out a life belt from a safe distance in an attempt to rescue her. No sooner had she been hauled up on deck than she started badgering the onlookers for alcohol, amazing all and sundry with her sheer pluck and courage.

In no time at all, the tilt had increased to forty degrees. Soon, people no longer knew whether they were going up- or down-stairs. People who slipped in the street found themselves not so much sliding as actually falling down the road. By now, the only people remaining in Marine City were the Mayor Fedora Last, the Chief of Police Miss Loyalty, and thirteen other women. The only man left was the carpenter Stubber Nasamule. Determined to see the end of Marine City, he'd made his wife and children leave for the mainland, while he himself enjoyed the sight of the City gradually sinking under the sea. He fashioned a rope walkway that allowed him to crawl back and forth along the road from his home to the supermarket, where goods could now be taken for free. He also made handholds and footholds here and there on other roads to prevent slippage. He even made some on request for the remaining women. Even then, he himself slipped on occasion, once sliding tens of yards. But he was always sure to keep the rope tied securely around his body. Even if he were to fall into the sea, he was confident of his ability to swim.

Some of the remaining women didn't need to trouble Stubber at all, relying on their own wits to devise means of motion. One of them found a way of moving from building to building using ropes. But such measures were out of the question for Fedora Last, on account of her obesity. Finally, she came to a decision and ordered Miss Loyalty to take her to the most northerly apartment building in Marine City. It was now clear that, once the tilt reached forty-five degrees, it would only be a matter of time before the city capsized completely. Under orders from Fedora Last, Miss Loyalty chained the Mayor's body to a water tower at the top of the building.

Actually, the government hadn't expected Marine City to tilt this far, and had tended to take a rather optimistic view of things. The assumption was that, once the sunken south-southwest section of Marine City's base reached the bottom of the bay – which itself should only be sixty metres deep, at the deepest point – the tilting would naturally stop. But when the angle approached forty-five degrees, there was now a very real possibility that the whole island could capsize. Nobody understood why the bottom of the bay had become so deep. Not even the author knew. Some speculated that the base had sunk into the mud layer at the bottom of the bay, and was gouging out the mud. But the mud layer couldn't possibly continue for a depth of several miles, and it was therefore decided, after all, that the reason was unknown. So, the debate now turned to urgent measures to prevent the City from completely turning over.

At last, the day had come when Marine City was predicted to capsize completely. An air force rescue team in a 26-seater V-107/A helicopter came to pick up the last survivors. One of its occupants was Rory O'Storm, who'd volunteered to persuade the remaining residents. The helicopter descended into the middle of the residential area and hovered at a height of two metres while staying more or less parallel to the ground. The rescue operation started. Realizing that to stay on the island would mean certain death, the thirteen housewives responded to persuasion and came out one by one. Stubber Nasamule followed suit.

It was almost midday. After passing forty-five degrees, the angle of inclination quickly started shifting to ninety degrees. Buildings began to make strange creaking, grating noises in unison, and objects began to fall at random onto the helicopter from buildings in the northeast.

The V-107/A had successfully picked up the thirteen women and Stubber Nasamule, along with two dogs and five cats, and was about to start its ascent, when Miss Loyalty, her body correctly inclined at 72.8 degrees to the south-southwest-by-west, came racing out of an apartment building to the northeast, popping away with her pistol, which she aimed at the helicopter's rotor. Rory O'Storm, judging her to be no longer human but some kind of demon, shot her dead.

The helicopter pulled away and set off towards the roof of the apartment building at the northeastern end of the City. The intention was to persuade Fedora Last, still chained to the iron frame of the water tower there, to give herself up. Rory O'Storm called out to her.

"Come any closer and I'll shoot!" she screamed back, brandishing a pistol that Miss Loyalty must have given her. "I'll have none of your meddling here!"

"Mayor. If you stay here you will die!" Rory O'Storm tried his hardest to explain. "Please leave with us. Marine City can always be rebuilt."

"Oh yes?!" the Mayor shouted back. She was looking up from what was virtually the summit of Marine City, which now protruded vertically from the sea on its side. "You men will just have a good laugh and say we told you so! Of course it won't be rebuilt!"

"The angle has reached ninety degrees. Mayor. In a few seconds you will be sinking upside down in the sea. It won't be nice at all."

"Shut up!" She fired her pistol at the helicopter.

Dwooooooooooooooooooooooaaaaaaaaaaaaaaaaaaaaarrrrrhhhh!

The collapse of the century had started. With a deafening roar, the northern half of Marine City plummeted towards the sea.

"I'm not going to die!" Fedora Last screeched yet, as she plunged seawards head first. "Even if I sink on this side, I'll float straight back up on the other side, me and Marine City. I'll show you!"

"It's not a waterwheel!" Rory O'Storm yelled from the helicopter, which continued to follow her down. "You can still save yourself with the rope. Throw the gun away. Don't waste your life!"

"Who says I'm going to die?! You fools! I'm not going to die, I am not! I'm going to float back up agebbo gabbo gobbo! Blublublublublub! Glugluglug, gluglug glugluglug!"

Upside down, Fedora Last disappeared under the sea. With that, the City capsized completely, sending up a massive column of spray hundreds of feet high.

Marine City floated upside down in the bay like a gigantic chocolate cake, its rust-coloured base exposed to view. After reaching an angle of 180 degrees, the City did not complete a turn of 360 degrees. It did not refloat itself. And Mayor Fedora Last was never seen or heard of again.

Bravo Herr Mozart!

The real name of the great composer Mozart was Joannes Chrysostomus Wolfgangus Theophilus Gottlieb Amadé Amadeus Mozart.

Mozart was born at the age of three. The reason for this is not known. He was born in his father's house at Salzburg – probably because he didn't have a mother.

It is said that, as soon as he was born, Mozart sat at a piano belonging to someone called Klavier and played a three-note chord. As we may judge from this surviving anecdote, Mozart only had three fingers.

As proof of his genius, we have the Nannerl Music Book, which Mozart composed for his sister at the age of four. This included eight minuets, designed to help his sister practise playing an instrument called the "Nannerl". Köchel names the composer of these minuets as a certain "Wolfgängerl". This was probably Mozart's doppelgängerl.

A friend of Mozart's father was a violinist called Schachtner. His violin was made of butter, which gradually melted, making its tone one-eighth lower than that of other violins. So Schachtner gave up and started playing the trumpet instead.

Once, Schachtner played his trumpet in front of Mozart. The boy was so shocked that he dropped dead on the spot. But he came back to life straight afterwards.

One day, when Mozart's father and Schachtner got together to play a trio, the four-year-old Mozart asked if he could join in. His father refused, saying he hadn't learnt to play the violin yet. Mozart had a tantrum, so his father reluctantly let him have his way. The child proceeded to play the second violin with his right hand and the first with his left. What's more, he played all six of Wenzel's compositions *at the same time.*

Mozart still didn't know how to use a pen when he was five. The score of a concerto composed by Mozart as a five-year-old is so splattered with ink, and this ink is so smeared over the page by the child's fingers, that it is unreadable. When he saw this, Mozart's father wept in despair. That's why, if this concerto were ever performed, it would truly be a miracle.

When he was six, Mozart was taken on a concert tour of Vienna by his father. There, he was invited to play for the Empress Maria Theresa and the Emperor Francis I at the Palace of Schönbrunn. During the performance, Mozart is said to have covered the keyboard with a cloth and played with one finger. It would seem that, by this time, Mozart only had one finger left.

There were a number of princes and princesses of Mozart's age in the Palace at this time. When Mozart slipped and fell on the polished parquet floor of the Palace, one of the girls helped him up. In his joy, Mozart promised, "I will surely make you my wife!"

The girl's name was Marie Antoinette. She took the promise seriously, and waited for him. But Mozart never came to claim his bride. She lost patience and went off to marry Louis XVI of France instead.

Even then, she still held a secret passion for Mozart. When he died in 1791, her grief made her provoke the people into starting the French Revolution. Stepping up to the guillotine herself, she ordered the executioner to behead her, thereby committing assisted suicide.

When he was eight, Mozart travelled to London. There, tutored by Johann Christian Bach among others, he composed a number of pieces including the 'Londoner Skizzenbuch', 'K19a', and 'Köchel-Einstein 15a-ss'.

Mozart received his first ever commission at the age of ten. He composed a piece called 'Licenza' for two patrons, Recitativo and Aria. But it's not very good.

In the following year, Mozart performed the 'Obligation of the First Commandment' for Apollo and Hyacinthus. Nobody seems to know exactly what this was.

In the autumn of Mozart's eleventh year, Maria Josepha, ninth daughter of the Empress Maria Theresa, was to marry King Ferdinand IV of Naples. When Mozart heard of this, he was furious (he'd mistaken her for Marie Antoinette). Though suffering from smallpox, he went back to Vienna to stop the wedding. Maria Josepha caught smallpox from Mozart and died.

Mozart seems to have had an amorous nature. As young as twelve, he fell in love with a vain, foolish girl called Buffa, with whom he is said to have been consumed from spring to summer. Of course, he had various obstacles to overcome here.

When he was fourteen, Mozart went to Rome. There, he was profoundly moved on hearing a piece called 'Miserere' in a well-known chapel. That same evening, he wrote a composition of his own. But it was exactly the same as the 'Miserere' he'd heard in the afternoon, and was therefore never recognized as his own work.

In Rome, Pope Clement XIV made Mozart a "Knight of the Golden Spur". But Mozart was physically weak. There is no mention of him performing as a knight after this, so we may infer that he refused the honour.

At the age of seventeen, Mozart again went to Vienna. There lived Joseph Haydn, who became engulfed in one of the whirlwinds that plagued the city. Mozart was also affected by it, and suffered serious injury. This whirlwind is known in German as "Sturm und Drang".

Mozart is thought to have had some kind of extrasensory perception. When he was twenty-one, he had a premonition that the soprano Josepha Duschek was about to pay a visit from Prague, exclaiming "Ah! Io previdi" (Hey! I saw it coming!).

At twenty-two, Mozart fell in love with all four daughters of a man named Fridolin Weber. Although little is known of Mozart's relationships with these four, common sense would suggest that it was merely an orgy, at most (sexual morals were not so strict in those days). Mozart's favourite was the second daughter, Aloysia, but in the end he married the third, Constanze. This would suggest very strongly that it had indeed been an orgy.

In the same year, Mozart composed the symphony known as 'K297', as well as 'Andante' and a prelude called 'Missing'.

When he was twenty-six, Mozart tried to marry Constanze. But she was whisked away to the palace of Friedrich Eugen, Duke of Württemberg. Overcoming a variety of hurdles, Mozart abducted Constanze, escaping with her from "the seraglio" and eventually marrying her.

But Constanze was a bad wife. She is said to have treated Mozart no better than a "goose of Cairo". It is not clear to what this refers, but Mozart apparently saw himself as a "deluded bridegroom".

Disillusioned, Mozart joined the secret society of the Freemasons at the age of twenty-eight, and took part in a conspiracy theory. He cantata'd his joy at this, while fighting off the CIA and the KGB. At one time he was a fugitive, pursued on a journey to Lied. But in November the organization was wiped out by the CIA. Mozart expressed his grief by composing the 'Masonic Funeral Music'.

Mozart fell ever deeper into poverty from this time on. He studied to be a magician, and tried to make ends meet by taking side jobs, like "theatre manager". But when his manservant Figaro upped and married in Prague without his permission, Mozart's financial fortunes reached an even lower ebb. He became dependent on a person called Chloe, went around seducing women and acting like a right Don Juan, wrote musical jokes for the NHS, walked the streets naked shouting "Eine kleine Nachmusik!" and summoned the God of Death by playing his magic flute.

Mozart lived to the age of thirty-five. We know this, because he died when he was thirty-five. After his death, he wrote a "Requiem" for the repose of his soul.

The Last Smoker

I'm sitting on top of the parliament building, resisting tear-gas attacks from air force helicopters that circle above me like flies. I will soon enjoy my very last cigarette, my last show of resistance. My comrade, the painter Kusakabe, fell to his death just moments ago, leaving me alone as the last smoker remaining on earth. At this very moment, images of me — highlighted against the night sky by searchlights down below — are probably being relayed live across the country from TV cameras inside the helicopters.

I've got three packs left, and I refuse to die before I've finished them. So I've been chain-smoking two or three at a time. My head feels numb, my eyes are starting to spin. It's only a matter of time before I, too, fall lifeless to the ground below.

It was only about fifteen or sixteen years ago that the anti-smoking movement started. And it was only six or seven years ago, at most, that the pressure on smokers really started to intensify. I never dreamt that, in such a short time, I would become the very last smoker left on earth. But maybe the signs were all there from the beginning. Being a fairly well known novelist, I used to spend most of my time at home writing. As a result, I had few opportunities to see or feel for myself the changes that society was going through. I hardly ever read the newspapers, as I abhor the journalistic style — it reminds me of dead fish. I lived in a provincial town, and my editors would come out to see me whenever the need arose. I tended to shun literary circles, and so never ventured into the capital.

Of course, I knew about the anti-smoking lobby. Intellectuals would often write articles stating their support or opposition in magazines and elsewhere. I also knew that the tone of the debate, on both sides, had gradually grown more hysterical, and that, from a certain point in time, the movement had suddenly started to swell while opposing arguments rapidly disappeared.

But as long as I stayed at home, I could live in splendid isolation from it all. I'd been a heavy smoker since my teens, and had continued to smoke without pause. Even so, no one ever admonished me or gave me any complaint. My wife and son tacitly put up with it. They probably realized that, for me to continue producing literary works and maintain an income as a fashionable writer, the consumption of huge quantities of cigarettes was absolutely essential. This probably wouldn't have been the case if I'd worked in an office, for example. For it seems that, from a relatively early time, smokers started losing out on promotion.

One day, two editors from a young people's magazine came to my house in the hope of commissioning an article. I showed them into my sitting room. One of them, a woman of about twenty-seven or twenty-eight, handed me a business card with this printed in bold across the top:

THANK YOU FOR NOT SMOKING

Apparently, this was not so uncommon at the time. More and more women were expressing anti-smoking sentiments on their name cards. But I was unaware of that. So you can imagine my indignation. Any magazine editor worth her salt should have known that a fashionable novelist such as myself would be a heavy smoker. Even if she didn't know it, handing a name card like that to someone who might be a smoker, especially when she was asking that someone to do a job for her, was completely out of order – even if the other person *wasn't* actually a smoker.

I stood up immediately.

"Regrettably, I'm unable to earn your thanks," I said to the stupefied pair. "For I myself am a chain smoker. I couldn't imagine even discussing work without a cigarette in hand. But thank you, anyway, for coming all this way."

The woman arched her eyebrows in twitching increments. Her colleague, a young man, hurriedly rose and started to entreat me. "Oh, well, you know, it's just that, please don't be angry, if we could just, you know…" he continued behind me as I left the room. It seems they also left shortly afterwards, arguing with each other on the way out.

I was somewhat perplexed by my overreaction. They had, after all, spent four hours travelling from Tokyo. And of course, I could have gone without a cigarette for an hour or so, if I had to. But why should I? It's not as though they were some kind of changelings who'd die if they breathed a bit of smoke. So I justified myself with the thought that, if I *had* agreed to talk to them without smoking, I'd have grown so irritated that our little *contretemps* would have seemed tame by comparison.

Unfortunately for me, this female editor happened to be one of the standard-bearers of the anti-smoking movement. She was so enraged by the incident that she started spreading malicious slander about me, in other publications as well as in her own. By extension, she also cast scorn on all smokers in general. Smokers were bigoted and pigheaded, obstinate and rude, arrogant and overbearing, selfish and obsessive, self-righteous and despotic – or so she said. Working with such people is fraught with difficulties and therefore bound to fail. As such, smokers should be banished from all workplaces. Reading this author's works is not to be advised, as the reader could become contaminated with his smoking ethos. All smokers are fools. All smokers are insane.

Eventually, I could remain silent no longer. It might have been all right if I were the only one, but other smokers were being insulted, too. Just as I was thinking of issuing some kind of reply, I received a call from the Chief Editor of a magazine called *Rumours of Truth*, for which I wrote a regular column. He urged me not to give in to this pressure from the newly empowered anti-smoking lobby, but to fight back against it. I quickly wrote my next submission to the magazine, which went something like this:

"Discrimination against smokers seems to have reached new heights. This results from a combination of extremism and the simple-mindedness of non-smokers. Anti-smoking proponents show an utter lack of understanding, precisely because they do not smoke. Mouth ulcers are cured by cigarette smoke. Tobacco soothes nervous irritation. Admittedly, people who don't smoke are healthy and have wholesome complexions. That's because many of them take part in sports. But they also smile for no reason. They don't think deeply about anything, and are totally uninteresting to talk to. Their conversation is superficial and their topics shallow. Their thinking is unfocussed and vague. They go off on a tangent without warning. They can't discuss any topic on more than one level. Their reasoning is not *inductive* but *deductive*. That's why they're so awfully easy to understand, yet, on the other hand, are always so quick to jump to hackneyed conclusions. When it comes to sport, they can prattle on endlessly, however little interest we show. But when the conversation turns to philosophy or literature, they fall asleep. In the old days, the air at long, difficult meetings would be thick with cigarette smoke. But now the conference room has been sanitized by air purifiers, ion generators and the like. Does that mean we can meet in relaxation? *Au contraire*. Meetings are over before they've started, or so I hear. Everyone's in such a hurry to leave. But of course – non-smokers can't bear long conversations, deep conversations, difficult conversations. As soon as the business at hand is over, or they know what they're supposed to do, they get up and go. They can't keep still. If someone detains them, they keep looking at their watches impatiently. But when they're angry, they just go on and on. What's more – whether male or female – they're all sex-mad. The more they take care of their health, the more they neglect to use their brains – at the expense of their health, ironically. In other words, they become imbeciles. What's the point of living such long, healthy lives if they're nothing but blockheads? Large groups of foolish old people would become a burden to the minority of younger people. Do they really mean to keep playing golf until they're a hundred? Tobacco was a truly great discovery – it has given people depth of feeling. Nevertheless, even journalists today are jumping on the anti-smoking bandwagon. What's that all about?! Newspaper editing rooms should be epitomized by murky clouds of tobacco smoke. Why are newspapers so uninteresting today? – Because the editing rooms are all too clean!!"

This article sparked a storm of protest as soon as it was published. Of course, originating from non-smokers, there was nothing particularly new about it. Some of it was simply idiotic – the writer would merely turn my argument on its head by replacing "non-smokers" with "smokers". These reactions were duly published in *Rumours of Truth*, where they were deemed suitably illogical to represent the views of non-smokers.

It was from about this time that I started receiving malicious phone calls and hate mail. The calls were simple abuse, along the lines of "So you want to die young, then? Moron!" The letters were similar, though sometimes rather witty – one, for example, contained a lump of tar and the message "Eat this and die!"

Soon, cigarette advertising was completely banned from all media. People's inclination to follow the crowd now came to the fore, and discrimination against smokers grew more overt. Though I spent most of my time at home writing, I would also venture out on occasion – to buy books, for example. On one such occasion, I shook in anger when I saw this sign in a nearby park:

NO DOGS OR SMOKERS

So now we were no better than dogs. That made me all the more defiant, and my will became so much more unyielding. Would I bend to such oppression? Was I not a man?!

A department store sales rep would bring ten cartons of cigarettes to my house once a month. They were the American brand More, of which I would consume around sixty or seventy a day. But then imports of foreign cigarettes were banned. Just before the ban, I stockpiled about two hundred cartons. These soon ran out, and I've had to make do with domestic brands ever since.

One day, I was obliged to travel to Tokyo, as I'd been invited to give an address at a literary event. The event was organized by a publishing house that I'd been indebted to for some years. So I asked my wife to reserve me a seat on the train.

"The fares for smoking seats have gone up by 20%," said my wife as she handed me the ticket. "And there's only one smoking car. The ticket-seller looked at me as if I were some kind of wild animal!"

I was utterly dismayed on entering the 'smoking car. The seats were falling apart and the windows covered with grime. Some were cracked for good measure, only held together by little patches of sticky tape. The floor was strewn with litter, the ceiling thick with cobwebs. In this filthy carriage sat seven or eight po-faced smokers. The gloomy strains of Grieg's Piano Concerto in A Minor filtered through the loudspeaker. The ashtrays by the seats were crammed full of cigarette ends, and had evidently not seen a cleaner for some time. On the doors at the ends of the carriage were signs saying "No passage to other carriages". The toilet at the rear of the carriage was just a hole in the floor, leading down to a vat. Peering through the hole, I could see a pile of human waste. There were no taps at the wash basin – just a tin cup chained to the wall, with a hand-operated water pump.

I was so incensed that I decided to cut my engagement and get out at the next station. From there, I returned home in a taxi. After all, if things were already this bad, who could know what awaited me at the venue, or the hotel?!

Urban tobacconists soon became ostracized by the communities they served. One after another, my local suppliers went out of business, forcing me to walk ever longer distances to make my purchases. In the end, there was only one tobacconist left in my vicinity.

"Don't tell me you're giving up, too!" I begged the elderly shopkeeper, adding, "But if you do, could you bring your remaining stock over to my house?"

And that's just what he did, that very same night. "I'm giving up," he said as he handed the lot over to me. It seems he'd been waiting for the opportunity to jack it in. When I said what I said, he'd jumped at the chance, gathered his stock and shut up shop.

Discrimination against smokers grew ever more extreme. In other countries, they'd already managed to ban smoking completely. We in Japan lagged behind as usual. Cigarettes were still being sold and people were still smoking them. Non-smokers saw this as a national humiliation, and started treating smokers as less than human. Some who smoked openly were beaten up in the streets.

There is a theory that the nobility of the human soul will always prevent this kind of lunacy from getting out of hand. I beg to differ. Opinions may vary on what exactly is meant by "getting out of hand". But looking back over the history of mankind, we find countless examples of such lunacy merely leading to greater forms of extremism, such as lynching or mob killings.

Discrimination against smokers quickly grew to the level of a witch-hunt. But it was hard to control, precisely because the discriminators didn't regard their actions as lunacy. Acts of human savagery are never so extreme as when they are committed in the name of a lofty cause, be it religion, justice or "correctness". In the name of the modern religion of "health", and under the banner of justice and correctness, discrimination against smokers soon escalated to the point of murder. A renowned heavy smoker was butchered in the street, and in broad daylight, by a gang of seventeen or eighteen hysterical housewives who were out shopping and two policemen. He'd refused to stop smoking despite repeated requests. It was said that, as he died, nicotine and tar spurted out of holes left in his body by bullets and kitchen knives.

When an earthquake set off fires in a densely populated part of Tokyo, a rumour was put about that they'd been deliberately started by smokers. So checkpoints were set up on the roads, and those trying to escape were stopped. If they were wheezing for breath, they were assumed to be smokers and executed on the spot. A sense of guilt, on a subconscious level, seemed to have given the discriminators their own paranoia.

When the national tobacco company went up in smoke and was forced to fold, it was the start of truly dark times for smokers. At night, gangs calling themselves the National Anti-smoking Front (NAF), their faces partly hidden behind triangular white masks, would roam the streets brandishing torches and setting fire to the few remaining tobacco shops.

I, on the other hand – milking the privilege accorded to a fashionable author – would instruct my editors to buy cigarettes for me, and continued to smoke as freely as before. "Pay me in cigarettes," I would say. "No smoke, no manuscript."

The poor wretches would scour the length and breadth of the land to find cigarettes that were still being sold, secretly, in remote country villages, or black-market contraband being trafficked in underworld "smoke-easy" joints. These they would present to me by way of tribute.

Nor did it seem that I was alone. Incorrigible journalists would occasionally produce features on celebrities who were still smoking. In their articles, they would list about a hundred people who, like me, declared themselves to be smokers and openly indulged in the habit.

"Which of these headstrong fools will be the last smoker?" ran one of their titles.

As a result, I was soon in constant danger, even at home. Stones were thrown at my windows, and suspicious fires would burn here and there around my walls and hedges. The walls became covered with multi-coloured graffiti, which was always renewed no matter how often I painted over it.

"SMOKER LIVES HERE"
"DIE OF NICOTINE POISONING, DIE!"
"HOUSE OF A TRAITOR"

The frequency of abusive calls and letters merely increased, most of them now consisting of unveiled threats. Eventually, my wife could bear it no longer. So she went off to her mother's, taking our son with her.

Articles headed "WHO WILL BE THE LAST SMOKER?" appeared in the newspapers on a daily basis. Some commentators even made predictions, and the list of names gradually shortened. But the pressure grew in inverse proportion to the declining number of targets.

One day, I telephoned the Human Rights Commission. A man answered in a brusque, dispassionate tone.

"We can't help you here. Our job is to protect non-smokers."

"Yes, but smokers are in the minority now."

"That's been so for a long time. We're here to protect the interests of the majority."

"Yes? Do you always side with the majority, then?"

"But of course. The very idea."

So I had no option but to protect myself. Smoking wasn't actually illegal yet. Instead, the lynchings became more violent (presumably out of frustration). I surrounded my house with barbed wire – electrified at night – and armed myself with a modified handgun and a samurai sword.

One day around this time, I received a call from a painter, Kusakabe, who lived not far away. Originally a pipe smoker, he'd switched to ordinary cigarettes when he could no longer obtain his favourite "Half and Half". Of course, he was one of the remaining twenty or so "smoking artists" who were always being targeted by the newspapers.

"That things should have come to this!" Kusakabe bemoaned. "I've heard that we will soon be attacked. The press and TV companies are inciting the NAF to torch our homes, so they can show pictures of our houses burning on the news."

"The infidels," I said. "If they come here first, can I escape to your place?"

"We're in the same boat, aren't we? If I'm hit first, I'll drive over to yours. Then we'll go up to Tokyo together. I know a safe house there. We have comrades there, too. If we're all to suffer the same fate, better to die glorious deaths together!"

"Agreed. Let us die magnificent deaths. Let them write in future school textbooks, 'They died with cigarettes in their mouths'."

We did laugh.

But it was no laughing matter. One evening just two months later, Kusakabe drove to my house covered in burns.

"They got me," he said as he parked his car in my garage, which was converted from a utility room in the main house. "They'll be here next. Let's get away."

"Wait a minute," I said, closing the garage door. "I'll gather up as many cigarettes as I can."

"Good idea. I've brought a few with me, too."

We were loading packs of cigarettes into the boot of the car when we heard a sudden commotion around the house. My porch window was smashed.

"They're here!" I said to Kusakabe, trembling with anticipation. "Shall we let them have it before we go?"

"Shall we? All right, let's. I've been itching to do this!"

We went into the dining room, which looked out onto the garden. A man was tangled in the electrified barbed wire on the back wall, his body making popping, cracking noises. I heated up a saucepan of oil I'd prepared earlier. Then I handed Kusakabe the modified handgun, and picked up my samurai sword.

We heard a noise in the toilet. I burst in. A man had broken the window and was trying to climb through. He must have jumped across from the neighbour's roof. I sliced his arms off at the elbow.

"................."

He disappeared from the window without a sound.

About a dozen others burst into the garden. They'd probably cut through the barbed wire. One by one, they started to prise open my shutters and windows. After a short discussion with Kusakabe, I went upstairs with the saucepan and poured boiling oil onto the garden from the veranda. The wretches started howling in agony. That was the signal for Kusakabe to start firing at random with the handgun. Terrified shrieks and screams.

They obviously hadn't expected us to be so prepared. The gang withdrew, carrying their wounded with them. But they'd started a fire near my front door, and the house was starting to fill with smoke.

"A parting gift for us smoke-lovers," Kusakabe quipped as he coughed. "But I draw the line at being burnt alive. Let's get out of here!"

"The garage door is very weak," I said as we got into the car. I sensed that there were people waiting for us in the driveway. "Just drive through it."

Kusakabe's car was a Mercedes Benz – built like a tank. I didn't have a car of my own any more. My son had taken it over recently, and he'd driven it off to his grandmother's.

The Merc started up, smashed through the garage door and roared onto the driveway. Then we turned into the street at the same speed. We seemed to have bulldozed through about a dozen photographers and reporters, clustered around my house like piles of garbage – but did we care?

"Well. That was fun!" laughed Kusakabe as he drove away.

I still don't know how we avoided all the road blocks on the way to Tokyo. The burning of our houses would certainly have been reported on television, and both the NAF and the police must have been on the lookout for us. But we drove on through the night, and arrived in the capital as day broke.

Kusakabe's safe house was in the basement of a luxury apartment block in Roppongi. There, we met about twenty comrades who'd also escaped after their country residences had been burnt down. This was originally a private club, partly financed by Kusakabe, and the owner was one of us, too. We vowed an oath of allegiance and resistance, honoured the god of tobacco and prayed for victory. The god of tobacco, of course, has no physical form. We merely raised the red circle of Lucky Strike, and worshipped this while puffing away.

I won't go into too much detail about our struggle over the next week or so, as it would be too tedious. Suffice to say that we made a fairly good fist of it. Our enemy was not only the NAF, along with the police and armed forces (which had merely become its tools). For now they were joined by the well-meaning conscience of the whole world, backed by the World Health Organization and the Red Cross. In contrast, the best support *we* could expect was from unscrupulous rogues who were continuing to sell cigarettes illegally. It would have hurt our pride as smokers to depend on them.

Eventually, the god of tobacco could no longer bear to see our plight, and sent assistants to help us in our hour of need. But they were only the dove of "Peace", the bat of "Golden Bat", the camel of "Camel", and the penguin of "Cool" – none of which were of much use to us. The last that came to assist us was a young superhero with gleaming white teeth, sent by "Smoker Toothpaste". At first, we thought he might serve some purpose. But soon we realized there was nothing behind his façade either.

"We lived through the horrors of war, survived postwar austerity, and for what?" asked Kusakabe. "The richer the world becomes, the more laws and regulations are imposed on us and the more discrimination grows. And now, we are not free at all. Why is that?"

All of our comrades had fallen, and only two of us remained. We'd been pursued to the top of the national parliament building, where we sat puffing cigarettes for all we were worth.

"Is that what people prefer?"

"I suppose it must be," I replied. "In the end, we'd have to start a war to stop this kind of thing."

At that moment, a tear gas canister, fired from a helicopter, hit Kusakabe full on the head. He plummeted down without a sound. The masses swarming below, merry with alcohol as if at a festival, sent up a great cheer and started to chant.

"Only one left! Only one left! Only one left!"

But I'm still here, a full two hours later, still resisting doggedly at the top of the parliament building. I'm quite proud of myself, actually. If I'm going to die anyway, I might as well use up all the energy I have left.

Suddenly, everything went quiet down below, and the helicopters disappeared. Someone was talking over a loudspeaker. I strained my ears to catch what he was saying.

"…won't we. But it'll be too late then. And what a terrible loss that will be. For he is now a precious artefact from the Tobacco Age. He should be turned into a natural monument, a living treasure. We must protect him. Will you help us? I repeat. We are SPS, the Society for the Protection of Smokers, created today for the urgent…"

A shudder went through me. Please, no! Don't let them protect me! This was the beginning of a new sort of cruelty. Protected species are doomed to extinction. They're turned into peepshow freaks, photographed, injected and isolated, their semen is extracted, and other parts of their bodies are messed about with in different ways. And what happens in the end? They just wither and die. But that's not all. After they die, they're stuffed and put out on show. Was that what I wanted? No. I'd rather die in my own way. I rushed forwards and jumped off the roof.

But it was too late. They'd already put out a safety net.

High above me, two helicopters approached with a rope mesh stretched out between them. Slowly, slowly, they descended towards me...

Bad for the Heart

My foreboding turned out to be correct.

Just as I thought, it was to inform me of my forthcoming "island duty" that the Department Manager called me all the way to the Reception Room.

Usually, "island duty" was reserved for unmarried researchers. But I have a wife and a three-year-old child.

Why did the Department Manager have to tell me in person? Because the Section Chief didn't know how to. It was a sign of the Section Chief's malice towards me. It was he who'd plotted this "island duty". I was sure of it.

I was to be posted to Pomegranate Island, a small island in the middle of the Japan Sea. It was about twenty miles off the coast of remotest Shimane Prefecture.

"Are there any telephones on the island?" I asked the Department Manager as I glanced over the map.

"The wife of the village headman is the switchboard operator. I'll have one installed in your office," he replied with a smile.

"You mean they've laid cables to the island?"

"God, no! Radio telephones, of course."

"Surely we don't have to go so far out to test water quality in the Japan Sea? We could do it on the coast. What about this place, Cape Ichizen? Couldn't we do it there?"

"Citroxin levels are unreliable on the coast. You get better readings out at sea. You should know that."

"There are still five or six single men in the Development Section. You don't have to send me."

"Ah, but they can't work alone yet. You should know that."

I refused to back down. "I've got a chronic illness."

"Yes, I know. Your heart problem."

"The Section Chief told you, then."

The Department Manager gave me a duplicitous look.

"No. It was Dr Masui." He was the company doctor.

"I don't think he knows anything about my illness. What did he say?"

"He said it's a nervous disorder."

"Not heart disease?"

"He said you yourself claimed it was heart disease," the Department Manager replied with a grin.

"In other words, he thinks I'm imagining it." I sighed. "That's why these quacks are no good."

"What does your own doctor say, then?"

I started to explain my illness to the Department Manager. As I'm always telling people about it, the words slip out effortlessly. And by nature, I tend to get quite worked up when I'm talking about it. "It certainly is a nervous disorder. But this cardio-angio-neurosis, as it's called, is not like other nervous disorders, nor is it an ordinary heart disease. It's a very complicated illness. Dr Masui knows nothing of neurological medicine. That's why he makes such irresponsible statements. My physician is Dr Kawashita. He knows all about both psychoneurology and internal medicine. I'm lucky to have met such a wonderful doctor. If I hadn't, I might have died of heart failure long since. No – I definitely would have done. Indeed, before I had the good fortune to meet Dr Kawashita, I went to a lot of different hospitals and argued with a lot of doctors, because all they ever said was that it was a nervous disorder. I mean, I actually have palpitations and get a gripping pain in my heart. Sometimes I can't even breathe. How could that be just a nervous disorder?! Dr Kawashita was the only one who correctly diagnosed it as cardio-angio-neurosis."

The Department Manager had listened to my tale with a bored look, but now lifted his hand to stop me in mid-flow. "All right, all right. Let's call it cardio-angio-neurosis. So what causes it, then?"

"In my case, it's apparently too much stress."

"Well, that's perfect!" He smacked the desktop with his hand, a look of hearty agreement on his face. "If you go to a remote island, there'll be no more stress or irritation from human relationships. You can take your time with the work – all you have to do is go and test the sea water a few times a day. You could see it as a kind of convalescence! Eh? What do you think? Hahahahaha!"

I was lost for words.

Well yes, I suppose I could see it that way. But what about the other cause of my illness – marital discord? My wife is of a purely hysterical nature. On top of that, she has showy tastes, and loves parties and socializing. She could never endure life on a remote island inhabited by a dozen or so fishermen. If she were forced to stay there, she would only become even more hysterical and torment me day and night.

But of course, it would have been unmanly for me to plead family circumstances to my superior, the Department Manager.

"Er…" I started nervously. "How long for?"

"Eight months."

"Couldn't it be a bit shorter?"

"It usually takes a year to monitor changes in citroxin levels. You should know that. I reduced it specially for you. Since you'll have to be away from your wife and child."

"Away?" I asked with widening eyes. "Can't they go with me?"

Now he widened *his* eyes. "Would you want them to?"

"Oh, come on. If I went alone, who would help me if I had an attack?"

"Well, all right, I suppose they can." He smiled again. "I hear your wife's quite a good-looking woman."

His implication was that I was worried about leaving her alone. And to an extent, he was dead right.

"Next year, the Development Section will split off from the Research Department and become an independent department of its own," said the Department Manager, suddenly looking serious. "The current Section Chief will become the Manager of the Development Department. And there'll be two new Sections beneath him."

"I see." I swallowed.

"I can make you a promise," said the Department Manager, nodding solemnly. "When you come back from the island, you will be one of the Section Chiefs."

"Hey. I've got island duty again," I reported to my wife on arriving home that day. "I didn't think it'd happen now that I'm married. But it seems it's my turn again."

For a few moments, my wife just stared at me blankly.

"Why didn't you refuse?" she asked at length.

"Well, I couldn't, could I. The Department Manager promised to promote me to Section Chief in return."

"You'll get promoted anyway, won't you? All the others who joined at the same time as you have been promoted long since. Some of them without doing island duty once!"

"That's because they're not in the technical line."

"But you're the only one! You're the only one who did island duty four times before you were married. So why do you have to do it again, now that you've got a family? Why on earth did you accept? Just how much of a pushover do you have to be?!" Her voice gradually rose in pitch as her words gathered speed. "That company of yours stinks. Can't you see? They're just using you! All the other wives will be laughing at me again. I can't show my face outside!"

Our three-year-old son, standing wide-eyed next to his mother, stared at her with a look of puzzlement.

"I did try to refuse," I said. "I explained about my illness."

"Oh, for crying out loud!" My wife looked up at the ceiling, gave out a long breath and shook her head in disbelief. "So now you've even told your Department Manager about your sodding illness. And as always, I suppose you went on and on and on about it. I suppose you were gesticulating all over the place, going on about your heart, your poor heart, exaggerating the whole thing!" She made her eyeballs bulge and distorted her lips in imitation of me.

"What do you mean, exaggerating? I always talk truthfully about it," I retorted indignantly. "How could he understand if I didn't explain?"

BAD FOR THE HEART

"How many times do I have to tell you? Just stop telling people about it! Tell *me*, if you like. But for God's sake, don't tell other people! Why do you think the Section Chief dislikes you, then? It's because you're always going on about your bloody illness! He must be sick to death of hearing about it. The moment he asks you to do anything, it's 'oh, my heart, my heart'. And whenever you think it's beating a bit funnily, it doesn't matter what you're doing, you have to make a great song and dance about it and rush out to the nearest hospital!"

"How do you know that?"

"Of course I know, it's easy! You're the laughing stock of the company, don't you get it? It's no wonder you never get promoted! This latest island duty is all because the Section Chief hates you so much he wants to get rid of you! Of course it is!"

"Don't you care if I die, then?" I yelled angrily. "Maybe you're right, maybe the Section Chief doesn't like me. But does that mean you have to talk like that too? Heart disease is a killer, you know. Of course, the healthy will always make fun of the sick. But I don't care. I'm looking after my health because it wouldn't be funny if I died. Why do you think I keep going to the doctor's? It's for you and the boy, of course!"

"DON'T BLOODY PATRONIZE ME!"

"What do you mean?" I hit the dining table with my fist and stood up.

"If you've got a heart problem, why didn't you tell me about it before we got married?" She stood up in turn and glared at me. "That's it! You tricked me, didn't you?!"

"What do you mean, tricked you?! I didn't have the illness then! It's come on since we've been married! What could I do about it?"

"So now you're saying it's my fault! And I suppose they're all saying that at your work, too! Bloody hell!" She was shrieking now.

"Hold on, hold on. Hold on." I quickly tried to return to the original discussion. "Let's not have another row! We're just going over the same old argument as always. I haven't told you where I'm going yet."

"What do I care where you're going?!" She stopped short and peered at my face. "Of course, you *are* going on your own, aren't you."

I was flabbergasted. "How could you be so heartless? You want to pack me off to a remote island on my own, in my state, with no doctor?!"

She laughed coldly. "Well, if you don't like it, you don't have to go."

"I'll be promoted to Section Chief when I get back. Aren't you pleased for me?"

Now her hair virtually stood on end. "PLEASED? NO! I'm not pleased at all! Maybe if you said 'Department Manager', yes! After all this time, you're the last to be promoted. Why the hell should I be pleased about that?!"

"Don't be ridiculous! How could I jump straight to Department Manager without being Section Chief first?! And I won't even get that if I don't go to the island!"

"God, you're so stupid!"

"What do you mean, stupid?" I kicked the chair over.

Our son is so accustomed to our rowing that he doesn't cry any more. He started playing on his own.

"Anyway, we're all going to the island together. Understand?" I said, breathing hard through my nose.

She looked at me aghast. "Do you want to turn our child into a barbarian?!" she said, performing her customary leap of logic.

"What's that supposed to mean?!"

"You don't stop to think of your family, do you. He's just started at private nursery school, hasn't he?! Do you know how hard I worked to get him in there?!"

"That was just for your vanity!"

"All right. So you think it's better for your son to have no friends, and to turn into an imbecile like some fisherman's boy, on some God-forsaken shit-hole of an island in the middle of nowhere, do you?! Just when he's started learning to read?" She burst into tears and ran over to hug the boy. "I'm sorry, poppet! It's only because your father is such a rotten good-for-nothing!"

"What's more important, then? His nursery school or my work?!" I bawled at her. "The only reason you don't want to go is because you won't be able to buy flashy clothes and go parading in front of everybody!"

"Oh, you hate that, don't you," she said, staring at me. "That's why you're going to drag me there with you. You just want to give me a hard time!" She stamped her foot on the floor. "No. I am not going with you! I'd go stark raving mad, stuck there on a lonely island with no one to talk to, with only an invalid like you for company! I'm definitely not going, all right? You can bugger off on your own. Go and have your bloody spasms. Serves you right. You can stew in your own juice for all I care!"

"Wha… wha… wha…" I wanted to shout back, but was suddenly unable to breathe. My eyes bulged as I gasped for air.

A sharp pain pierced my heart. I screwed up my face and crouched on the floor clutching my chest. My heart was clearly palpitating. I moaned helplessly and felt a cold sweat coming over me.

"Oh look, he's having another one." She stood over me with a twisted smile on her mouth. "Funny how it always happens when he's losing an argument. What a very convenient heart problem."

Still wheezing for breath, I stretched out my hand towards her. "M-my pills, w-would you get m-my pills."

"Get them yourself," she said, and started clearing away the dinner things.

I rolled sideways along the carpeted floor. "In my, in my j-jacket pocket. W-would you get them for me."

Our son got up and looked down at me. "Daddy not well!"

"Oh, leave him. He only wants attention." She stomped off loudly into the kitchen.

Terrified by the sharp pain and the fear of death, I crawled along the floor and managed to reach the coat pegs as wheezing sounds still issued from my throat.

"All right, all right. Well done." Sighing, my wife came back out of the kitchen, took the bottle of pills from my jacket, and threw it down in front of my nose. "Good performance. I nearly believed you."

"And so, you see, I need eight months' medication," I told Dr Kawashita the next day, having taken the morning off to go to his clinic.

"Well, yes." Dr Kawashita pulled a wry face. "I could give them to you, but…"

"You've got to!" I pleaded. "They'll be my only hope on a remote island without a doctor!"

"But you'll take them all at once, won't you." He scratched his head vigorously. "The problem is that you make no effort to remove the cause, but just keep taking the medicine. That's no good at all."

"No, it's not true. I am making an effort. I've stopped smoking and drinking coffee, as you advised. I avoid strenuous exercise and work of a highly urgent and responsible nature as far as possible," I said with a bow of the head. "And of course, I've stopped having sexual relations with my wife."

"What?" He lifted his face and stared at me. "Altogether?!"

"Yes, altogether. Well, that comes under strenuous exercise, doesn't it?"

"As I've said many times before, no visible symptoms can be observed in your case," the doctor said with a long sigh. "It's not good to dwell on your condition too much. The worst thing for you is marital discord. If you've stopped having intercourse with your wife altogether, that could be another cause of marital discord."

"Surely you're not going to say I'm imagining it too?!"

"I'm not saying that. You are definitely sick. But anxiety will only make your condition worse. And then you'll merely grow more anxious. It's a vicious circle. I don't want to frighten you, but if that happens, even a regime of complete rest and a change of air won't work. You need to relax, and try not to get angry. That's the best cure."

"But my wife makes me angry. I can't help it."

"Will your wife accompany you to the island?"

"Of course."

"You see, this is your perfect chance for a complete convalescence." He screwed up his face. "Is there no way you could go alone?"

"You're joking! I couldn't leave a skittish woman like that on her own. Who knows what she'd get up to."

"Distrust between partners, suspicions of infidelity, these are things that can directly aggravate your condition, you see."

That hit a raw nerve. "Are you saying I'm jealous?" I said loudly. "How can I help it? She's a wanton woman, I'm telling you!"

"All right, all right. Calm down." The doctor hurriedly tried to pacify me. "That's exactly what I mean. You mustn't allow yourself to become so agitated!"

"Can I have the medicine?"

"Well, if you promise not to waste it, I'll let you have eight months' supply. But don't come to me saying you've used it up and could I give you some more. This is all you're getting. Do you understand?"

"I understand."

"Serpentina alkaloid," he said to the nurse before turning back to me. "Whatever you do, don't take too many. Your blood pressure isn't very high, so if you exceed the dose it could be life-threatening."

"Yes, I understand."

Huh, he's only trying to frighten me, I thought. Once I'd got the pills I could do what I liked with them!

The rule in my company, Marine Chemical Resources Development, is that, once a decision has been made to send an employee to an island or coastal observation point, the work has to start within a week. But this only applies to single employees. I was given special dispensation of two weeks in which to prepare, as I'm a family man. And on the final afternoon of those two weeks, I boarded a small steam ferry to Pomegranate Island from Cape Ichizen with my wife and child. The ferry crossed to the island and back once a day.

"What? WHAT?! What sort of island is that?!" my wife shouted at the top of her voice as we approached Pomegranate Island. We could now see the whole of the island before us. "What kind of shape do you call that?!"

In the middle of the island was a mountain shaped like an

upturned helmet. The top of the mountain was split wide open like a pomegranate exposing its obscene red insides.

"You've got to be joking! I can't live on an island that looks like that!!" my wife shrieked at me in a state of shock. "Why of all places do we have to live on an island that's got its top split open?"

"How could I have known?!" I shouted back. "I've only seen it on the map. Nobody told me Pomegranate Island was an island with its top split open!"

"Aha, ahaha, ahahahaha!" Our son pointed at the island and laughed merrily.

"It's a volcano, that's what it is! What are we going to do if it explodes? The whole island will be wiped out!"

"Are volcanoes shaped like that?!"

"It's a bloody volcano, I tell you! Of course it is!" She started to sob. "What am I going to do? I wish I'd never married you. I had another proposal after we were engaged, I'll have you know. Now he's been posted to Europe with his family. What a mistake it was to choose you!!"

"It's because you say things like that and make me angry that my condition gets worse," I said slowly, deliberately, breathing deeply to control my rage. "Dr Kawashita has said it many times. Marital discord, and particularly quarrelling, is very bad for my heart. Some of his patients have even died of heart failure during rows with their wives."

"Well, if you're so scared of dying, hurry up and divorce me, then! All you ever say is Dr Kawashita this, Dr Kawashita that. He's nothing but a ruddy quack!"

"He is not a quack!" I screamed. "Do you want me to get angry and die?"

"Are you dying then? ARE YOU?" she screamed back. "Go on then, die! Then I might believe you!"

"H-how... h-h-how—" Her logic was so absurd that I could find no words in reply. "How could you say—" I could hardly breathe. A prickling pain pierced my heart.

"It's the company that's trying to kill you by sending you to this island! They want you to die. They've no intention of promoting you. Of course they haven't." She stamped her heels noisily on the deck.

"Stop… please st-stop." I clutched my chest and sat on a bench. "My p-pills, please, my p-pills. In the c-cabin. In my bag. In my b-bag."

She tutted, and peered down at me with a look of disgust on her face.

"Daddy not well again," said my son.

"Come on, let's leave him. Let's go," she said icily, without expression. She took our son's hand and hurried off to the after-deck.

I was beside myself with rage. The palpitations started and I stopped breathing altogether.

"Uhhh… uhhh… uhhh…"

Moaning, clawing at the air with fingers bent rigid, I twisted and contorted my body until, at last, I reached the cabin. I opened my bag with fitful hands, took out the medicine bottle and swallowed three tablets without water. The doctor had instructed only two at a time, but two were no longer enough.

Once I'd regained my composure I peered at the bottom of the bottle. There were only four or five tablets left.

Suddenly struck by a feeling of unease, I rummaged around inside the bag. I wanted to make sure the package containing the eight months' supply was still there.

It wasn't.

I hastily tossed aside the suitcase and emptied the contents of my wife's bag all over the cabin. But there was no sign of my medicine.

"Where's my medicine?" My heart was starting to beat like a drum.

"What's the matter with you?" my wife asked, looking at me coldly. I'd raced out of the cabin with my hair all over the place.

"My medicine!" I yelled. "The big package with my medicine in it. What have you done with it?"

"How should I know?" She gazed out across the sea. "It's in your bag, isn't it?"

"It's not in my bag. It's not in yours either. What have you done with it?" I screamed. "WHAT HAVE YOU DONE WITH IT?"

Frightened by my unusually savage appearance, my son clung tightly to his mother.

"Would you keep your voice down? Look, you're scaring him. And you're upsetting the other passengers." Actually, a solitary old woman on the after-deck was the only other passenger.

"Never mind that. You were shouting yourself just now, weren't you? Answer my question. Where have you put the package with my medicine in it? If I don't have that medicine, it could hinder my chances of staying alive!"

"It could hin-der his chan-ces of stay-ing a-live, he says," she repeated to the boy with a snigger. "What grand expressions he uses. Answer his question, he says." She turned to look at me with spiteful eyes. "Who the hell do you think you're talking to?"

"I'm sorry. I apologize," I said more calmly, trying not to accept the provocation. "Could you please tell me what you did with the package?"

"What package."

"It was about this big, wrapped in brown paper. It had eight months' supply of medicine in it. I've only got four or five tablets left in my bottle. I need to refill it, you see."

"There. Why couldn't you have said it like that before," she said like a schoolteacher. "That package. Yes. I put it in a trunk with our winter clothes and sent it by Daitsu."

As Daitsu were the most reliable carriers in the country, I was somewhat relieved. But would the trunk arrive before my medicine ran out?

"You shouldn't have done that without asking me," I said in a plaintive voice. "I've only got four or five tablets left."

"If they're so important to you, why didn't you look after them yourself?!"

"And when will Daitsu deliver the trunk to the island?"

"They said it would take four to five days. That was four days ago, so it should be there by tomorrow."

I'd have to make sure I didn't have an attack before the next day.

As we arrived on the island, an old man came to meet us on the ferry landing stage. He said he was the village headman, and took us to the observation point, where I would live and work for the next eight months. Near the coast about a mile out of the village, it stood on sandy ground below a cliff. It was made of wood, measured about thirty by thirty feet, and was of course newly built. It would probably be destroyed at the end of the observation period. Though crudely fashioned, it had a large carpeted room at the back, and looked much more comfortable than I'd expected.

"Well, we should be able to make do with this," I said.

Standing in front of the village headman, my wife said nothing.

The observation equipment had already arrived. I started unpacking and assembling it as soon as the headman had left and my wife had started cleaning. It was well into the night by the time I was finished.

My wife came on to me that night.

With the uncertainty of a new environment, she probably needed to immerse herself in an activity that involved monotonous repetition, something that felt familiar. I shared that feeling, but of course I didn't make love to her. I might have suffered a spasm if I had. I reminded her that I only had four or five tablets left. But she just repeated the same old complaint as always.

The next day, I carried the observation instruments to the rocky beach and set them up at six points. It took a whole day.

There was no Daitsu delivery that day.

"It hasn't arrived!" I complained to my wife.

"It'll probably come tomorrow," she answered with her customary indifference.

"You've got the receipt from Daitsu, haven't you."

"I wonder. Did I bring it? Look in my handbag. If it's not there, I'll have left it at home." As irresponsible as ever.

I hurriedly emptied the contents of her handbag onto the table, and hunted for the receipt. I was relieved to find it there, crumpled into a ball.

But there was no Daitsu delivery the following day either. After completing my observations I went down to the ferry landing stage to check. The ferry had already left, and there was no sign that it had brought any kind of baggage. This was driving me mad. I hurried back to the observation point and picked up the telephone.

"Hello?"

"Hello, yes? What can I do for you?" said an old woman's voice at the other end.

I'd been told that the village headman's wife operated the telephone exchange. The village headman himself was at least seventy. So the woman on the other end must have been his wife.

I took care to speak politely. "I'm sorry to trouble you, but may I make a call to the mainland?"

"The mainland, you say? Oh! Yes, the mainland." For some reason, she sounded quite thrilled. "Yes, of course. What number?"

Reading from the receipt slip, I repeated the number of the Daitsu City Branch to the stupid woman several times.

"Oh yes, yes, I've got it now," she said in great excitement. "Please replace your receiver and wait for me to call."

I waited in a state of mounting irritation for about fifteen minutes, until the phone finally rang.

"Hello? Yes. Well, at last we have a connection," the old woman said cheerfully.

"Daitsu." The girl's voice sounded awfully distant.

"Yes, hello? My name's Suda. I gave you a trunk to ship on the 6th, but it hasn't arrived yet."

"One moment. I'll put you through to the Dispatch Office."

Next, a young man spoke. He sounded even more distant. "Hello?"

"Hello?"

"Er, hello? We have a bad line here. Hello?"

"Hello? Yes, my name's Suda. I gave you a trunk to ship on the 6th, but it hasn't arrived yet."

"Ah. Hold the line. I'll put you through to the Duty Clerk."

Next, a middle-aged man spoke. I repeated the same thing to him.

"Really. Well, I'll look into it," said the man, as if it were too much for him. He obviously had no desire to look into it at all.

"Will you look into it now, please?"

"What, now?" the man said in a sullen tone, followed by silence.

"It contains something important that's urgently needed. Actually, it's medicine. Without the medicine, someone could die."

"Really. Just a minute." He seemed to be looking, albeit reluctantly. "Er, what was the name again?"

"Suda."

"Shudder?"

"No, Suda."

"No shudder?"

"Er, Suda."

"Er shudder?"

"S for Sparrow. U for Unicorn. D for Donkey. A for Ant."

"...Eh?"

"S for Sparrow—"

"Mr Sparrow?"

"S for Sparrow. U for Unicorn—"

"Mr Uniform?"

"SUDA. The name is Suda. Suda."

"Mr Suda?"

"Yeeessss. That's right."

"Oh yeah. Here it is. Item received on the 6th. One trunk, was it."

"That's the one. That's the one!"

"Sent to... how do you read that?"

"Pomegranate Island."

"Yeah, Pomegranate Island. Well, yeah, it's already been sent."

"...What?"

"We've already sent it out."

"Hello? Hello?"

"Yeah. Hello."

"I'm actually calling from Pomegranate Island now."

"Really." He wasn't even slightly impressed.

"And it hasn't arrived yet."

"That's funny. It should have done."

"Yes."

"It should be there by tomorrow."

"That's what I've been thinking for the last two days."

"But it'll arrive by tomorrow. No problem."

"And what will you do if it doesn't?"

"What do you want me to do?" He was laughing.

"Couldn't you trace it for me?"

"Trace what?"

I was beginning to lose my patience. "I would like you to trace the whereabouts of my trunk."

"Well, once we've sent it out, it can't be traced."

"Surely it can. You must know the shipment route. Could you please telephone and check."

"Could who please telephone and check?"

I snapped, momentarily. "You, of course! No, not necessarily you. It doesn't matter who. Could someone please look into it?"

"Well, no, actually. We're very busy with other shipments here."

"I'm busy too! That trunk is important to me!"

He laughed again. "And our shipments are important to us."

"It's a matter of life and death!"

"Really." He thought I was exaggerating, of course.

"Hello?"

"Yeah."

"Would you mind telling me your name."

"Murai," he answered grudgingly.

"Well, Mr Murai," I said in a tone of authority, "could you please check out all the points along the route. I'll call you back later."

"All right then. Yeah, OK, I'll check them out. It must be serious if it's a matter of life and death, eh?" He suppressed a laugh.

I slammed down the receiver in great annoyance. "Jesus. How rude can they get."

"What's the matter?" asked my wife next to me.

"The Daitsu people. Their attitude is abysmal. As if it's more than their job's worth! Who the hell do they think they are?!"

"What do you expect? They *are* the best in the country. And I hear the recruitment exams are really hard. They only hire people

184

from top universities, you know." She cast me a sharp sideways glance. "They're the élite."

Her sarcastic tone made me all the more annoyed. "And that gives them the right to be arrogant, does it?"

"Well, yes. They're not bothered about a piffling little trunk. They specialize in hauling heavy machinery, construction equipment, that kind of thing. Their main business is delivering steel girders in the right order when a railway bridge is being built. Mobility, that's what they're all about. So it's no wonder they pooh-pooh our insignificant household effects."

"If you knew that, why the hell did you use them?"

"Oh come on. Who else is going to transport a paltry trunk to the middle of nowhere?" she asked with a derisive smile.

"They've got a monopoly?"

"Correct."

"Damn them!" I brought my fist down on the table. And my heart started to palpitate immediately. I quickly took out the medicine bottle and swallowed two tablets. Only three left now.

For a few minutes, my wife seemed lost in thought. Then she looked up at me. "Maybe they've deliberately delayed the trunk, out of spite."

"W-why?" I stared at her. "Do you know something I don't?"

She answered with a serious expression, as if to stoke my anxiety. "Well, I had a bit of a set-to with the Daitsu driver. He came on his own to pick up the trunk, and asked me to help him carry it. I said why didn't you bring someone with you, carry it on your own, that's your job. Then he gave me a really nasty look."

"What was his name?"

"It should be on the receipt," she said with a smirk.

There was no Daitsu delivery the next day either. I went to the ferry landing stage with my wife. The only thing to come off the boat was a group of five students who'd come to the island on holiday. They were all male. My wife immediately started chatting to them as if she'd known them all her life.

She said she wanted to buy something at the local Co-op, so I went back to the observation point on my own. Our son, who'd been having his midday nap, woke up and started howling. I managed to get him back to sleep, then phoned Daitsu. It took half an hour for Murai, the one I'd spoken to the previous day, to come to the phone.

"Yep."

"It's Mr Suda on Pomegranate Island. We spoke yesterday?"

"Right."

"The trunk still hasn't arrived."

"That's funny. It should have done."

"Of course, you did look into it, didn't you."

"Well, yes. Your trunk should eventually arrive at the Shimizu Branch. You could phone to see if it's there yet."

"For goodness' sake! That's what I wanted *you* to do! Never mind. I don't know why I should do it, but I'll call them. I haven't got time to mess about. Would you let me have the number." I wrote down the number he gave me. "By the way, Mr Murai. I understand my wife had a little misunderstanding with the driver who came to pick up the trunk. It's possible he might have deliberately held the trunk back, out of spite."

"No, no, that's not possible!" He laughed.

"I assure you, it is possible. Would you please check it out. And I'll contact the Shimizu Branch."

Murai replied with exaggerated courtesy. "Yes, sir. I'll be sure to check it out." Of course he would do no such thing.

I replaced the receiver, and had just asked the village headman's wife to connect me to the Shimizu Branch when my wife came home.

"Still on the phone? That'll cost a packet."

"Who cares? I'll charge it to the company." That gave me an idea. "How did you settle the bill with Daitsu? Payment on arrival?"

"Uh-uh. In advance."

"You should have made it payment on arrival. I could have used that as a bargaining tool."

"Don't be childish. They don't give two hoots about the payment, do they?!"

"Do you have to keep saying things like that?"

She seemed to have a spring in her step.

I was put through to the Shimizu Branch.

"Yes, hello, this is Mr Suda speaking from Pomegranate Island. Has a trunk arrived for me yet?"

The voice on the other end was gravelly, like a fisherman's. "Hold on a sec. I'll have a look." Five minutes later, he returned to the telephone and continued in his gravelly voice: "No, nothing's arrived." At least the provincial employees were a little more polite.

"I had it sent from the City Branch, you see. They say it should be there by now."

"Well, if it hasn't arrived, it hasn't arrived. We have to deliver everything as soon as it comes in, otherwise we'd be overrun with parcels. We deliver 'em as soon as they come in. So we aren't going to keep anything back, are we."

"No, I suppose not."

The man with the gravelly voice hung up abruptly. There was little doubt that the trunk hadn't arrived.

I was waiting to be connected to the City Branch for the third time, when my wife emerged from the back room in skimpy swimwear.

"Why are you dressed like that, at your age?" I asked. "Are you going swimming on your own?"

"Uh-uh. Those students who arrived today are camping down by the beach. They invited me over, so I said I'd go."

"No way!" I shouted. "You're not cavorting around half-naked with a group of young men when your husband's facing a life-or-death crisis!"

"Oh dear. I do believe you're jealous."

"I'm not jealous! It's simply that distrust between partners or suspicions of infidelity are the very worst things for my condition. You're not to go!"

"As I thought. You're jealous," she laughed. "You drag me to this hellish island, then have the nerve to tell me what to do and what not to do? Take a running jump!"

"If you must go, take the child."

"Certainly not! He'd show me up," she said on her way out.

My whole body was shaking with rage, when my call came through.

Murai came to the phone, so I let rip at him. "The Shimizu Branch say the trunk hasn't arrived. Where the hell is it?!"

"Really. That is worrying," he said in a wholly unworried voice. "Of course, it might be better if we knew whether it went by rail or road. If it went by rail, it would arrive at the Yabuki Branch. If by road, it would go to the Itagaki Branch. I know! Why don't you try calling the arrivals desk at Itagaki? If they haven't got it, it must have gone by rail, so it could be at Yabuki. Er, the phone number of the Itagaki Branch is—"

"Isn't that your job?!" I roared. "Take some responsibility, for Christ's sake!"

"No need to shout. Hahaha!"

"It's not funny! If you don't search for my trunk, I'll ask the police to investigate it!"

"Really. But it's bound to be somewhere on the way, isn't it."

"And I'm asking you to find out where!"

"Hello?" Suddenly, the coarse voice of the village headman's wife interrupted our call. "I'm sorry, but are you going to be on the line much longer? I've quite a few other people wanting to make calls."

"Shut up! I'm still talking!" I yelled.

"I wonder, could you please be brief?"

I could hear Murai laughing.

"Shut up! SHUT UP!" I screamed at the top of my voice. "I'm still talking, I said! I'm still talking! I'm still toh-toh-toh-toh—" I suddenly found it hard to breathe, and clutched my chest.

"Is something the matter?" the old woman asked nervously. "Hello? Is something the matter?"

I replaced the receiver and hurriedly looked for my medicine bottle. I had stopped breathing altogether. My eyes were bulging, my body was twisted and bent backwards. I opened the medicine bottle with shaking hands and swallowed down the last three tablets without water.

. . .

"My medicine's run out," I complained to my wife in a tearful voice that night. "What am I to do? I told the man at Daitsu that I'd get the police to investigate it, but he didn't seem to care!"

"Well, he wouldn't, would he," she replied, sniggering. "After all, they're corrupt from the top down in that company."

"Yes…" I remembered an incident from some years back.

She wanted it again that night. In fact, she seemed more aroused than usual. Probably because she'd been flirting with those young students.

"No, no, no," I cried. "I've no medicine left. What would happen if I had an attack? I would surely die."

"All right then!" she shrieked hysterically. "Because tomorrow, I'm going to be unfaithful with one of those sweet boys!"

"Why do you torment me by saying things like that?" I pleaded in falsetto. "Don't say such things, please! You should know that sexual activity is bad for people with heart disease. Are you trying to kill me?!"

"I'm saying you don't have to do it!"

"But then you'll go and do it with someone else!"

"Huh. Not much of a man, are you."

"All right. If that's what you're saying, I'll do it for you." I put my hand on her.

She pushed my hand away. "You don't have to feel obliged."

"I don't feel obliged. I really want to make love to you. Honestly." More or less ready to die, I forced myself to embrace her.

Perhaps because it had been such a long time, I was finished in no time at all.

"What?! Is that it?!" my wife said in obvious dissatisfaction. "You deliberately finished quickly to protect your heart. I can't stand this any longer. I'm going to be unfaithful tomorrow. I'll have it off with all five of them, that'll show you!"

"Please don't! Please don't!" I pulled the sheets over my head and sobbed in sheer misery. My heart was already starting to palpitate after all that strenuous exercise and aggravation. I couldn't even shout at my wife as I would usually have done. "I think I'm going to die. I'm dying. I think I'm dying. Yes, I'm dying."

The trunk still hadn't arrived by the next day. Work was out of the question.

I telephoned Murai at the City Branch again. "It's Mr Suda from Pomegranate Island."

"Well, hello! Hahaha. Has your trunk arrived, then?"

"Of course not. That's why I'm calling you."

"Yeah. Yeah, of course."

"My medicine has at last run out."

"Medicine? What medicine?"

"The medicine for my heart problem."

"Really."

"The next time I have an attack, there won't be any medicine."

"I'm sorry to hear that."

"Do you know where my trunk is?"

"No. I don't."

"Did you try to find out?"

"Really."

"Did you try to find out?"

"Find out what?"

"Where the trunk has gone."

"Who?"

I gave a great sigh. "All right, I'll do it. Please give me the numbers of the Yabuki and Itagaki Branches."

I wrote the numbers down and phoned both branches. Neither of them had my trunk.

I asked for another long-distance call, this time to the Kawashita Clinic.

A nurse answered. "Kawashita Clinic?"

"Hello, my name's Suda. I'm one of your patients."

"Sorry? We have a bad line here."

"May I speak to Dr Kawashita?"

"I'm afraid he's not here."

"Oh dear. Could you tell me where he is?"

"He's away at a conference."

"Oh. A conference. Do you know where it is?"

"Sapporo."

"Sapporo?"

"That's right."

"Well, actually, you see, Dr Kawashita gave me some medicine, but it's been lost, you see, and I wonder if perhaps you could urgently send me some more, please?"

"You're breaking up. I can't hear you. Hello? Hello?"

"Hello? Yes. I would like you to send me some serpentina alkaloid urgently, please."

"Celluloid?"

"No, no. Serpentina alkaloid. That's the name of the medicine."

"Medicine? What about medicine?"

"I want you to send it urgently, you see."

"I can't issue medicine without the doctor's instructions."

"Yes. Of course."

"Pardon? What did you say?"

"Er, hello? I wonder if you could tell me where Dr Kawashita is staying in Sapporo?"

"Wear what?"

"What hotel is he staying in?"

"What to tell?"

"No, what hotel?"

"This isn't a hotel. This is the Kawashita Clinic. A hospital."

"Yes, yes. I know that. But Dr Kawashita, where is Dr Kawashita staying in Sapporo?"

"Ah, I see. Yes. Just a minute. Er, it's the Queen Hotel."

"Do you know the telephone number?"

I wrote down the number, then asked for another long-distance call to Sapporo. I'd been talking so loud that I was out of breath and sweating profusely.

I was connected to the Queen Hotel in Sapporo. The line sounded even more distant, so I had to shout at the top of my voice. At last, I was put through to reception.

"Oh, you mean *that* Dr Kawashita?" answered the faint voice of a man at the other end, when he'd at last understood what I was saying. "Dr Kawashita the doctor? Yes, he's with the police right now."

"The police? Why's he with the police?"

"Haven't you seen the papers? A woman was horribly murdered here last night. Three doctors who were attending the conference, including Dr Kawashita, are helping the police as key witnesses. So I can't really say when they'll be coming back, I'm afraid."

Without access to television or newspapers, I was completely unaware that such an incident had happened. If the doctor was being questioned by the police, this would be no time to discuss medicines, even if I did make contact. I abandoned the idea and replaced the receiver.

There was no sign of my trunk the following day either. Or the day after that. Ten days had passed since the trunk was sent. That day, the village headman's wife called to inform me, in a roundabout way, that the whole village was starting to notice my wife's immodest behaviour with the students.

Another five days passed. I was completely neglecting my work, spending whole days making long-distance phone calls here and there. Having finally lost patience with me and my complaining, whining and moaning, my wife took our child and returned to the mainland. Together with the five students. On the ferry.

Each time I argued violently with this person or that on the telephone, I thought I was going to die. I had palpitations eight times and stopped breathing four times. On three occasions, I was attacked by an intense heart pain that nearly made me lose consciousness. Each time, I fell and writhed on the floor in fear of imminent death.

At last, on the seventeenth day, there was a call from the Shimizu Branch to say the trunk had arrived. I'd asked them to call me as soon as it turned up.

"So, will it be here today?"

"Today's ferry has already left, hasn't it. So it'll be on tomorrow's," said the gravelly voice.

"Why has it taken so long?"

"Because it came by road."

"Why wasn't it sent by rail?"

"How should I know," he said, hanging up abruptly again.

The next day, I was waiting at the ferry landing stage a good hour before the ferry was due to arrive. A typhoon had passed from Kyushu to the Korean Peninsula, and the seas were rough. It wasn't raining, but the wind continued to gather force as I waited.

At last, some thirty minutes behind schedule, the ferry came into view.

"It's here!" I danced for joy at the end of the jetty. "That's the one! That's the boat that's carrying my medicine!"

"But he can't possibly berth here!" said the village headman, who'd come to stand behind me with several other villagers in their concern over the stormy weather.

"W-why's that?" I asked in surprise.

"Because of the typhoon," one of the villagers replied.

"That's right. With the waves this high, if he tries to berth he could be smashed against the jetty and capsize," the village headman explained.

"Don't be ridiculous!" I screamed. "I'm at the end of my tether, I tell you! I can't wait any longer! All right – if the boat can't berth, I'll swim out to it!" I took off my jacket.

"Impossible!" The village headman and the other villagers hastily tried to hold me back. "Don't do it! You'll drown! No, before you drown, you'll be smashed against the jetty and die of heart failure!"

"What do I care?! My heart can do what it likes! I need that medicine!" I shook myself free of their grasp and plunged deep down into the angrily billowing waves.

And that was when my crazy adventure started. I abandoned my family, packed in my job, crossed seven seas and traversed five continents in pursuit of a single package of medicine. I swam the English Channel naked, ran the Sahara Desert barefoot, fought off natives blowing poisoned darts in dense tropical jungle, grappled with a polar bear on the Arctic ice, and was caught in a gunfight between international agents trying to snatch my medicine on the Trans-Siberian Railway. Because that, you see, was my only way of staying alive.

I still haven't found my medicine.

Salmonella Men
on Planet Porno

It was Yohachi, the odd-job man, who brought the Team Leader's message. He wanted us all to attend an emergency meeting because Dr Shimazaki, an authority on botany and the only woman in our Research Team, was pregnant.

I looked up from my microscope. "Why must we have a meeting just because she's pregnant?" I asked.

"How should I know?" Lingering for a moment near the door of the lab, Yohachi opened his gap-toothed mouth and laughed coarsely. He was surely about the same age as me, but looked more than ten years older.

"Tell him I'll be right over," I said, turning my attention back to the eyepiece.

"He said if you didn't come straight away, I was to drag you there myself," Yohachi announced in his thick, rude voice.

"God! He must be in a hurry," I said, and reluctantly left my seat.

My ecosystems research lab, which also served as my living quarters, was a small makeshift structure near the edge of the Research Base. The Base was at the foot of Mount Mona, where up to ten similar buildings lay scattered about. In the middle of them stood the Research Centre, a two-storey building measuring about forty by forty feet. It was in fact a hastily erected affair that consisted only of the Team Leader's living quarters and a Meeting Room. Mount Mona, so named by the first expedition to reach the planet, was a low-lying mountain formed primarily of andesite. When a stiff wind blew at night, the hollows and crevices on the mountainsides made a noise that sounded like a woman moaning – hence the name.

I locked the door of the lab and went outside with Yohachi. Not that there were any burglars up there – but with so many freakish plants and creatures around, one couldn't be too careful.

"Who's the father then?" I asked Yohachi as we walked along.

Short enough already, Yohachi made himself shorter by hunching his back as he walked. He looked up at me with a sideways glance and grinned. "Who knows? Maybe it's you, mate."

"Not me," I answered straight-faced, then thought for a minute. Yes, I was fairly sure.

A little orange sun began to set behind Mount Mona. It was the season when night and day alternated every two hours on this planet called "Nakamura" in the Kabuki solar system. Both the planet and the solar system had been discovered by Peter Nakamura, a second-generation Japanese who was a big fan of Kabuki theatre. There again, back on Earth it was more commonly known as "Planet Porno", for which it was famous. The planet was inhabited by humanoid natives who lived in a country called Newdopia, about fifty miles west of the Base. They looked exactly the same as humans, with one major difference – they went around permanently naked.

It suddenly came to me. "It must be you," I said. "You've been sleeping with Dr Shimazaki!"

Whereupon Yohachi's expression was transformed. Lewd furrows appeared in the corners of his eyes, his mouth grotesquely distorted with lecherous imaginings. It was horribly distressing to see.

"I wish I could, mate!" he replied with an air of deepest torment. "I fancy her all right. God I wish I could." He made a writhing motion, licked his lips – along with the saliva that flowed over them – and seemed on the verge of tears. "*God* I wish I could."

Yohachi's lechery was renowned throughout the Base. He would have nosebleeds if he didn't have sex at least twice a day. In fact, he was sharing his quarters with a middle-aged woman he'd brought with him from earth. I'd always assumed she was his wife, but that appeared not to be the case.

Yohachi sighed once more. "I wish I could."

"So it's not you then."

"I wish it was, mate."

If it wasn't Yohachi, who on earth could have impregnated that thirty-two-year-old, gentle, fair-skinned, unmarried, well-rounded beauty of a woman, Dr Suiko Shimazaki? Still without a clue, I opened the door to the Research Centre. Yohachi, for some reason, bounded off towards his quarters.

"I was about to crack the feeding habits of the false-eared rabbit!" I complained to the Team Leader on entering the Meeting Room. "Do we really have to debate the ins and outs of private sex acts by Team members here in the Centre?"

With the others yet to arrive, the Team Leader sat alone in the Chairman's chair, his shoulders hunched around his thick neck as usual. "Firstly, this is no private matter," he started. "Secondly, we don't yet know whether it could rightly be called a sex act."

I stood open-mouthed.

Before I could ask whether it was possible for a woman to become pregnant without engaging in a sex act, in walked Dr Fukada, the physician, and Dr Mogamigawa, the bacteriologist.

"There's something there all right. It can't be a phantom pregnancy," reported Dr Fukada. "But it's impossible to tell with radiology alone what exactly it is. She's in her fourth month."

"She's been pregnant four months without knowing it? What sort of woman is she?!" I said, almost shouting. "Or perhaps she was deliberately hiding it?"

Ignoring my outburst, Dr Mogamigawa, an utterly humourless, solemn, stubborn old man who refused to recognize anything other than natural science, grimaced as he produced a weed that resembled a type of fern and placed it on the table. "This obscene plant was mixed up among the samples collected by Dr Shimazaki. I found it in her collecting case."

I jumped up. "What? Widow's incubus?! What's that doing in these parts? It's only supposed to grow west of Newdopia!"

"Correction. West of Lake Turpitude," Mogamigawa said, glaring at me. "Dr Shimazaki went to the lake to collect plants, but failed to notice that she'd collected the widow's incubus along with the other samples. The microspores of the widow's incubus must have penetrated her body. As you know, the androspores of this obscene plant stimulate the ovarian cells of higher vertebrates, and independently cause the growth of new individuals in utero."

"But Dr Shimazaki is not a widow," said the Team Leader.

Mogamigawa simply turned away in disdain, as if to say, *What has that to do with anything*. Dr Fukada took over instead.

"It was tentatively called widow's incubus by a member of the First Expedition," he explained. "Actually, it doesn't matter if the host is a widow or not. It will attempt parthenogenesis with any woman, as long as she isn't a virgin. Parthenogenesis literally means virgin generation, but in this case perhaps we should call it non-virgin generation. Ahaha. We don't yet know why it fails to stimulate the ovarian cells of virgins, but it may have something to do with the quantity of estrogenic hormones secreted. And of course it should be no surprise that Dr Shimazaki is not a virgin," he said with a smile. "After all, she *is* thirty-two. It would be harsh to cast aspersions on her just because she isn't a virgin."

"Hold on, I'm not casting anything on her," said the Team Leader, stirring in his seat. "Well, there are only four of us – but let's start the meeting anyway. Dr Shimazaki herself has declined to attend, on the grounds of embarrassment. Well, that's only natural, considering how shy and demure she is. The geo-mineralogists are out surveying that obscene cloystone at the Hokomaka Pass on Mount Arasate."

"As the matter demands immediate action, we should act right away. Ah! I appear to have said much the same thing twice. How embarrassing," said Fukada, who, having written some thirty tedious novels as a hobby, posed as a man of letters. "Ahem. Proceeding to the main issue, pregnancy caused by widow's incubus reaches full term in ten earth days. So, to amend the statement made by Dr Sona just now, Dr Shimazaki was pregnant for only four *days* without knowing it. In the two previous cases involving earth women, a member of the First Expedition miscarried on the seventh day, and a female doctor attached to the Base Construction

Team rather recklessly aborted her own pregnancy by curettage on the third day. But in Dr Shimazaki's case, curettage is already out of the question, and we have no way of knowing whether she can miscarry or not. There is every chance that she will in fact give birth. However, Dr Shimazaki herself says that she does not want to."

"Well, she would say that, wouldn't she. Having a child fathered by a weed called widow's incubus would bring disgrace to her long family line of notable scientists."

"May we keep this discussion on a scientific level?", said Mogamigawa, glaring at me again. "It is inconceivable that the androspores of widow's incubus, having entered the body through the respiratory organs, would then proceed directly from there to the uterus. Rather, they merely give some kind of acid stimulus to the woman's unfertilized ovum, and thereby induce the growth of a new individual. As such, the widow's incubus has not directly fertilized Dr Shimazaki per se, and therefore cannot be said to have 'fathered' anything. All will be revealed when she gives birth, but I feel sure that the new individual will only have chromosomes from the mother's side. It's normal for human individuals born by parthenogenesis to lack a reproductive capacity, as Professor Yoishonovitch Sano states in his *History of Transparent Embryogeny in Humans*."

"Well yes, that would be the normal way of thinking," Fukada started in counter-argument. "But things aren't always normal on this planet, or to be more exact, *things tend to veer from the normal towards the obscene*, if anything. There is every possibility that the spores of widow's incubus could reach the uterus via the respiratory, digestive or circulatory organs, or what have you – without biodegrading, mind – and then find some means of infiltrating the uterus. Parthenogenesis is a perfectly normal method of reproduction in the animal kingdom, even on earth. So it wouldn't be unthinkable for something as preposterous as embryonic fertilization by plant spores to occur on this infamous 'Planet Porno'. When I said there was 'something' inside Dr Shimazaki's uterus, what I meant was that it doesn't necessarily have to be a human embryo."

Mogamigawa's face was still set in a grimace. "In principle, I agree with you when you call this an obscene planet. But I heard that the foetus miscarried by the female in the First Expedition did indeed appear to be human."

"However—"

"The problem, however," I intervened, hoping to speed the discussion along, "is neither the nature of Dr Shimazaki's pregnancy, nor the identity of her foetus. Surely, it is how to prevent it from reaching full term."

"Well, on that subject," the Team Leader said with a nod in my direction, "I think there are two methods available. One is to remove whatever it is from her womb by Caesarean section."

"We have no equipment for that," groaned Fukada. "Of course, it can still be done, but I don't like doing it. And the burden of opening Dr Shimazaki's abdomen would be too great to bear."

Fukada was attempting to shirk responsibility as usual. Mogamigawa cast a contemptuous eye in his direction, then turned to me. "Would you happen to know how the Newdopians prevent pregnancies caused by widow's incubus?" he asked. "Or what measures they take when a pregnancy occurs? They must surely fall victim to it."

"Yes, I think they do. The vegetation around Newdopia is characterized as having communities, or plant divisions, or anyway very large quantities of widow's incubus. But since humans cannot enter Newdopia, we don't yet know how the natives deal with such cases."

The Team Leader leant forwards. "Then again, the second method I was considering was, in fact, for someone to go to Newdopia and somehow find out about it from the natives. It would also have value as scientific research, so it would be like killing two birds with one stone, as they say."

"But they won't let us in," I said with a shake of the head, remembering how we were flatly refused permission to enter on a previous research mission. "Unless it's someone who shares their mentality, that is. They're pretty good at reading our minds, you know." I turned to face Dr Fukada. "The quickest way would be for you to perform a Caesarean section, after all."

Fukada immediately started to panic. "Well, yes, in the barbarian era they did such operations very crudely by hand, but now, well, it's only performed under fully automated conditions using computer systems, and so, that is I mean, as a doctor, I don't particularly, well, they don't teach such things at medical school, and..."

Mogamigawa looked up at the ceiling as if to say, *So you can't do it then.* I was equally disappointed.

"According to one report, some members of the First Expedition entered Newdopia and saw what it was like," said the Team Leader to revive the discussion. "How did they manage that?"

"Because it was the first time the natives had seen human beings, I suppose. They didn't realize that we were such an obscene race, and just let them in without thinking. By that, of course, I mean obscene from their point of view."

"Obscene? They're the obscene ones!" Mogamigawa said, wrinkling his cheeks in annoyance. "As far as I've heard, they openly have carnal relations with each other, outdoors in broad daylight, and they don't much care who the partner is! Nor do they care where they do it – in the street, public squares, community halls, anywhere, great numbers of them together at the same time!"

"That's exactly my point," I replied, popping up a finger at Dr Mogamigawa. "It's that very attitude, the attitude that sex acts are obscene and should be hidden from the eyes of others, that appears obscene to them. Looking at it from their point of view, I suppose they would feel distracted or inhibited if we watched their acts with that kind of attitude."

"Are you saying you don't find such things obscene?" Mogamigawa gave me a look laden with antipathy.

I blushed slightly. "No, I don't find such things obscene."

"In that case, why can't you get in there?"

"Because I am obscene. Well no, in my case, I find it interesting and enjoyable to watch such things as an onlooker, call it voyeurism, peeping or whatever. But if you asked me to do such things in front of people, I suppose I would feel embarrassed, unnatural, self-conscious, and I wouldn't be able to go through with it. They can see right through my mental framework, and that's why I would be refused entry."

"In other words," said the Team Leader, appearing to have hit upon an idea, "the only earth humans who would be permitted to enter Newdopia are those who have a highly progressive attitude to sex?"

"Well yes, but from the natives' point of view, that 'progressive attitude' would apparently not be progressive at all. That is, people who are said to have a progressive attitude to sex tend to link sexual liberation to anti-establishment movements, rebellion against the 'old powers', criticism of government control and the like. From the Newdopians' point of view, such people cannot really be said to be pursuing or extolling sex acts at all. Apparently there was a member of the Sexual Liberation Alliance in the First Expedition. The Newdopians rejected her because she only wanted to take advantage of their behaviour to justify a low-level social movement. Anyway, she took to her heels and ran when she was approached by a Newdopian man who resembled a bear, I heard."

"So just what sort of person can get in?" asked the Team Leader in a rather throwaway tone.

"Well, of course, the kind of person who has no metaphysical conception of the sex act, but who at the same time has an endless supply of powerful philanthropic urges towards the sex act itself."

"In other words, then..." Mogamigawa widened his eyes and raised his voice in a tone of thorough disgust. "Someone who's happy to have sexual intercourse with any partner, no matter who?!..." He stopped and scratched his head. "Why am I talking so loudly? Despicable. How low have I fallen since coming to this planet!"

The Team Leader suddenly adjusted his position and stared out to space. "Hmm. Well, we have a person of just that description, do we not."

I looked at the Team Leader aghast. "Surely you don't mean Yohachi?..."

"Who else," replied the Team Leader, fixing his gaze on me. "Yohachi is surely the only person at the Base who has the mentality needed to enter Newdopia."

"Impossible!" Mogamigawa shook his head as if to add, *The very idea.* "Even if he managed to get in, with his inferior intelligence he wouldn't discover anything for us at all."

"However, Dr Mogamigawa," the Team Leader said abruptly, in a bid to persuade him, "even if he has no knowledge of medicine or biology, surely it isn't beyond him to ask how they prevent pregnancy?"

"If Yohachi goes to Newdopia, we'll never see him again," I said with a grin. "Apart from anything else, Newdopian women are said to be universally beautiful – far beyond the likes of earth women. Didn't the report say 'The women were all like angels'?"

"What a banal expression," said Fukada, turning away.

"Yes, but someone else could go with him," argued the Team Leader. "He could wait near the Newdopian border and give Yohachi instructions from there. If the information Yohachi brings is unclear, he could be sent back repeatedly until an intelligible answer is received."

My head sank. "You want me to go, don't you."

"Correct," the Team Leader declared coldly, before turning to Mogamigawa. "And I think a knowledge of bacteriology will come in handy too. Could you accompany them, Doctor?"

Mogamigawa nodded casually. "I could do that. If we take the survey ship, we'll be there in about an hour."

"However," interrupted the Team Leader, shifting uneasily in his seat. "We only have one ship, and it's currently being used by the geo-mineralogists."

"So you could contact Dr Nayama and order him to return immediately."

"In fact, I was speaking to him by telecall just now," the Team Leader said with a pained expression. "He says they won't be back for another two days. As you know, he's an obstinate so-and-so. He won't take orders from anyone."

"Of course, you did tell him how urgent the situation is."

"Of course. But it was like water off a duck's back. 'Let her give birth, then just dump the thing somewhere,' he said."

"Very amusing," Mogamigawa said with a sigh. "Then we shall go by hovercar."

"What?!" I gasped. "The hovercar will only take us as far as Lake Turpitude. It can't travel over water. And we can't go round the lake, as there's the Sea of Newdopia to the north, and sea from the tip of Cape Onania to the south." As I spoke, I felt rising anger at the studied silence of Dr Fukada. If only he would perform a Caesarean section, this problem would not have existed in the first place. Surgeons were increasingly unable to perform operations manually; as they themselves said, it was all thanks to advances in medical science. But what good are scientific advances if they cause such inconvenience? "If we go, we'll have to take the hovercar as far as Lake Turpitude, then make some kind of raft from the vegetation around there, cross the lake, go through the marsh to the west of the lake, then walk the remaining twenty or so miles to Newdopia."

Dr Mogamigawa groaned. "Is that the only way?!" Evidently sharing my thoughts, he turned to glower at Fukada with a look that said, *Quack!*

Fukada shifted uncomfortably in his seat and attempted to excuse himself. "Of course, I should go. But as you know, I have a bad leg, not to mention my chronic condition."

"Nobody is asking you to go, my friend," Mogamigawa said sharply. Fukada cast him a look of petulant indignation, then fell into a sullen silence.

Nobody said anything for a while.

At length, Fukada could take it no longer and rose from his seat. "Well, I have work to do. Excuse me."

Once our incompetent friend had left the room, the Team Leader let out a huge sigh. In our disgust, Mogamigawa and I had lost all inclination to speak.

The groaning voice of a woman riding on a wave of ecstasy came blowing in on the wind from Mount Mona.

"What an obscene sound," cursed Mogamigawa. "A mountain that makes a noise like that should be called Mounting Climax, not Mount Mona." His eyes bulged. "What am I saying?!" He scratched his head. "Dear me. How low have I fallen."

I took a long puff from my cigarette and started to speak as calmly as I could. "From my one experience of walking from Lake Turpitude to Newdopia and back, it won't be all that hard to make a raft and walk there. The main reason why I really didn't want to go there on foot again was because of the nightmarish flora and fauna we encountered on the way. Not to mention their habitats. Of course, I myself should be well-accustomed to the outlandish habitats of bizarre life forms on alien planets. But even I could not remain apathetic to their sheer obscenity, based on scientific interest alone."

"Er – you needn't mention that now," said the Team Leader in some haste.

I shook my head. "I'm sorry, but I have to warn Dr Mogamigawa of these things before we go. It may help to lighten the blow."

"Are they really so obscene? I've heard rumours, but…"

"Well, most of them are plants and creatures that also exist around here, but over there they've formed biocenoses to the point of overpopulation. The plants grow in multi-layered communities, among which the animals form complexes while maintaining relationships of peaceful coexistence. For example, species of algae that are only occasionally found in these parts have formed whole communities in Lake Turpitude, which is arguably their physiologically optimal habitat. There's clingweed and bleedweed, not to mention fondleweed."

"Not fondleweed! It's obscene!" Mogamigawa repeatedly banged both fists on the table and contorted his body. "Only recently my wife went to a lake not far from here and bathed in the water. After a few moments she began to look drowsy, and came out looking utterly dissipated. There was fondleweed in that lake! It's obscene," he muttered once his agitation had abated. "I should never have brought my wife to such an obscene planet!"

"Lake Turpitude is also full of strange creatures. It's literally swimming with flatback hippos, eleventh-hour crocodiles, gurgling alligators, and what have you."

"Are they dangerous?"

"No. They're not dangerous, but they come and do obscene things. Besides the larger animals, there are also swarms of matchbox jellyfish and other weird creatures. We'll have to build the raft sturdily, as it'll be no joke if it capsizes."

"I'll wager there's something in the marsh too. Is there something in the marsh too?" Mogamigawa asked, trembling with trepidation.

"There are communities of forget-me-grass there."

"Not forget-me-grass! It's obscene!" Mogamigawa repeatedly banged both fists on the tabletop and contorted his body. "Only recently I was collecting species of grass for culture tests on perforating bacterial pathogens, and that plant was mixed in amongst them. I forgot what culture tests I was supposed to be doing! That was just with one specimen. If we have to cross a whole field of forget-me-grass, who knows what we'll forget. We might even forget what we've gone there for!"

"Perhaps you should make a note of it in advance," said the Team Leader.

"What if we forget how to read?"

The Team Leader laughed dismissively. "It causes temporary amnesia, not senile dementia! Honestly, it can't be that bad."

"Wasn't there a jungle too?" Mogamigawa looked at me with fear in his eyes. "What's in the jungle?"

"There are communities of sheath and mantle, characteristic of woodland borders, lying between the jungle and liberated vegetation zones such as fields of forget-me-grass. Mistress bine grows there. It's a type of lichen that hangs from the branches of the itchy scratchy tree. As for animals in those parts, the main ones are the panting hart, the false-eared rabbit, the grindhog, the gaping hooter and the collapsible cow. For birds we have the penisparrow, for insects the screeching cicada. Unclassified species include the relic pod, and finally, one that's heard but never seen, the wife waker."

"Not the wife waker! It's obscene!" Mogamigawa banged his fists madly on the tabletop and scratched his hair. "If one hears its ghastly cry while in bed at night, one is sure to have an erotic dream! It wakes my wife, then she wakes me. I should never have brought her to such an obscene planet!" He put his head in his hands.

Serves you right for not trusting her on earth, I thought.

Mogamigawa lifted his head. "And what's in the jungle ahead of that?" He was gripping the edge of the table with both hands. "Some unspeakable abominations, I suppose?"

"Actually, I don't know," I said with a sigh. "The first time I went, it was a research trip and we weren't in such a hurry. The jungle was dark and eerily foreboding, even during the day. It was like a pandora's box – we had no way of knowing what ghastly horrors it might hold. We certainly weren't brave enough to go in, so we made a detour."

"'Dark and eerily foreboding'. 'Pandora's box'. 'Ghastly horrors'. Must you use such provocative expressions?" the Team Leader said in grouchy irritation. "You're an ecologist, aren't you? Where's your spirit of enquiry?! Not only will these be the very places to find clues for elucidating habitats, but they're also treasure troves of new species for alien biology, are they not?"

Go yourself then, I thought, casting him a reproachful glance.

"And this time I suppose we'll have to go straight through it," Mogamigawa said dolefully.

The Team Leader turned to face him, nodding vigorously. "Yes! Yes! But even then, you're sure to make some new discoveries!"

I had to agree. Too many, if anything.

By the time we'd discussed other details, such as our itinerary and what to take with us, dawn had broken. First, a pink sun appeared over the distant horizon beyond our window, then, about fifteen minutes later, the orange sun we'd seen setting earlier also started to rise from the same point. These two formed a 'spectroscopic binary', two stars that look like one from a distance, with a very small interval between them. The pink sun was the principal star, the orange one the companion. Though slightly different in colour, when seen side by side they looked just like a pair of woman's breasts. This earnt them a variety of names, among them 'golden globes', 'heavenly orbs', and 'cupid's kettledrums'.

Mogamigawa and I decided to spend the two hours of daylight making preparations, then to catch some sleep for the ensuing two hours of night. We knew we would need to store up energy in advance, as sleeping would not always be an option on our journey.

The Team Leader had already called Yohachi and handed him his weighty mission. Needless to say, Yohachi was delighted.

It was still dark when I stepped out of my research laboratory after less than two hours of sleep. Outside the Centre, Yohachi was already loading baggage onto the hovercar while Mogamigawa shouted instructions.

"Look here! Load those more carefully, would you? Look, that case is full of culture-medium slides! Don't put the microscope at the bottom, man! Put food at the bottom!"

My own baggage consisted of a single collecting case containing insect jars, dissection equipment and the like. I had wanted to take a trapping cage for small animals too, but it would have been impossible to carry such things on foot. For detailed study, I could borrow Dr Mogamigawa's sophisticated electron microscope.

The three of us boarded the hovercar in front of the Team Leader, who had come out to see us off. I would drive, with Mogamigawa in the passenger seat next to me and Yohachi in the back with the baggage. I switched on the repulsion force engine, whereupon the vehicle rose about three feet off the ground.

"Take care now," the Team Leader said perfunctorily. "I look forward to a splendid catch."

Mogamigawa snorted. "And you, sir, look after things while we're away. If Shimazaki gives birth before we return, watch that quack of a doctor, will you? If you leave him to his own devices, there's no knowing what he'll get up to."

I turned the vehicle due west and started off. It was an easy drive, as there was little rainfall in this area and the terrain consisted mainly of savannah-type grassland. Our frequent visits to the lake to fetch water had created a natural pathway, along which the hovercar sped at 100mph. Soon the golden globes rose over the horizon, and the suns started to shine down on us in the open-topped vehicle. There was no wind, the air was warm. Tall frizzly acacias grew here and there, while screeching cicadas – little insects like caddis flies – shrieked and whooped gaily around the treetops. Small crimson birds called penisparrows populated the air. The penisparrow was a terribly obscene bird whose head bore a striking resemblance to a penis. Meanwhile, the unclassifiable species known as the relic pod hung from the lower branches of the frizzly acacias.

"The weather's fair, the air is fresh," said Dr Mogamigawa. "If only we could ignore all these loathsome plants and creatures, it would actually feel quite pleasant out here."

"Yes," I agreed. "The temperature's comfortable, humidity's low, we're perfectly content and healthy, the scenery is good, the time is morning, about ten in the morning, frizzly acacias flutter in the breeze, penisparrows dance in the air, screeching cicadas shriek and whoop, relic pods hang from the branches, the golden globes reign in the heavens. All in all, a truly obscene world."

As I finished speaking, I laughed aloud. Mogamigawa looked at me as if I'd lost my mind.

"Sorry. It started going funny in the middle."

"A word of caution. We are scientists. Please take care to retain your sanity at all times."

Personally, I was more concerned about *his* sanity from now on, but I kept that thought to myself.

As we approached Lake Turpitude, the ground became increasingly covered with ferns and gymnosperms. The smaller ones included bric-a-bracken, cloven hare's foot, black-and-whitebeam, animephedra and sagging palm. Larger ones included the foolhardy tree-fern and the burly sequoia. Besides these, there were numerous clusters of ferns and tree ferns that had yet to be named, either by previous expeditions or by Dr Shimazaki.

Mogamigawa alighted from the hovercar, which I'd brought to a halt just ahead of the lake, and surveyed the scene around him. "What a plethora of fern species," he said.

"Dr Shimazaki says it's adaptive radiation of flora. Ferns have specialized into many different forms, and there are now several thousand species, apparently."

"That must make them difficult to name. Of course, Dr Shimazaki would never give them obscene names, would she." Mogamigawa looked out over the deep green surface of the lake, which remained ominously quiet for now. "I wonder why they had to specialize to that degree. In such a narrow geographical area."

"Well," I said, tilting my head. "If they were animals, I could think of a plausible explanation, judging from the environment. Since most of the higher vertebrates around here are herbivores, it may have something to do with their eating habits."

"Are we going to build this raft then?" asked Yohachi.

"Oh yes. Could you fetch the electronic saw?"

"It'll take a while, mate," he said resentfully. "The other gentleman put all his own things on top. The saw is right at the bottom."

"Look here! Stop moaning and get a bloody move on!" Mogamigawa bellowed. "*Tempus fugit*, man! What'll we do if the suns set while we're still on the lake?!"

Yohachi and I started cutting wood. There were various species of pine and cedar, which the members of the expedition had half-jokingly named supine, overcedar, and so on. But those would have taken too long to fell, so we concentrated on cutting tree ferns, which we bound together with rope to form a rectangular raft about twelve foot square. By the time we'd transferred the baggage onto the raft, camouflaged the hovercar under fronds of fern and launched the raft onto the lake, the suns had already started to set.

"Only thirty minutes to nightfall!" said Mogamigawa in dismay as he eyed his wristwatch, having done nothing himself but constantly hustle and bellow at us. "Can we cross to the other side in thirty minutes?"

"Yes, if we all use our poles together," I replied with an ironic grin.

He pulled a sullen face. "Are you expecting me to use my pole?"

"Yeah, just like you do with your wife every night," Yohachi whispered in my ear.

We had brought three collapsible plastic poles with which to propel the raft. We extended them to a length of about fifteen feet, took one each and climbed aboard. As we pushed our poles into the edges and bottom of the lake, pockets of air came bubbling up to the water's surface around the raft, accompanied by a reddish-brown mud. We pulled away from the lake's edge.

Every now and again, blood-red algae would come up entangled on our poles.

"That's bleedweed," I said. "Makes my skin crawl every time I see it."

"If there's so much bleedweed here, there must also be a good number of matchbox jellyfish," Mogamigawa said as he cackhandedly manoeuvred his pole. "They'll be surfacing any moment now."

Before I could say "*Well postulated*", a swarm of rectangular jellyfish that resembled large translucent matchboxes came floating up to the surface and eagerly huddled around our raft belly-side up, mouths agape and tentacles swaying.

"Swimming upside down as usual. What an obscene creature."

"Also known as the jacuzzi or missionary jellyfish."

"I did some research on these once," said Mogamigawa. "They have ectodermal reproductive glands and appear to eat bleedweed, as well as various species of vegetable plankton."

"Do they sting?" asked Yohachi.

"Well, considering how very obscene they are, they're obviously going to sting, aren't they," said Mogamigawa, staring at Yohachi maliciously. "Why not try grabbing one?"

"They only sting before reproducing," I explained to Yohachi, then turned back to Mogamigawa. "And when they do, it doesn't really hurt but is a rather pleasant feeling. Why do you think that is?"

"That's precisely my point," he replied sourly. "Their pre-reproductive nematocysts contain poison, like that of earth jellyfish. I'm analysing this poison now, but it seems somehow to display anaphylaxis. That is, the first sting only has a mild effect on the ejaculatory centre, but with increased frequency the resistivity is lowered, finally leading to ejaculation. It's the opposite of immunity."

"Have you tried it out?" I said with a snort of laughter. "Oh. Sorry."

Mogamigawa gave me a murderous look.

"Let's catch a few of them, then!" said Yohachi.

A gentle splish-splashing noise could be heard. I looked back towards the shore, which was already about fifty yards behind us.

One by one, a colony of gurgling alligators, which appeared to have been basking on mudflats some distance from our launch point, were starting to slip into the lake.

"Do you think they're coming after us?" Mogamigawa said anxiously.

"But of course," I answered as I vigorously thrust my pole down to the bottom of the lake. "And in some numbers. Let's make haste!"

The alligators, somewhat smaller than the earth variety, started to approach our raft in groups. Although some seemed to have concealed themselves underwater, dozens of them swam just under the water's surface, showing only the tips of their snouts, their eyes and the tops of their bony backs, which resembled dorsal fins. They closed in on us at speed, making no sound in the water except the lazy gurgling noise of breath flapping out of their nostrils.

"If they all come here, the raft will capsize!" Mogamigawa shrieked while frantically working his pole. "What do they want from us?!"

"Our chastity," I replied. "They have a habit of mating with other species."

"If they drag us underwater we'll drown!" Mogamigawa wailed. "Isn't there anything we can do? How did you get over this last time?"

"By getting to the other side quickly. The opposite shore is the territory of eleventh-hour crocodiles…"

Just at that moment, the alligators approaching underwater must have risen to the surface, for the raft suddenly listed to one side. We all lurched with it.

Mogamigawa crouched down on the surface of the raft to prevent himself from falling. "These must all be females, then?" he asked.

"Some are male, some female," I answered, also squatting on the raft. I had hurriedly withdrawn my pole, which they'd tried to wrench from my grasp with their gaping mouths, and was now holding on to it for dear life. "They can't tell the gender of other species, so they just try to mate with them anyway."

"But it's usually only the male that displays courtship!"

"Yes, but on this planet both males and females display courtship. We know that attractants such as sex pheromones have hardly any effect between individuals of the same species, which means that they don't mate much among themselves. They compensate for this with a strange innate releasing mechanism, whereby they chase other species as if hunting prey."

"Won't the species then become extinct?"

"No. Excessive inbreeding is more likely to cause extinction. Especially on this planet, where the animals have hardly any natural enemies."

"Why don't we try it out?" said Yohachi, using his pole to bash an alligator as it tried to crawl onto the raft. "It might feel good."

"Idiot. If it's a male, your anus will be ripped apart," I said, then gasped in relief when I saw the opposite shore only thirty feet away. "Thank God! Eleventh-hour crocodiles!"

Slightly larger than the gurgling alligators, groups of eleventh-hour crocodiles were crawling into the lake from swamps near the shore.

Pushed up from below by the alligators' snouts, our raft continued to tilt wildly. We clung onto our baggage to avoid being shaken off, and waited for the eleventh-hour crocodiles to arrive.

"But it's out of the frying pan into the fire, isn't it?" said Mogamigawa, shaking with fear.

"We'll escape while they're fighting," I replied.

The eleventh-hour crocodile at the head of the group snapped at one of the gurgling alligators. The pair corkscrewed their bodies and leapt six feet into the air as they grappled with each other. A massive spray of water flew up, and at last, the mother of all battles started around our raft.

"Now!" I yelled.

We desperately worked our poles to escape from the carnage.

"That's quite a battle," said Mogamigawa, turning back to watch the action goggle-eyed. "Many of them will surely die."

"No. What you're seeing is a 'ritual contest', as they say in ethology. It's the same as when males of earth species fight over the females. The difference on this planet is that they're not fighting over females but over the spectators, creatures of other species that simply watch the action from the side. They're waiting to yield their chastity to the victors." I was punting along for all I was worth, but let out a cry when I saw the far bank approaching. "Oh no! What a fool I've been! There's a pod of flatback hippos near here!"

Mogamigawa raised his voice in alarm. "Those unearthly creatures?! Good God, it'll be no joke if we're ravished by *them*! Which way should we go?"

"Let's skirt the shore southwards. Hey, Yohachi – look out!"

Before I could finish, a number of flatback hippos surfaced around the raft, showing only their flat rectangular backs.

"Take that!" I shouted.

"Take that!" yelled Yohachi.

"And take your bestial desires with you!" added Mogamigawa.

We thrust our poles into the backs of the flatback hippos in a mad frenzy. Their soft backs were covered with fine crêpe-like wrinkles resembling the mesh of a reed mat. With each manly thrust, the ends of our poles would penetrate the skin and slide into the thick fat on their backs. But it didn't appear to hurt the hippos at all, for they continued to close in on our raft undeterred, oblivious of their gaping wounds. A very small quantity of white fat oozed out of the round holes made in their backs by the poles. As I continued to thrust, I wondered if perhaps they actually enjoyed having this done to them…

The hippos' backs now had so many holes in them that they began to resemble honeycombs, a truly sickening sight. I decided to stop thrusting the pole and started smashing them over the head with it instead. But merely being hit on the head wasn't going to make these hippos desist. They continued to look up at us ruefully, their eyes bloodshot with carnal lust, some diving down below the raft while others waited for a chance to crawl up onto it.

"*Aaargh!*" Yohachi had plunged his pole into a hippo's back with such force that he was unable to pull it out again. As he clung to the end of the pole, he was lifted off the raft and hoisted about three feet into the air vertically above the hippo's back. "HELPPPP!!!" he cried, eyeballs bulging.

Our raft, surrounded on three sides by flatback hippos, was gradually buffeted along the shore away from Yohachi. The hippo that had Yohachi on its back also continued to chase, but lagged somewhat behind the others under Yohachi's weight. The gap between us gradually widened as a result, though we remained at the same distance from the shore.

"Is it all right to leave him like that?" Mogamigawa asked.

"The main thing is for us to reach the shore," I replied. "Then we can throw him a rope."

At that moment, one of the hippos must have stood on all fours in the shallows directly beneath us, for the raft started to tilt at an acute angle.

"As I thought – we should have made the raft of pine or cedar," I shouted, frantically gathering up the baggage to stop it falling into the water. "We'll be up a creek if we fall off now. The water round here is full of fondleweed!"

"But we're men, and we're wearing trousers, are we not? We will surely not be fondled so vigorously," said Mogamigawa. "This is no good at all. We'll capsize at this rate. You take the machinery and equipment, and I'll take the food. If the raft capsizes, we'll wade ashore with the bags on our backs. We'll just have to force our way through the fondleweed. *Audere est facere*, my friend!"

"Right."

The raft moved closer to the shore. Dusk was starting to close in.

With the flatback hippos still standing beneath us, the raft had tilted to an angle of about forty degrees. We slid down its surface with the baggage on our backs, landing thigh-deep in water.

"Run! Run or be fondled!" Mogamigawa hollered as he started to race bow-legged through the water. I followed behind. The flatback hippos were still grouped on the other side of the raft, and as they could only waddle through the shallows with their slow thumping feet, there was no danger of them catching us.

We reached the shore safely without being molested by fondleweed, then turned back in relief to look at the lake. The flatback hippos had given up chasing us. Instead, they were now homing in on Yohachi from all sides. Some started to clamber up onto the hippo that had Yohachi's pole stuck in its back.

"Quick, fetch the rope!"

I went to get the rope out of the baggage, but it was too late. Yohachi's trousers, along with his pants, were instantly snapped off by the gargantuan mouths of the flatback hippos.

"That's it – I'm off!" Yohachi shrieked. He boldly leapt off the pole and bounded towards us, completely naked from the waist down, using the heads and backs of the hippos as stepping stones, then plunged straight into the lake and began to run towards us waist-high in water.

I braced myself. "Hey – he's running through the fondle-weed…"

"Come on, he's a man! Even if it fondles him, it won't be that bad."

No sooner Mogamigawa had spoken than Yohachi started to slow down. His eyes assumed a haunted look, and he gasped oppressively as he walked the next two or three steps. Then a half-smile came over his face as he issued a loud cry, bent his head backwards, and in that pose fell flat on his face in the water.

"It's got him!" Mogamigawa shouted aghast. "The fool! He should have kept his trousers on!"

As I watched, I shook at the horrible thought of what the swarming fondleweed might be doing to Yohachi under the water. The surface started to bubble feverishly, then Yohachi's face appeared, followed by his upper body. He started towards us with an expression of complete exhaustion, staggered up onto the shore with white trails of semen hanging from his still erect member, and collapsed at the water's edge panting furiously.

"I wonder why the flatback hippos remain unharmed by this fondleweed," Mogamigawa mused as I nursed Yohachi. "They eat fondleweed, so they must always be physically surrounded by it."

"No, even the flatback hippos are fondled. Or to be more exact, they only know where their food is when it starts to fondle them. Of course, they must have the occasional orgasm while they eat."

"Really? Now I begin to understand," Mogamigawa said with a

nod. "Once, Dr Shimazaki asked me to test the water quality near a spot where fondleweed grows. There I discovered large quantities of helical bacteria breeding on protein, potassium and calcium. The fondleweed evidently absorbs these substances once they've been degraded into inorganic matter and excreted by those bacteria."

"So the process goes something like this. First, fondleweed fondles the flatback hippos, and the males ejaculate. Bacteria reproduce by eating the protein and other substances in their semen. The fondleweed then absorbs the degraded excretions of the bacteria and transforms them into vegetable protein, which the hippos eat. In other words, it's a tripartite regenerative cycle – right?"

"Well, yes, although of course there are other species of bacteria that live on the excretions of the flatback hippos."

Undeterred by Mogamigawa's challenging expression, I continued to argue in the growing belief that we were about to make a discovery – a clue to understanding the laws that governed ecosystems on this planet. "On the other hand, since fondleweed forces the flatback hippos to ejaculate, this must create environmental resistance to increases in population size, weakening the fecundity of the species as a whole. This in turn provides negative feedback that prevents the fondleweed from being completely consumed by the hippos. In other words, what we have here is a regulating biotope for these three species. After all, with no pronounced seasonal variation in climate on this planet, organisms would go through population explosions followed immediately by extinction if left unchecked, wouldn't they."

"You seem overhasty in your desire to make judgements, but you shouldn't jump to conclusions, my friend. Even if that happened to be true in this case, don't forget that this is merely a single cybernetic system within the wide, open space of an entire planet. We don't know how it links with others."

As Mogamigawa continued to speak with his customary glare, Yohachi tottered shakily to his feet.

"I think I'm all right now," he said.

"So you should be. Pull yourself together, man. What's two or three ejaculations?!" said Mogamigawa.

Yohachi gave him a withering look. "Anyone else would have passed out, or even died. I came seven or eight times!"

The suns had already set. But for us, it was time to be on the move, as we had to cross the marsh right away. It would have been sheer lunacy, after all, to go through that dark and eerily foreboding jungle at night.

We let Yohachi carry most of the baggage, while we ourselves took only the experimental observation equipment that we thought might come in handy on the way. With that, we entered the marsh. I took the lead with Mogamigawa following behind.

"Anyway," I said as I walked on ahead, "the relationship between those alligators, the matchbox jellyfish and the bleedweed could also be seen as part of a multi-species regenerative system similar to that of the flatback hippos and the fondleweed, could it not. Unlike the earth varieties, the alligators are not carnivores but eat bleedweed and other algae. And besides, they're mammals, aren't they? What completely ridiculous names the expedition members gave these creatures. The false-eared rabbit isn't even a rabbit, for Christ's sake!"

"Well, there are still cases of such risible names being fabricated by amateurs. More than that, though, aren't nearly all the higher vertebrates on this planet mammals? What happened to all the lower-order reptiles, amphibians, et cetera? Did they all die out like the giant reptiles on earth during the Mesozoic, do you think?"

I was stuck for words. If I'd said what I'd been thinking for a while now, it was certain that Mogamigawa would once again look at me as if I'd lost my mind.

I changed the subject in the nick of time. "However, the very fact that most species of higher-order animals are mammals and, although very different in appearance, are so similar as to be related to each other, means that mating between species is possible, even if they can't actually reproduce. Although of course, if a small animal like the false-eared rabbit were to mate with one of those flatback hippos, it would probably die of organ rupture."

"I wonder if the hippos actually go looking for other animals to have it off with," Yohachi said loudly as he walked along at the rear, a mountain of baggage piled high on his back. "After all, they're always being done over by that fondleweed, aren't they. And by the way, it's really fantastic being done over by that fondleweed."

"What Yohachi just said is correct," I continued regardless. "All higher-order vertebrates have an innate releasing mechanism that incorporates the activity of mating with individuals of other species. However, flatback hippos usually herd together with individuals of the same species, and the expression of the mechanism is suppressed by the fondleweed. In any case, many species would be killed if the hippos mated with them. The mechanism is only released through stimulation when higher vertebrates of other species approach them."

"Why is it," Mogamigawa groaned, "that all higher-order vertebrates on this planet are essentially programmed with an obscene and moreover unproductive urge to mate with any partner they find? You seem to be saying that it's somehow incorporated in their genes as information." He spoke in a muffled, lewd tone, and seemed to be twisting his lips as he continued. "What's more, they're all so remarkably similar to common earth animals, like the hippopotamus, alligator, rabbit or cow. That makes them seem even more obscene, to us earth humans. Why is that, I wonder."

"Well, I don't know about 'obscene', but as a phenomenon it's probably adaptive concentration. To give an example, long ago on earth there were lower-order marsupials that lived only in Australia and surrounding areas. In other words, they only developed after the separation from Eurasia, and underwent adaptive radiation in that isolated location. There they diverged into a variety of forms. However, each of these creatures, known as epitherians, was amazingly close in appearance to higher-order eutherians that existed in other parts of the world. It was a process of parallel evolution. For example, a kangaroo resembles a jumping hare, a Tasmanian tiger-wolf is much like a wolf, a northern marsupial mole is akin to a mole, a koala is likened to a bear, a rabbit-eared bandicoot could be mistaken for a rabbit, a common brushtail possum is not unlike a fox, a dasyure is uncannily similar to a cat, an opossum resembles a mouse, and so on. Though completely different species, the only visible difference between them is that the former have pouches while the latter don't. Now that we've started making scientific surveys on other planets, Professor Fujioni Ishiwara claims that this adaptive radiation or adaptive concentration, or whatever, is linked to genetic-information carriers in life forms on each planet, and has a vastly broad scope of application. I'm opposed to his theory on the *Law of Universal Orthogenesis*, though."

"I asked why they're so obscene," Mogamigawa said with more than a hint of irritation. "Just as all marsupials are characterized by having a pouch, all the life forms on this planet are characterized as being obscene. Is that what you're saying?"

"I'm saying they're not obscene!" I said caustically, growing more than a little irritated myself. "If anything, I'd say the characteristics of this planet are that all higher vertebrates are herbivores and that there is a complete absence of a food chain here. Not only are there no predators, but also, since population sizes are stable, there is very little conflict between individuals of the same species, i.e. mutual interference. That's how I'd characterize the characteristics! There again, it might have nothing to do with population size, but the fact that these species have absolutely no aggression."

"Ludicrous! What species has no aggression?!" Mogamigawa ranted, parading his basic knowledge of ethology. "If they lose their aggression they will also lose relationships between individuals. If relationships between individuals disappear, they won't even be able to reproduce. The same is also true of humans, after all."

"Ah, but this planet is special in that respect," I countered. "I believe the aggressive impulse is incorporated in the erotic here. Think about it. Animals often bite each other's necks when copulating, or chase or grapple with each other in foreplay, don't they. In other words, they do things that, at first sight, seem like aggression when mating. So wouldn't you agree it's impossible to make a clear distinction between the two impulses? And for the animals on this planet, the erotic impulse is amplified, since there's no need to show aggression, either to heterogeneous or to homogeneous individuals. So they try to mate with individuals of both types."

"Huh. Freudian dualism," Mogamigawa snapped. "You take a classic theory like that and apply it to the animal kingdom! And you believe all that, do you?"

"Not all of it, naturally!" I snapped back. "But if I could say one thing, the destructive impulse revealed by Freud in his later years, well, Freud wasn't even serious about that himself. But he came up with a bipolar theory because there were some things he couldn't explain with libido alone."

"And so you postulate the existence of animals that have nothing but erotic desires? Fool!" he roared. "You've been tainted by the obscenity of the creatures on this planet!"

"The obscene thing again?!" I roared back. "Are bacteria not obscene, then?"

"Bacteria are not obscene! What are you talking about?! The bacteria on this planet are the same as those on earth. They're not obscene in the slightest. They reproduce homogeneously, as they should, and if we attempt successive subculture of multiple species, they fight each other, as they should, and the losers are wiped out. That is as it should be. Or what are you saying? That your Jungian theory also applies to the bacteria on this planet?!"

"It's not Jungian! It's... someone else-ian..."

"Well, it matters not, but why doesn't, what, the thing that only affects higher-order animals, why doesn't it affect bacteria too? See! You've got it all wrong. Habitual... whatsit... would have to be, as it were, interrupted... and all that. Wouldn't you see that as odd?"

"But bacteria and those, what was it, higher, yes, higher-order thingies, they're different... aren't they?"

"No, they're not!"

"I'm not saying that, you know, everything on this... on this planet has to be... kind of... uniform... the... you know, genetic stuff... it doesn't have to be the same..."

"And that's what's odd, is what I'm saying."

"That's right. It's odd."

"What are you talking about?"

"What are *you* talking about?"

"Hold on. What exactly were we talking about?"

We somehow sensed that something was not quite right and, without knowing what it was, stopped dead in our tracks. We flashed our torches at the dimly star-lit scene around us.

"It's a field," I mumbled. "We're in a field of that, you know, what-do-you-call-it."

"Forget-me-grass," said Yohachi.

"Let's get out of here!" wailed Mogamigawa as he dashed past me, stumbling over the weeds and hollows in the ground as he went. "If we stay here doing... what-not... then we'll... whatever!"

"That, you know, that thing, it's gradually getting more, you know!"

I had a vague feeling that we'd been arguing about something, but I couldn't remember what it was about. Proof enough that we were in the middle of a community of forget-me-grass. Our powers of thought or memory were rapidly disappearing – what could be more unsettling than that? I quickened my pace until I was virtually running.

We continued for about a mile after emerging from the field. The Algernon effect had receded, but our amnesia remained. By the time our memories at last started to return, dawn had broken and the golden globes were already in full view. Trees grew sparsely in the surrounding terrain, false-eared rabbits hopped in and out of the undergrowth, and the odd collapsible cow stood munching grass here and there.

"Er, Doctor," I called out to Mogamigawa, who still walked on ahead.

"Yes," he answered in apparent relief. His voice was soft, quite in contrast to his previous tone. "Would you like to continue our discussion?"

"Yes, I would."

"I see. Well, debate is certainly important, is it not."

"Not debate, exactly. I was just wondering how forget-me-grass affects the animals on this planet, and wondered if we could discuss that."

"Have you had another idea, then?"

"Will you listen? Just now we were having a debate. Well, actually it was closer to an argument. If it had escalated any further, we would have been fighting."

"And?"

"The forget-me-grass prevented us from doing that. And oddly enough, our debate was about aggression."

Mogamigawa stopped and turned round, staring me hard in the face. "Are you saying that the forget-me-grass stops animals on this planet from attacking each other?"

"Well, it may partly explain that phenomenon, at least."

"But look around you!" He gave a sweeping wave with one hand to divert my attention to our surroundings. "There's not much forget-me-grass around here, is there. So we're not affected by it at all. Only when one's in the middle of a field of forget-me-grass does memory loss occur. Surely it would be impossible for genetically programmed aggression to be erased just like that?"

"Nevertheless, not only is forget-me-grass distributed all over this planet, but there are also communities of it scattered in various parts. Furthermore, all the higher vertebrates on this planet are herbivores, which means that, unlike us, they're always munching that grass. We know the false-eared rabbit eats it, at the very least. And it's also been found in the excretions of other animals."

Mogamigawa stared at me again. At length, he turned back to survey the scene around us, walked over to a specimen of forget-me-grass growing several feet away and pulled it up by the root. He returned muttering to himself. "It may be caused by pollen toxins, or the composition of gas expiration. I'll take it back to analyze it with Dr Shimazaki. Put it in your collecting case, will you." He held up the specimen as if it were a poisonous snake and thrust it towards me.

We hurried on further ahead. Although we wore earth watches, we were confused by the two-hourly alternation of night and day, and had no clear perception of the time or date. In any case, making haste was the best policy.

A false-eared rabbit scampered across our path from right to left and hopped into a clump of grass.

"So what about the false-eared rabbit then?" asked Mogamigawa. He had evidently been mulling over my counter-argument as he walked on, and now spoke with some relish, as if he'd at last discovered his justification.

"What about it?" I retorted.

"It grows nine to eleven ears on its head. Only two of them are real, and the rest are, er…"

"False."

"That's right, it has seven to nine false ears. If you grab them, they come off like lizard's tails, but don't grow back. Surely, this proves that the rabbit has natural enemies?"

"Certainly, it has natural enemies. But, with respect, it's only humans who catch rabbits by grabbing their ears. Look at the gaping hooter, a large creature that has no nose. It's a herbivore. Bearing in mind that the Newdopians eat rabbits and, in fact, the false-eared rabbit is the only meat they eat, the false ears could be seen as a mechanism to prevent capture by humans."

"Are the natives really the only carnivorous vertebrates on this planet, then?"

"Yes, as far as I know. But of course, we don't know what we may meet in the jungle."

Mogamigawa grimaced.

Trees were gradually increasing in density, a sign that the jungle was close at hand. On the previous mission, we had started our detour around the jungle from this point. The trees were not only bizarre in appearance but also had names to match – frizzly acacias and itchy scratchy trees, dripping deutzia, and more. Relic pods already hung in clusters from the branches of the frizzly acacias. Mistress bine lay on the branches of the itchy scratchy trees, like a terrestrial version of the fondleweed. Screeching cicadas shrieked and whooped in ever-growing clamour, and there were increasing numbers of grindhog, panting hart and gaping hooter, the equivalent of earth squirrels, deer and monkeys. The occasional collapsible cow would suddenly stick its neck out from the shadow of a tree ahead of us, making us practically jump out of our skins.

The collapsible cow had a face that scarcely resembled a cow, with a body that was much smaller than a cow's but looked more like a wild boar. It was called a "cow" merely because it ruminated. Not to say that it ruminated with four stomachs, as a cow does. It would keep its front legs still and move only its hind legs forwards, thus contracting its trunk like an accordion. This would have the effect of compressing its stomach, forcing the contents out into its mouth. Next, it would keep its hind legs still and only move its front legs forwards, stretching its trunk until it looked like a dachshund. Actually, I was quite keen to dissect one to see what its skeleton was like.

Mogamigawa resumed our dialogue. "Whether in water, on trees, on land, or underground, they've all undergone adaptive radiation that makes them almost identical to earth species, but, unlike the latter, they're all herbivorous mammals. Moreover, as *you* would have it, they're not merely mammals but actually primates, or, if not, then higher-order creatures very close to that. Don't you think that's odd?"

"Not really. After all, even reptiles in the Mesozoic underwent adaptive radiation. For example, the triceratops resembled a rhino-ceros, the pteranodon a bird, the brontosaurus an elephant, a certain theropod a tiger, and the ichthyosaur a fish."

"No, no. That's not what I'm saying. Why are there so few lower order mammals, reptiles or amphibians, as I mentioned just now? There don't seem to be any fish either, nor birds, except that darned penisparrow."

I held my tongue. It was clear that if I'd spoken my mind openly, we would only have started another argument. And it would have been much worse than the previous one.

Still Mogamigawa persisted. "Just now, you said you were opposed to Ishiwara's theory on the *Law of Universal Orthogenesis*. If I remember correctly, he said that 'Organisms on all planets, not only those in our solar system, evolve from bacteria and algae in the broad sense to intelligent life forms, in accordance with a major law of orthogenesis that pervades the entire cosmos.' You would disagree with that, would you?"

Now I felt compelled to reply. "Yes, but he went on to say that 'There are life forms which, in appearance, seem to differ from planet to planet. This is merely an embodiment of the Law, to a certain degree of probability, depending on environment and conditions.' My view is that there could be a planet that doesn't fit that principle. Depending on its environment and conditions, of course."

"More twaddle!" Mogamigawa snarled in his customary way of intimidating his opponent as a precursor to shouting. "Utter tripe! What on earth are you talking about?! No matter what synthetic culture medium we use for our research, the first thing to appear will be bacteria, followed by protozoa that eat the bacteria. The excretions of the protozoa become nutrients on which algae multiply. Then, and only then, will the first multi-cell organism come into being and the symbiotic system stabilize. Whatever the environment or conditions, the cycle of succession in living organisms is always from small to large, from microbes to flora, from flora to fauna. I have never witnessed an ecosystem on any planet that has any other form of succession. Evolution is always the same. Only when there is something to eat can something exist to eat it. It is utterly unthinkable that the birds came first, followed by the insects and seeds that are eaten by them."

"So you're saying the idea that humans came first is nonsense?"

"But of course!"

"Even so, a friend of mine has the following theory. First there was man. A being that regressed from man became the common ancestor of humans and apes. That being evolved into an ape, and a being that regressed from the original being became the ancestor of the insectivores, and so on and so on, until finally single cell protozoa were formed. In other words, a theory of reverse evolution."

"Ha," Mogamigawa scoffed. "Of course, he cannot be serious, but it's a pity he didn't make the argument more intriguing all the same. He's a scientist, is he?"

"A psychoanalyst. Yasha Tsuchini. It was he who discovered the universal human desire for a regression theory. He claims that the theory of evolution is what humans find most problematic, since they always want to believe in the superiority of the human race. The regression theory is one of the myths that lie deep and unnoticed in the bosom of modern man. This applies equally to biologists, he says. Their theories are merely the reverse of an intrinsic belief in human supremacy, as witnessed in the claim by Professor O.E. Kenzabroni that 'Humans who take the side of animals are extremely cruel towards other humans'. To give a more concrete example, even Konrad Lorenz, who won the Nobel Prize for biology some centuries ago, sometimes seemed to extol the superiority of the human race precisely because he was a neo-Darwinist."

"And yet he was an evolutionist. All right, he supported discrimination based on eugenics, but what's wrong with arguing the superiority of the human race?"

"Nevertheless, even some modern biologists who've been influenced by Lorenz say there could be no such thing as evolution, since everything is determined genetically. According to them, adaptation is achieved through population dynamics in all species."

"Yes, I know about them. Fools to a man!" Mogamigawa started to shout again. "Incorrigible anti-evolutionists will always appear in one guise or another. You make it sound as if all evolutionists are conservative while regressionists are universally progressive. Or perhaps the modern trend is in that direction anyway. Well, I can't accept that. Come to think of it, there are even some bacteriologists who argue that humans evolved from single-cell protozoa. Take the theory of 'Devolution' proposed by Professor Edmond Hamilton of SFM University. He suggested that intelligent beings that were actually single-cell protozoa from the galaxy Altair, hundreds of thousands of light years from our own galaxy, created a civilization through telepathy and came to earth, the 'poisonous planet', billions of years ago, where they gradually regressed, subdivided into lower and lower forms of life, and finally produced the lowest, most grotesque life form of all – man. You're one of those fools, are you."

"Surely Hamilton's claims are meant as a rebuttal of the 'black superiority' of evolutionists who regard the human race as the ultimate product of evolution, the highest natural creation in the cosmos. You see—"

"Not all evolutionists are discrimination theorists, you know!" yelled Mogamigawa. "Even among humanoids, there are some telepaths, like all of the Newdopians on this planet, but only a fraction of humans on earth. Now that intelligent humanoid beings of a higher order than earth humans, in a sense, are being discovered on different planets, evolutionists who maintain such an antiquated approach—"

"Er, sorry to interrupt, gentlemen," Yohachi said sardonically from the rear. "We're in the jungle, in case you hadn't noticed. Hadn't we better be careful? Just now there was a huge spider dangling above your heads, wondering which of you to go for!"

Darkness had suddenly fallen around us, and I'd assumed that the suns had retreated behind clouds. In fact, we were already inside the jungle, a tertiary mixed forest.

"Ah. That was probably a nursery spider," I said as I continued along an animal trail. "Please be careful, Dr Mogamigawa. This area is full of itchy scratchy trees. We may have to edge past them sideways." Already starting to itch under their influence, I was beginning to feel irritated myself. That sensation of shuddering just before having sex started to creep up my spine, and I sneezed twice in quick succession.

"*Aaaaaaaargh!*"

Mogamigawa had become horribly entangled in mistress bine, which had bound him fast to the trunk of an itchy scratchy tree and instantly covered his body with bluish-green lichen. "Quick, man! Get the knife out, quick!" he screamed at Yohachi with a half-crazed expression, panting with increasing ferocity. "*Aaargh! Aaargh!*" A look of sheer rapture started to spread over his features.

Yohachi grinned as he slowly pulled a knife from his pocket; then, waiting for the perfect moment when Mogamigawa's frenzied screams reached their gasping climax and his body slumped down limply, brandished the knife and cut the mistress bine into pieces.

"Why didn't you cut it sooner, man?!" Crumpled in a heap on the ground, Mogamigawa glared up at Yohachi reproachfully. "You did that deliberately, didn't you!"

"Come, did you?" Yohachi let out his vulgar laugh.

"Shut up!" Mogamigawa clambered to his feet with renewed vigour, as if to show that he hadn't just ejaculated, and shouted loudly again. "Come on then! Let's be off, *quam celerrime*! Otherwise we'll still be in this obscene jungle when it gets dark!"

It was obvious to see that he was merely putting on a show. Even I was cringing at the thought of the abominable creatures that lay in wait for us ahead.

"Yes. Let's make haste!" I called in falsely high spirits, quite at odds with the quaking in my heart. But no sooner had I started off than I screamed loudly and fell flat on my back. A gigantic nursery spider had slid down from the trees in front of my eyes, brought its weird lemur-like face close to mine, then gripped my face tenderly with its folded, hairy front legs and seemed about to kiss me.

"Chase it away, for Christ's sake!" I shrieked, virtually foaming at the mouth as I lay prostrate on the ground.

"It's gone," said Yohachi. "You scared it off when you screamed."

"Was that really a spider?" asked Mogamigawa behind me when we'd started off in trepidation once more. "It had four legs, did it not. More like a cross between a lemur and a spider monkey, I'd say."

"It is almost certainly not a spider. After all, one characteristic of this planet is that there are hardly any insects at all, except for those screeching cicadas," I answered as I waded through the undergrowth. "I can't say anything for sure until we catch one, but I think they're either mammals or something close to that. Its hands were warm."

"So what's behind the name, then?"

"Nursery spider? It was named by a chap called Hatsumi, a member of the First Expedition. He loved making puns, and it was he who named most of the species on this planet. But he came across so many bizarre life forms that, when quizzed about the names back on earth, he often couldn't remember why he'd named them."

"How thoroughly irresponsible."

"Indeed. But there must be some meaning behind the name."

We heard a flapping, rustling noise of something violently beating the leaves of the trees above us. A flying creature skimmed over our heads, its large warm body smacking against my instinctively raised hand.

"*Graarrghh!*" the thing squawked, then fell to the ground and scuttled off into the undergrowth.

"A penisparrow!" Yohachi shouted in amazement. "A whopping great penisparrow! The size of a cat! The king of all penisparrows!"

"No. That wasn't a penisparrow," I said, still somewhat stunned. "It had fur, and its call was different too. It either glides by stretching the skin on its sides like a flying squirrel, or else it has membrane wings like a chiropteran, I'd say."

"I don't believe it," Mogamigawa muttered grumpily. "We keep seeing creatures that do nothing but support your famous regression theory!"

I was little inclined to go over the whole regression theory again. On the other hand, if we had something to debate, perhaps we could distract our minds from our mounting terror. So I started again. "The regression theory is difficult to establish because it assumes that humans suddenly appeared out of nothing. But let's say the Newdopians are intelligent humanoid beings that came here from some other planet. By that I don't mean some major species migration, but something like, well, you remember back in the Second Green Revolution on earth, when all those obnoxious hippies were herded onto spaceships and banished beyond our galaxy. The Newdopians could be their descendants."

"Based on what, pray?"

"Based on the fact that they haven't spread all over this planet but are limited to one location. Perhaps they knew about their ancestors, and for that very reason predicted that, sooner or later, intelligent life forms similar to themselves would visit them from another planet. That's why they created a proper country as they have done here. They did refuse us entry, after all. And we may not be the first beings to have visited Newdopia from another planet."

"And you're saying that all the mammals on this planet could have regressed from them?"

"That's right. I mean, look at those!" I indicated a group of three gaping hooters sitting in line on a nearby tree, flaring their exposed nostrils as they looked down at us. "Give them noses, and they'd look just like Newdopians, don't you think?"

"Well, I've only seen the natives on photographs. But hold on – what about the flora then? Are you saying they existed on this planet from the beginning?"

"Yes, at least the algae. And there were probably also fauna, up to about the stage of multi-cell protozoa. It's conceivable that the original ancestors of the Newdopians carried food provisions in the form of chlorella or such like. They must also have brought parasites with them. That would explain the discontinuity between higher- and lower-order fauna, and the fact that there are many gymnosperms but only two or three species of angiosperm among the flora. In other words, the fauna have not yet regressed as far as reptiles or fish, while the flora have yet to evolve as far as angiosperms."

"I'm sorry, but it doesn't explain anything of the sort," said Mogamigawa. "Otherwise how can you accommodate the screeching cicada, an insect? Also, considering your adaptive radiation of gymnosperms, it's abnormal for there to be so few species of higher order vertebrates. If they're all mating so heterogeneously, I would have expected new species equipped with genetic plasticity to be crawling all over the place. And there's also the puzzle of how the fecundity of the Newdopians and higher vertebrates is kept in check, inter alia."

"Actually, the screeching cicada is merely an extremely primitive form of insect, despite the name. On earth it would be about the equivalent of the protoblattaria or primitive cockroaches that appeared in the Carboniferous period. Whether it evolved from a crustacean, or from one of the earliest arthropods like the trilobite, it must have subdivided into various forms when it came up on dry land. As such, we should see other types of insects here. I don't know why that's not so, but I'd say the most plausible explanation is that all the other primitive insects died out, for some reason, leaving only the screeching cicadas to adapt and survive. It may sound ridiculous, but their cry so resembles the shrieking voices of young women that it sounds highly erotic, and this may have helped them adapt to the overriding ambience of eroticism on this planet. Their cry so intensely stimulates sexual urges, you see."

"It's unscientific, I admit, but I've also started to feel the same way. I mean, this planet may be a world in which only indecent life forms are allowed to exist," Mogamigawa said with a sigh, seeming to lack energy after his violation by mistress bine.

"Sssh!"

I signalled to Mogamigawa and Yohachi to keep their heads down, and hid myself in a thicket of evergreen fern. Beyond the thicket lay an open clearing that appeared to be the dead centre of the jungle. There, a number of animals were writhing around in highly furtive activity.

"Are they mating?" whispered Mogamigawa, who'd crawled along the ground to join me.

"Clearly."

"The female resembles a small bear…"

"And the male looks like a mountain goat. The other two seem to be a cross between a tapir and a pig."

"What are they doing?"

"Waiting their turn, probably," I answered, sickened by the sheer outlandishness of it. "I've never seen any of these before. They must live permanently in the jungle. I can't remember hearing names that would answer to any of them, either."

"I doubt such an obscene sight could be found on any other planet," muttered Mogamigawa with a look of nausea. He hurriedly started to crawl back. "Let's be off. I don't wish to see any more of this."

Noticing the sound of rustling leaves as Mogamigawa brushed against the evergreen ferns, the two creatures that resembled tapir-pigs reared up on their hind legs and turned towards us.

"Oh no! They've spotted us!" exclaimed Yohachi.

The two tapir-pigs both sported massive erections. No sooner had they discovered us than their bloodshot eyes started to glisten, as if they assumed us to be new objects for their sexual gratification.

They began to waddle towards us on hind legs, hips jerking and lower bellies thrust forwards, revealing their swollen members. Their appearance reminded me of a certain type of middle-aged man who's so starved of physical affection that he turns into a sex-crazed monster. Nothing could be more repugnant to the eyes.

I set aside my fear and prepared to run. But the blood drained from my face when I saw another seven or eight animals suddenly emerge from the undergrowth around the dead centre. The tapir-pigs weren't the only ones that had been waiting their turn to mate – these others had also been lying in the thickets quietly biding their time. They were all creatures that I'd never seen before in the two months since I'd been on this planet. One looked like a horse, another resembled a dog, another an elephant, another a sloth and another looked like nothing on earth. The weirdest of them all resembled a massive gaping hooter, but was even closer in appearance to a human. They all stood on hind legs, displaying erect penises and panting heavily as they yielded themselves to their burning carnal desires and started to approach us. No words could describe the dread that filled us at that moment.

"*Naargh!*"

"*Hyaargh!*"

"Here they come!"

We started to run for all we were worth. It was as if we were being pursued by the demons of vengeance for spying on the Walpurgis night feast. We felt like dead men already, and had lost all sense of our bearings. All we could do was to keep running, gasping and wheezing for breath as we imagined what might happen to us if we stopped or fell, those demonic beasts ravishing us from behind, their blood-red members thrust deep inside of us. Just when it seemed that our hearts would leap out of our mouths, it was Mogamigawa who at last flopped down onto the ground in exhaustion, then Yohachi on top of him, and finally myself on top of the two of them.

"Noooooooooooooo!" Mogamigawa, evidently mistaking us for the beasts, leapt up waving his arms about madly like a man in the throes of death, and tried to run off again. He was about to collide with an itchy scratchy tree that stood in his path, but howled with fright when he saw its trunk. "*Wha! Gnngggnngg! Frphhhghh! Drrgrrrnnn!*" No words of significance would emerge from his mouth.

A tapir-pig had become entangled in mistress bine on the trunk of the itchy scratchy tree, and had died as it remained fastened there. Its exposed face had started to decompose and its eyeballs had fallen out. We shuddered at the ghastly sight of its agonized features, and slumped to the ground petrified with terror.

"That's odd," I said with a tilt of my head when I'd recovered my senses and found my tongue again. I pointed at the carcass of the dead tapir-pig. "Mistress bine only has gripping force initially, but eventually it relaxes its hold. So a creature as large as that should be able to disengage itself easily. And anyway, this individual is a male. Surely, the animal would have lost its usefulness once it had released its protein, and the mistress bine would have returned to its usual dangling state…"

"Perhaps he gave himself up voluntarily?" suggested Yohachi. "Perhaps he got such an unbearable itch from the itchy scratchy tree, and because he didn't have a partner, went to rub himself on the plant. Then he couldn't stop doing it, and as more and more of the plants came to give him one, he eventually used up all his energy and died. That's what I reckon."

"Hmm. You may have something there," I said, looking him up and down. "But what made you think that?"

"I dunno," he laughed. "That itchy scratchy tree has been making me itch like hell for a while now. I wouldn't mind getting tangled up in that plant myself!"

"You've already ejaculated seven or eight times and still you say that?!" said Mogamigawa with a frown. "How utterly disgusting!"

"I wouldn't be surprised if all the animals in this jungle, including the ones that were mating just now, have their sexual desire aroused by the itchy scratchy tree," I said with a nod to Mogamigawa as I got up. "It's just one big orgy around here. Let's get out, quick!"

In the blind panic of our flight, we'd strayed off our linear course through the jungle. I set off once more at the head of the group with compass in hand.

As we continued to push on westwards, we stumbled across a

truly heart-rending scene. A female gaping hooter had collapsed at the foot of a sagging fern palm and, with thighs spread wide, was in the process of giving birth. The baby's blood-drenched head and shoulders were already protruding outside the mother's body. I stopped walking and lowered my head to watch.

Mogamigawa edged close to me and whispered in my ear. "Aren't we right in the middle of an animal trail here? Why give birth in such a wide-open space, when it doesn't even live here?"

"Because it has no natural enemies, of course," I replied. "But look at the baby's head! It doesn't look anything like a gaping hooter – it's a much larger creature. More like a hybrid between a gaping hooter and that bear-like thing we saw earlier."

"The mother's certainly having a hard time of it."

"Yes. The baby's too big and she will probably die. Look how badly she's bleeding."

"In that case, the baby will also die. There'll be no mother to feed it, and no surrogate mother either, as it's a hybrid."

"Yes, naturally." I stretched my back, then went over to examine the newborn before turning back to Dr Mogamigawa. "Hybrids like this must be born and die all the time in this jungle. Poor wretches! Right, let's be on our way. It'll be dark soon."

"Wait a minute!" yelled Mogamigawa, placing his palm on my chest to hold me back. "Take a look at *that*!"

A nursery spider, hanging on a thread that emerged from its backside, came sliding down from the trees directly above the prostrate body of the dying mother. We watched its behaviour closely, wondering what it was planning to do.

Though a mammal, the nursery spider seemed to have a number of silk-spinning glands in its backside, from which it produced a silk-like thread. This thread must have been formed by mucus secreted from those glands, instantly congealing on contact with air, and was found on closer observation to consist of several strands. If there were only one, it would have broken with the weight of the nursery spider alone. The spider descended onto the mother's body with all four legs; then, after appearing to sniff around it, crawled across to the newborn hybrid by its side.

Suddenly, the spider popped the blood-soaked newborn into its mouth and stood up on its hind legs. Then it appeared to be using its front legs to scoop forwards the thread, which was continuously secreted from the silk-spinning glands on its backside, winding it very nimbly around the body of the newborn in its mouth.

"It's preparing to eat it later," murmured Mogamigawa with an air of excitement.

"But the nursery spider is not supposed to be a carnivore," I whispered back. "I think we're about to discover the meaning behind the name. Let's watch a little longer."

The suns started to dip, and a ray of orange light fell diagonally onto the floor of the jungle, vividly illuminating the figure of the nursery spider as it continued its surreal activity.

At length, my jaw dropped when I realized what was being created in the arms of the nursery spider. "A relic pod! So that's what they are! Newborn hybrids cocooned in the silk of the nursery spider and hung from the branches of trees – for whatever purpose. If only I'd studied the relic pod earlier, I could have discovered so much! But instead, I classified it as unclassifiable and wasted my time examining the ecology of animals closer to hand!"

"That was certainly inattentive of you," agreed Mogamigawa.

In no time at all, the nursery spider had wound its silk around the newborn in the shape of a pear, leaving only a single hole at the top – probably for air. Then it grabbed a few threads that protruded from around the neck of the pod, slung them over its shoulder in true swagman fashion, and started to climb the nearest tree.

"If the aim is not to eat it, it must be to rear it," I said as we started off again. "It cocoons the newborn in silk to return it to the 'womb', as it were. The newborn grows inside the cocoon until it can stand by itself. So there you are – now we know why they're called nursery spiders."

"But where is the merit in so doing?" asked Mogamigawa. "Rearing hybrid young brings no prima facie benefit to the host."

"That's true," I replied with a tilt of my head. There could surely be no life form on any planet that would engage in such pointless activity outside the major goal of preserving its own species. "Once we're out of the jungle, let's cut a relic pod from a tree and open it up. We may discover something."

When we at last emerged from the jungle, night had fallen once more. We switched on the girdle lamps that hung from our waists, and continued westwards through a belt of woodland margin over gently rolling terrain.

We came to a shallow river that flowed some five miles down from the mountains in the north, and decided to set up camp on its rocky shore. With our many exertions so far, we had started to feel slightly inebriated. There was more oxygen in the air than on earth, making our fatigue all the more extreme.

"You go on to Newdopia by yourself now. The border is right over there," Mogamigawa commanded Yohachi. "You know what you're supposed to do, don't you. We've told you often enough."

Yohachi guffawed. "I'm a man, aren't I? You needn't tell me what I'm supposed to do."

Mogamigawa scowled. "Not that, you fool!"

I pointed at Yohachi's nether regions. Having been relieved of his trousers by the flatback hippos, he was wearing nothing but his spare pair of pants. "Take your clothes off," I said. "You'll have less trouble getting in if you're completely naked. You can carry your baggage on your back."

"All right. I'll do that." Yohachi merrily hummed a tune as he undressed himself.

"What's got into him?" Mogamigawa said as an aside.

Completely naked but for a canvas bag containing a telecall and other requisites tied around his head, Yohachi splashed into the river with gaily dancing steps, waded over to the other side and disappeared into a grove of trees.

"What a cheerful chap," Mogamigawa said with a wry smile before easing himself onto the ground.

I went to find a sandy area and lay down there. Well might the Newdopians live their lives permanently naked – the climate was pleasant and there were no pestering insects, leaving one to sleep in peace without even needing a blanket.

"He's cheerful all right. He can have sex as often as he wants in there," I said with a huge yawn. And no sooner had I spoken than the dark demons of sleep descended on me.

I awoke after only two hours, unable to bear the dazzling light shining down from the two suns. That was the problem with this planet. Most people, on first arriving here, had their biorhythms disturbed and suffered badly from sleeplessness.

I boiled some rice in a mess tin, opened a can of Sakata Land Horned Beef and ate my dinner. As I was brewing some coffee with water from the river, Mogamigawa, who'd disappeared from his sleeping place, returned with three relic pods hanging from his arms.

"Let's open them right away. I really must know. Do you have any scissors?"

"I do." Taking a pair of dissection scissors from my collecting case, I snipped one of the relic pods open in a straight line from the hole at the top to the base.

Inside the cocoon was a hybrid creature, curled in fetal position with eyes still closed, surrounded by a liquid that resembled amniotic fluid. It was probably formed when the inner surface of the silk cocoon had dissolved. The creature had the body of a nursery spider and the head of a tapir-pig.

"A cross between a nursery spider and a tapir-pig," I said. "So the parent must have turned its own hybrid newborn into a relic pod."

"Hmm." Mogamigawa snorted in a way that suggested disagreement, then signalled to me to open the other two cocoons.

The other two relic pods contained not hybrids but juvenile nursery spiders with eyes already open and hair on their bodies. They grew excited and let out unearthly cries when they felt the outside air. I exchanged astonished looks with Mogamigawa.

"The wife waker!"

"So that's where the noise comes from!"

"Look here, Sona," said Mogamigawa, using each hand to prevent a juvenile nursery spider from escaping as he scrutinized their bellies. "For what possible reason would a nursery spider cocoon its own young in silk and turn them into relic pods? When they're not even hybrids?"

"Because that's how they rear their young? They can't distinguish between their own young and, say, hybrids produced by other creatures. If they see a baby, their first instinct is to wrap it in..." I stopped in mid-sentence and stared wide-eyed at Mogamigawa. "In other words..."

He nodded. "I think these juveniles may have no reproductive capacity. Could you examine them for me? Use my electron microscope if you like."

"All right."

I didn't need the electron microscope, for it was clear to see that the juveniles had no sex organs. What's more, the sex organs of the other relic pod – the cross between a nursery spider and a tapir-pig – were severely reduced and looked more like vestigial organs.

"First generation hybrids with no reproductive capacity all mutate into nursery spiders," I said with a sigh. "How did you know?"

"I simply imagined that the spiders might raise the young of other species because they cannot reproduce by themselves," Mogamigawa said rather proudly. "Also, I felt that the niche of the spiders in the jungle was abnormally high. Each time I looked up, I would invariably see a nursery spider in the trees above me. I thought that it must therefore be the dominant species. And when we saw that the relic pods were in fact produced by nursery spiders, I became convinced of it when I considered the sheer quantity of relic pods hanging from the branches of the trees."

"To think that such a thing could be possible!" Gazing at one of the open relic pods, I dipped the tip of my finger into the thick, slimy solution inside it.

"The fluid must provide a stimulus that triggers spontaneous metamorphosis, you see. It causes evolutionary regression to the nursery spider, which seems, to all appearances, the lowest life form on this planet. It often happens among lower-order organisms – an anomalous metamorphosis that causes a once evolved species to regress back again under external stimuli. If you had it your way, the reverse evolution theory should apply to this planet, shouldn't it. Ergo, the nursery spider must be preventing any further regression or divergence of species. Or in other words, anomalous metamorphosis on this planet has become what Goethe called 'normal metamorphosis'."

"This seems increasingly like an artificial ecosystem, doesn't it," I mused.

"I've started to see the Newdopians in a slightly different light myself. They seem after all to have a highly advanced spiritual culture, as well as a grasp of science and technology," Mogamigawa agreed. "Of course, it's virtually impossible to create a totally artificial ecosystem, but they must have started the reverse evolution of higher-order species and had the technology for suppressing species divergence. Or even if they didn't, they must at least have known that any higher-order species that devolved from themselves would inevitably be able to coexist peacefully, as befits their own planet. And in fact that's exactly what happened. Furthermore, even lower-order species and plants evolved until they could be incorporated into the ecosystem of these higher-order vertebrates. Or perhaps those species alone were not eliminated but underwent adaptive radiation."

"Rather than having technology as such, perhaps they merely applied a reverse logic to the theory of evolution," I added. "That is, on planets where the theory of evolution applies, there always exists a predator-prey relationship. Even man, the 'terminal animal', inevitably needs an aggressive instinct, which makes him destroy his environment, start wars and so forth. In that case, conversely, if we could create a planet to which the regression theory applies and where only relationships based on libido exist, it should be possible to maintain a peaceful environment. Instead of a Thanatosian 'eat or be eaten' ecology, we should be able to create an Erosian ecology, in which all living things love each other. Being pacifists, the original colonists must surely have been convinced of that. Considering the dubious nature of Freud's dualist theory in his later years, even I have started to think that this erotic ecology may more closely warrant the title of orthodoxy in our cosmos."

"Well, I don't know where they came from. But I've no doubt they must have learnt a lot from the egregious errors of their home planet," said Mogamigawa, waxing oddly lyrical. "Perhaps that planet surprisingly resembled the earth."

I felt the same. We looked at each other and laughed with one voice.

"Isn't it about time we contacted Yohachi?" I said as I finished my coffee and took out the telecall. "He may have done it so much that he's forgotten what he's there for."

"That sounds likely," said Mogamigawa.

"Yo!" Yohachi's voice as he answered the telecall was bounding with cheerful energy. In the background, I could hear the spirited sound of five-beat music.

"So you got in all right? It sounds very lively there. Are you in a dance hall?"

"I'm at an open-air arena. They're doing ballet on the stage. I've never seen anything so fantastic in all my life!"

"Idle bugger!" Mogamigawa snatched the telecall from my hand and bellowed into it. "Have you asked them how to contracept pregnancy by widow's incubus and abort the fetus, man?"

"Yeah. I've asked."

"Well, come straight back here then!"

"Can't I watch this a bit longer? You see it's... well... it's just fantastic!"

"No you may not!" bawled Mogamigawa. "Or do you mean to keep two eminent scientists such as ourselves waiting idly by in a place like this? That would be the biggest mistake in the history of science, I can tell you. Though I can't expect you to take responsibility for that."

"I can't quite hear what you're saying, but anyway, yeah, OK, I'll be on my way soon," said Yohachi, and with that he terminated the telecall from his end.

Night fell once more. When it was starting to grow light again, Yohachi at last returned. After his carnal excesses, I was fully expecting him to look completely spent – but on the contrary, he appeared utterly exhilarated. He strolled up from the river with a

relaxed gait, water dripping from his naked body. Even the look in
his eyes had changed.

"Seems you were well-received!" I said with a grin.

Yohachi shook his head with an expression of sincerity, though
still with a look of elation on his face. "I wasn't particularly well-
received, but I wasn't driven away either. We always go on about
'entering' their country, but there was no border of any sort, and
it was at night. So I just walked in amongst them, and was soon
surrounded by a lot of naked men and women who were trying to
ask me something. The moment I tried to speak, they seemed to
know immediately what I wanted to say, which saved me a lot of
trouble, I can tell you. They even started to take words out of my
head and put them together until they could speak earth language
themselves. They seemed to know straight away what I was there
for, and soon they were all laughing their heads off."

"And did they tell you what we asked?"

Yohachi nodded at Mogamigawa. "I don't know if you'd call it
'telling', but one of the men just said this: 'Ah. Well, all you have
to do is have sex with the women here, then go back and have sex
with the one who's pregnant'."

Mogamigawa turned to me with a look of bewilderment. "What
on earth can he mean?"

"And what happened then?" I asked, leaning towards Yohachi
with mounting curiosity. "Did you have sex with the women?"

"Oh yeah," Yohachi replied with the same earnest expression
on his face. "The men quickly lost interest and buggered off. But
the women hung around for a bit. They were all so beautiful. And
naked. I just couldn't wait to get stuck in. I already had a hard-on
and was chomping at the bit. Then one of the women led me to
a nearby park and let me do it with her on the grass. After that I
did it with, oh, God knows how many. Twelve or thirteen? But
I still didn't forget why I was there in the first place, all right? 'I
mustn't forget what they tell me,' I thought, 'I must remember it
correctly.' So I repeated the same questions to four or five women.
One of them said this. The women in this country are often raped
by those penisparrows in their sleep. I mean, the birds stick their

heads into the women's... you know. That's the penisparrow's kind of, er..."

"Habit?"

"Habit, yeah. This woman said the penisparrow carries a sort of infection caused by, er, something-ella, and so more than half of the women in Newdopia have been, you know, they've been..."

"Infected?"

"Yes, infected by that, er, whatever it was. So then it also infects the men. And the, er, something-ella eats the, er, something of the widow's incubus, the... er..."

"Spores?"

"Yeah, it eats the spores of the widow's incubus, and that stops them from getting pregnant. And even if they do get pregnant, they just have to have sex with a man who's got the infection, and then they can get rid of it easily."

"I want to know more about this infection," Mogamigawa said to Yohachi. "Let me examine you."

Yohachi grasped his overworked member, which now hung down limply. "Yeah, sure. Go ahead."

"No, no. That's not enough. I'm asking you to masturbate, strum your banjo, grease your pole, whatever. I need a *specimen*, man."

"I don't really feel like doing it now," Yohachi grumbled, but still managed to squeeze out a quantity of semen onto Mogamigawa's glass slide. Mogamigawa immediately started to observe it under his electron microscope.

"And anyway, what happened then?" I asked, drawing closer to Yohachi. "Tell me more."

"It was around midday, I think. All of them, even the old people and children who hadn't appeared much till then, and all the young men and women as well, they all went haring off together. 'What's going on?' I asked the woman I was having sex with at the time. She said it was a ballet performance. So I followed them all to the open-air arena." Yohachi's eyes suddenly started to glisten. "I have never seen such a fantastic sight in all my life. There was no scenery, no lighting, just dozens of naked men and women dancing together on the stage. And they were actually having sex as they danced and jigged around. When they brought the lower parts of their bodies together, the man's erect penis would actually go inside the woman. The join between the two of them would turn into a kind of support, so they could both hold hands while the woman, with her face upwards and leaning back, would twirl around and around. Ah. I could never find the words to explain how wonderful it was." Yohachi slapped one knee one after the other in frustration. "Then the men would line up in a circle. The women would line up in another circle around them. The men would start by dancing with the woman facing them, then with the next one."

"Aha. Like changing partners."

"The man would lift the woman high into the air from behind. The woman would stretch out her arms and legs in mid-air and arch her body backwards. The man's penis would go inside the woman again. Then he would change to the next woman and lift her up in the same way. And he would go inside her as well. And so he would pass all the women in the outer circle round to the next man. And the music, I even started to appreciate that music, which I hadn't really noticed until then. It really moved me. Ah. How it moved me. And I started wondering why we can't do that kind of thing on earth. Why doesn't anybody think of such a wonderful ballet on earth, or even try to? I felt so happy. No one was looking at me like I was a dirty old man, no one called me obscene or perverted. Far from it, they showed me such a wonderful kind of art. When I thought about it, it seemed like the ultimate kind of love, a kind of art that couldn't ever be bettered, and I was so moved by it that I actually cried," Yohachi said with tears in his eyes. "What we call sexual intercourse on earth, it's something sordid, something you have to do hidden from prying eyes. It's seen as obscene, dirty, sometimes even as a crime, and you get taken away by the police and frowned on by society even if you just describe it in words or pictures, let alone do it in front of people. But here it's done in broad daylight and out of doors, openly, the most beautiful natural thing a person could do, and it's performed as a kind of art. That moved me to tears. Come to think of it, it's only natural that this kind of art exists. Don't you think it's strange for a society *not* to have such beautiful art? Well anyway, what went through my mind as I watched the ballet was that anyone who doesn't understand the beauty of this can't be called human any more. If someone from earth watched that ballet and said it was obscene or something, that would be someone who can't understand love or art or anything. But, in fact, most people on earth would be like that person. Realizing that made me cry even more. It all got muddled up together – my feeling of bitterness at being looked down upon till now, the sadness of those earth people, and my happiness and emotion at being able to watch that ballet. In the end, I was bawling my head off." Tears were streaming down his face.

That Yohachi could speak with such eloquence, such enthusiasm, when he was usually so taciturn and poor at expressing himself, proved how deeply he'd been moved. The realization of this helped me to share some of his emotion.

My gaze was still fixed on Yohachi's face when Mogamigawa called over to me, his eye still on the microscope.

"Sona. Come and look at this."

When I looked into the eyepiece, I saw, swimming there in a sea of semen, some flagellar bacilli that were clearly distinct from the spermatozoa.

"What are these, then?" I asked.

"A type of salmonella," answered Mogamigawa. "On earth, this bacillus is well known to cause typhous diseases in humans, as well as food poisoning and gastroenteritis through infection from the excreta of birds and mammals. But that's not all. There's a type of salmonella bacillus that has no effect on humans but causes miscarriage in horses, i.e. equine mycotic abortion. This one seems to be parasitic on penisparrows and infectious to humans, causing what we might call 'human mycotic abortion'. That's what it must be."

"In other words, the Newdopians have been controlling their population with the aid of salmonella and the penisparrow. Hmm. I had wondered why there isn't a population surplus with all this sexual activity going on," I said as I continued to watch the movement of the salmonella bacilli. "Yohachi has always wanted to sleep with Dr Shimazaki. Now he'll have to, to infect her with salmonella. Lucky bastard!"

Mogamigawa groaned morosely. "Why should a fool like that be given such an enviable task? No, there's a quicker way. Dr Shimazaki could masturbate using the penisparrow as a dildo," he said, then blushed when he sensed my burning glare on his face. "Er, of course, I'm not saying that out of jealousy, no no no. It's because I doubt Dr Shimazaki would wish to be violated by such a man."

"I'm not so sure. I reckon she'd prefer that to some unnatural method like masturbating with a penisparrow. Especially if she saw him as he is now…"

Mogamigawa glanced back towards Yohachi, then brought his mouth to my ear. "Don't you think the look on his face has changed?" he whispered conspiratorially.

"Yes. That's the face of someone who's been awakened to art. The gleam in his eye is completely different," I answered. I started to collect up my things, which lay scattered about on the river bank. "Well, anyway, why don't we leave the decision to Dr Shimazaki?"

"Yes, I suppose we could," Mogamigawa said with little conviction as he idly packed away his electron microscope. "Damn that Yohachi! How could he have better looks than me?!"

A whole day would soon have passed since our meeting at the Research Centre. In that case, Dr Shimazaki would soon be entering the sixth month of her pregnancy, in earth terms. Whatever was gestating inside her captivating midriff had to be aborted as soon as possible, and for that it was imperative that we return quickly. It was hard on the elderly Dr Mogamigawa, as we'd only slept a total of four hours in about a day and half. But as soon as we'd gathered up our baggage, we immediately set off for the Research Base.

As we neared the jungle, night fell once more.

"I refuse!" exclaimed Mogamigawa, who'd been trailing behind with little enthusiasm until then. He parked his backside on the ground and started to fret like a spoilt child. "Of course I'm tired anyway, but going through that jungle at night would be my vision of hell. Who knows what hideous monstrosities will appear? I'm not going in there, and that's the end of it. Why don't we just sleep here for two hours until it grows light again? Eh, Sona? Won't you?" In the end he was almost begging.

"All right, let's do that," I said. "To be sure, I don't think the jungle will be any less terrifying than it was before."

We decided to take a nap at the foot of a frizzly acacia tree, from whose branches hung a line of relic pods, in a hollow just ahead of the jungle. I knew that having frequent catnaps would merely deprive us of deep sleep. That was particularly bad for the brain activity of scientists such as ourselves, not to mention our physical well-being. But it really couldn't be helped in our present situation.

I was starting to doze when Yohachi shook me awake.

"What is it? I'm trying to sleep! I was just about to drop off!"

"You've been asleep more than two hours already, mate!"

I opened my eyes to find that it was already broad daylight.

"I can't find Dr Mogamigawa," said Yohachi.

"He must be collecting something in the vicinity."

"I don't think so." Yohachi took me to the spot where Mogamigawa had been sleeping, and pointed at the ground.

The footprints of several creatures had disturbed the sandy surface there. The buttons from Mogamigawa's clothing lay scattered around, but the bag containing his electron microscope lay undisturbed in its original position. I was convinced that creatures from the jungle had abducted Mogamigawa during the night.

"Hurry!" I shouted, almost screaming at Yohachi. Mogamigawa may have been a pig-headed old man, but I admired his enthusiasm for research and his virtuous morality. It would have been just too awful if he'd been gang-raped by large creatures and his internal organs had burst. I felt sorry for him. We quickly lifted the baggage onto our backs and headed towards the jungle. "Look there," I said. "The tracks continue this way. Don't lose sight of them."

We immediately lost sight of the tracks under a deposit of dead fern leaves. We then turned towards the dead centre, where we'd seen the creatures having their orgy on our outward journey.

Mogamigawa's bloodstained clothes lay torn to shreds in the middle of the dead centre.

"His pants are here too," said Yohachi with an air of insouciance. "The animals must have taken turns to use his ageing body as the object of their pleasure."

"Could you stop talking like that?" I snapped as I surveyed the scene around us. "I just hope to God he's not dead."

For the next half hour or so, Yohachi and I searched the vicinity of the dead centre, occasionally calling out to each other to prevent us from getting separated. Wherever they'd hidden themselves, we could see no sign of a single creature, let alone our dear colleague.

I returned to the dead centre, wondering how I was going to explain it to Mogamigawa's wife on our return, and how I would berate the Team Leader for forcing an old man on such a dangerous mission. Yohachi was just standing there, looking up vacantly into the trees.

"He'll obviously be lying on the ground naked," I said. "There's no point in looking for him up there."

Yohachi ignored me and started talking, as if to himself, still looking up pensively. "He must have been stark-naked... There was blood on his clothes... In that case, if one of them spiders had found him lying on the ground unconscious, what would it have thought?" He slowly turned to face me. "It would have thought he was a big animal that had just been born. In that case, what would it have done? Wrapped him up in one of them cocoon things, of course. Wouldn't it?"

For a moment I was flabbergasted. "What on earth gave you such a far-fetched idea?" I asked. Then I realized. I hurriedly turned my eyes to the object of Yohachi's gaze.

Above our heads, a massive relic pod, large enough to contain a collapsible cow, was hanging down from the middle of a stout branch.

"You're saying that could be Dr Mogamigawa?" I leant backwards, held my breath and stared up at the relic pod.

"Let's climb the tree together," I said after coming to my senses a few moments later. Yohachi remained as unperturbed as ever. "We'll pick it up together and bring it down carefully. If he's inside, we obviously won't want to drop it."

Yohachi pushed my heavy backside from below as I climbed up ahead. I really had put on a lot of weight in middle age. I crawled along the branch in a snail-like fashion and, on reaching the little air hole of the relic pod, peered into it. It was pitch-dark inside and there was nothing to be seen, nor any sign of movement.

I shouted into the air hole. "Doctor Mogamigawa! Are you in there?"

At that, the swollen base of the huge relic pod suddenly started to squirm and wriggle restlessly. A sound like the obscene cry of the frequently heard wife waker, but several times louder, was emitted from the air hole like a steam whistle, reverberating all around us. The sound was so intense that I instinctively put my hands to my ears and nearly fell from the branch.

"*Yeeuurrgghuuukkkmmmaunnnnnngghhherereeuurghhhhh! Yeeeeuurrggh! Yeeeeuurrggh! Yeeeuuurrrnnnnnnngggghhherereeuuurghhhhh!!!*" The wife waker continued to scream what sounded like obscenities for several minutes, before at last starting to speak in intelligible earth language. "Oh, so sorry. Is that you, Sona?" It was the voice of Dr Mogamigawa. "When I tried to speak just now, nothing but that funny noise would come out. I even surprised myself, to be fair."

"Dr Mogamigawa!" Relieved to hear him speaking with such apparent good cheer, I signalled to Yohachi to come and join me in the tree.

"Well, I *am* glad you found me, I must say. I suppose you've imagined what happened, but I've had a pretty rough time of it, I can tell you. Wahahahahaha!" Confined there in the pod, Mogamigawa spoke with a blithe gaiety that suggested the opposite of a "pretty rough time". "Now, would you let me out of here sharpish, as it were? Otherwise the stimulus from the liquid in here will transform the rest of me into a nursery spider, and we wouldn't want that, would we!"

The rest of me?... I had a terrible foreboding. With Yohachi's help, I quickly hoisted the relic pod up onto the branch, cut the thread that tied it fast, and brought it down from the tree. We were soaking in sweat. "Are you all right in there?" I called. "I'm going to open the pod with my scissors now."

"Yes, would you mind? I'm fine, have no worries there. My desire to return to the womb has been sated, and I've had a good sleep inside the old amniotic fluid. Perhaps that's why I feel in such high spirits! Wahahahahahahaha!"

I cut open the relic pod with the scissors, then watched open-mouthed as Dr Mogamigawa crawled out. In no more than two hours, his metamorphosis had advanced with astonishing speed. Only his head remained unchanged. In fact, it would be truer to say that he was now a nursery spider with the face of Dr Mogamigawa. Four spindly limbs protruded from the side of his trunk and bent under his belly in the fashion of a four-legged spider. His trunk was flat, and his whole body was covered with soft-looking light-brown hairs. Wart-like protuberances, probably his silk-spinning organs, had already broken out near his anus. His penis had shrivelled to the point of non-existence.

"Dr Mogamigawa…" I at last managed to squeeze out in a strained voice. "W-what's happened to you? W-what hideous thing have you become?"

"Pardon? Oh, *this*." Mogamigawa started to crawl around like a spider as he surveyed the changes in his appearance. They didn't appear to shock him so much at all. "Well, as long as I still have my mind, I really don't care what happens to my body. Actually, I feel jolly good and fresh, as if I've been reborn. After all, there's nothing more precious than one's health, is there! You arrived at just the right time, old chap. If the transformation had advanced any further, my mind would have become the same as a nursery spider's. What simply perfect timing! Heeheehee!" His flippant tone suggested that even his personality had changed. He hopped onto the trunk of a nearby tree with a sprightly leap and turned his head downwards. "Look! I can even do this."

In utter confusion, I turned to Yohachi for help. "Yohachi. What shall we do?"

Yohachi calmly returned my stare. "Do about what, mate? If you mean the professor, what can we do but take him back to the Base?"

That was the problem. Taking him back would be all right, but how would we explain it to his wife? If she saw her husband transformed into a spider, she might have an apoplexy. She might drop dead on the spot. Then again, it would be next to impossible to explain his condition without letting her see him. "*I'm very sorry, madam, but your husband has been turned into a spider."* She was never going to believe that – she would think we were joking.

Mogamigawa was frolicking about, revelling in his ability to move his reborn, flexible body just as he wished. "Dr Mogamigawa?" I called.

"*Yeeeeuurrggh! Yeeeeuurrggh!* Oh, sorry! *Mea culpa.* It comes out like that when I start talking suddenly. What is it, my friend? You're wondering whether you should take me back to the Base? But of course you should. You needn't worry one jot about my wife. She can cope, I assure you. The main thing is that I'm so full of energy! My mind is crystal-clear. Now that I've lost my sexual functions and my sexual desires, I'm liberated from obligatory sex with my wife, not to mention concern or jealousy over her infidelity. That means I can devote myself to my research and enjoy life on this wonderful planet. So yes, my dear Sona, I can hardly wait to get going! *Carpe diem,* as they say! Wahahahahahaha!" He climbed the tree as he spoke, then roared with laughter as he slid back down in front of our eyes, on a thread that emerged from his backside. "Wahaha! Wahahahahahaha! Wahahahahahahahahahahaha!"

This was no longer the Mogamigawa of old. That's how it seemed to me. It was someone else. Or perhaps some new species of creature.

The three of us, or should I say the two of us and one spider, set off for the Research Base in accordance with Mogamigawa's wish. The now arachnid Mogamigawa scurried along the ground ahead of us. It may seem hard to believe, but he didn't appear to see anything remotely wretched or absurd in his condition. Paying no heed to my muddled thoughts, he continued to speak without pause.

"You know, this may be a kind of retribution against my former self, a kind of *quid pro quo.* I used to think that the humanoids and animals on this planet, even the natural phenomena, were all obscene. But what splendid retribution! This planet has transformed me, a conservative, opinionated old man who abhorred anything erotic, into a nursery spider, a creature that has no sexual capacity and is, at it were, the ideal host for me. In doing so, it has released me from sex and incorporated me into the ecology of this planet

– *mirabile dictu*! That's right. I am no longer human. I am a creature. Well, Sona my friend? What name would you give to this new creature? Hmm?"

I could find no words with which to reply, and simply continued walking in silence. Instead, Yohachi, whose face now exuded a kind of sublime saintliness, answered on my behalf. "*Mutatis mutandis*," he said in the austere, solemn tone of a divine revelation.

"I see, yes, I see. *Mutatis mutandis*. Indeed yes, I have mutated into a spider and the spider has mutated into me, yes indeed. Wahahahahahahahahaha. What an excellent name. Oh look. We've left the jungle now. Soon we'll be in the field of forget-me-grass. What fun. How wonderful it is to walk as freely as this, to hop and jump like this. But more than that, I'm no longer burdened by the pressures of sex, which were clinging to me doggedly and refused to desist even in my sixties. I will never again be troubled by mistress bine, fondleweed or the itchy scratchy tree. This planet is exactly like heaven to me now. No, no. This planet really is heaven, is it not? Newdopia may be a paradise where totally naked deities have created a country. This planet is a paradise of love! It has the magical power to make not only Yohachi and myself but all humans adapt and conform, sooner or later, provided they live here long enough. From now on, I can continue my research without constraint. But occasionally I will go out to the jungle to save unfortunate newborn hybrids that have been separated from their dead parents. I will cocoon them with my silk and change them into relic pods. Yes – I will dedicate myself to the instinct of love! I will live here for the rest of my life. Look! Is that a field of forget-me-grass I begin to see in the distance? What joy. What joy. And after the forget-me-grass, there's Lake Turpitude. What fun. What fun. Wahahahahahahahahaha. Wahahahahahahahahahahahahahahaha. Waha. Waha. Wahahahahahahahahahahah. Wahahahahahahaha-hahahahahahahahahahahahahahahahahahahaha. Wahahahahaha-hahahahahahahahahahahahahahahahahahaha."

ABOUT THE AUTHOR

Born in Osaka, Yasutaka Tsutsui is particularly well-known for his science fiction. After graduating from Doshisha University, he founded NULL, a science-fiction magazine. His short story *O-tasuke* (*Help*) won him the recognition and respect of Rampo Edogawa, "the father of Japanese mystery writing." During the 1970s Tsutsui began experimenting in a variety of styles, from slapstick and black humour to various kinds of metafiction. Winner of many awards, including the Izumi Kyoka Prize, Kawabata Prize and Yomiuri Literary Prize, he was decorated as a Chevalier des Arts et des Lettres by the French government.

A NOTE ON THE TYPE

This book was set in a version of the well-known Monotype face Bembo. This letter was cut for the celebrated Venetian printer Aldus Manutius by Francesco Griffo, and first used in Pietro Cardinal Bembo's *De Aetna* of 1495.